A Gift of Thought

Sarah Wynde

COPYRIGHT NOTICE

A Gift of Thought is a work of fiction. Names, characters, places, and incidents are the product of the author's imagination. Any resemblance to actual persons, living or dead, events, or locales is coincidental.

Cover photograph: www.shutterstock.com

Cover design: Wendy Sharp

Visit me on the web at **sarahwynde.blogspot.com/**

DEDICATION

To our ghosts

Linda Labar Sharp
November 24, 1942 – August 6, 2011

Malcolm Ferrier
December 23, 1930 – September 6, 2011

Sharon Mirr
July 28, 1954 – November 23, 2011

Michelle Saunders-Zurn
April 4, 1967 – February 5, 2012

We miss you

TABLE OF CONTENTS

Copyright Notice...2

Dedication 3

Chapter One...7

Chapter Two 19

Chapter Three 25

Chapter Four..35

Chapter Five...50

Chapter Six..66

Chapter Seven..79

Chapter Nine 102

Chapter Ten 119

Chapter Eleven...133

Chapter Twelve 147

Chapter Thirteen 161

Chapter Fourteen...177

Chapter Fifteen...188

Chapter Sixteen 200

Chapter Seventeen 213

Author Note 218

Acknowledgements...219

CHAPTER ONE

The airport was already decorated for Christmas.

If Dillon had still been alive, he would have said something wry and sarcastic about the materialism of contemporary American society, about Christmas as an excuse to sell stuff, about cheap glitter being no way to celebrate light into darkness.

As it was, he kind of liked it.

He wished he knew what he was doing in the Orlando Airport on the day after Thanksgiving, though. The crowds were crazy. The lines wound back and forth, back and forth, through the huge open space with the gigantic screen of arriving and departing flights. As a ghost, Dillon didn't have to worry about standing in line, of course, but he was following his father, Lucas, and he didn't want to lose him in the chaos.

For the first few years of his afterlife, Dillon had been trapped in the place he died: the backseat of a black Ford Taurus. He supposed he was lucky. At least he hadn't died in a car accident. Eternity stuck in a smashed-up wreck sitting in a junkyard wouldn't be fun.

Instead, he'd died while hiding out in the car trying to jumpstart a psychic gift. Most of his family had one—his grandpa and his Aunt Nat could see the future, his dad could read minds, his Uncle Zane could find anything—and he'd been tired of waiting for his own to show up. He'd thought the prescription pills he'd stolen would make him hallucinate. Instead they killed him. He'd had plenty of time to think about what a stupid way it was to go.

Last winter, though, he'd met a woman, Akira, who could see and talk to ghosts. She'd introduced him to some other ghosts, including Rose, who was pretty much his best friend now. Akira had also, although it was sort of an accident, broken his tie to his car. He was no longer trapped. He could go anywhere, do anything.

He was a little nervous about it.

Oh, sure, he was a ghost, so it wasn't like anything really bad could happen. He couldn't get cold or wet or hungry. And he was already dead, so nothing could kill him. But he'd seen that there were dangers for ghosts in the world, and Akira had told him stories. He just didn't know whether he'd recognize trouble when he saw it.

Plus, what if he got lost? What if he got stuck somewhere and couldn't get home again? What if he ran out of energy and faded away?

Being dead had done nothing to make Dillon less anxious.

Still, he was determined. Life—or afterlife—had to have more to offer than watching television with Rose or hanging out at Akira's lab while she worked. Despite all that might go wrong, Dillon was going to travel with his father for a while.

Okay, so maybe traveling with your father didn't sound ambitious.

But as fathers went, Lucas was the mysterious type. Dillon didn't really know him. He'd been raised by his grandparents, and for most of his life Lucas had been a "swoop in for an action-packed weekend before disappearing again" father.

Not that Dillon was complaining. He hadn't even seen his mom since he was a month old. She'd dropped him off at his grandparents so they could babysit and never came back. Dillon didn't really blame her for leaving. She'd been awfully young, his dad even younger. He didn't like to think about it, but when Dillon died, he'd already been older than his dad was when Dillon was born.

A wide-eyed little boy in Mickey Mouse ears was staring at him. Dillon paused and grinned at the perplexed look on the boy's face, wondering if the boy could actually see him. Then he realized that Lucas had gotten several people away and hurried after him.

It wouldn't be a big deal if he got stuck at the airport, he told himself. His home town, Tassamara, was hours away by car, so it'd be a long walk. But, hey, he had nothing but time. Still, he'd rather not lose his dad quite so early in their trip.

He wondered if he should send his dad a text to ask where they were going.

That was the other thing Akira had done for him. She'd helped him find a way to cope with the worst part of being a ghost: not being able to communicate with anyone. After much practice and many destroyed electronic devices—his Aunt Grace bought them in bulk when she learned what he was trying to do—Dillon had succeeded in manipulating his own ghostly energy to send text messages.

It wasn't as crazy as it sounded. Grace found stories of ghosts who tried to communicate using radio waves. Supposedly someone had even invented a device that let spirits combine audio clips to send messages, although it didn't seem to work very well. Akira had a theory that the digital signals used by cell phones, computers, and e-readers required less power and were easier to create than audio transmissions, but Dillon didn't care how it worked as long as it did.

Unfortunately, long conversations were out. Dillon could send a few words, even sentences, but his energy was limited enough that he hadn't bothered to ask where they were going that morning. Anywhere would be more interesting than his car.

Still, he was surprised to wind up in a public airport. His dad traveled a lot but not usually on commercial flights. The family company, General Directions, owned several planes: one fancy corporate jet that could cross oceans and a few smaller private planes for shorter hops. What was wrong with using one of them?

Lucas swung his bag onto the conveyor belt, and placed the contents of his pockets into a plastic bin. In the requisite security ritual, he slipped out of his shoes, and dropped them and the coat he was carrying into another bin. Pacing forward barefoot, he stepped through the gate of the metal detector, the bored TSA agent barely registering his presence. But as Dillon followed him, the detector started beeping wildly.

Oops.

The guard waved Lucas back while Dillon waited on the other side of the detector. If Akira had been here, she might have explained what happened scientifically, but it looked like his ghostly electromagnetic field energy messed with the metal detector. Next time, he'd walk around.

Lucas walked through the detector again, his expression revealing nothing of his thoughts. Dillon wondered whether his dad realized what had happened and that Dillon had set off the machine. This time the detector was silent.

Too silent, Dillon realized, as the guard frowned and gestured to another uniformed man. While the second security officer ran the handheld wand over Lucas's clothes, the first held out a hand for his travel documents.

Lucas passed them over without comment, then smiled and said to the guard in front of him, "Busy day today. You guys should get holiday pay."

"That'd be nice, wouldn't it?" said the guard, finishing with his scan and straightening up.

He stepped back and away, and glanced at the first guard who shrugged and handed Lucas's paperwork back with a casual, "Here you go, Mr. Murray. Have a safe flight."

Murray?

Lucas's last name was Latimer, just like Dillon's.

As they walked away from the security checkpoint and boarded the monorail that would take them to the gate, Dillon's mind was racing. Why was his father traveling under a fake name?

What the hell was going on?

*****

Guarding Rachel Chesney was a pain in the ass.

Sylvie kept her face impassive, her hands tucked behind her back, while she listened to Rachel's father rant. To keep her mind occupied, she considered exit strategies. The room only had one door to an outside hallway: could she get her charge out of one of the two tall windows if she had to?

Probably not while Rachel was puking, she admitted to herself. Not without a climbing harness and much more time than they'd have if armed intruders were banging on the door.

So in the absence of a quick escape, how would she defend the space? The suite had an entry foyer, small, but if she lifted the sofa onto one end, she could shove it against the door. It was a sleeper sofa, so it'd be heavy, but it looked doable, and it would definitely slow down incoming assailants.

With Rachel already in the bathroom, huddled against the toilet, Sylvie would have to put her back to the bathroom door and take out the enemy head-on. Probably better to drag Rachel into the living space and move her behind the bed, Sylvie decided. No one would get upset about a little vomit on the floor if they were under attack.

Not the way her father was already upset about her very public puke in the hotel ballroom, anyway.

"What do you have to say for yourself, Ms. Blair?" Raymond Chesney finally snapped. His usually pale, benevolent face was flushed with fury, and the brown eyes behind his round glasses were blinking rapidly.

Oh, goodie, he's going to let me speak, Sylvie thought, before saying, expressionless, "As I told you when you hired me, sir, I'm a bodyguard, not a babysitter."

"You're supposed to take care of her!"

"Close protection on a teenage client requires the establishment of a trusting relationship." Sylvie didn't let her eyes drop from their focus on the glint of Chesney's glasses. It was a trick she'd learned that let her look as if she was maintaining eye contact. Raymond Chesney was a wealthy man and a force to be reckoned with in Washington. She shouldn't—wouldn't—let him bully her. "I can't do my job if I'm viewed as an adversarial authority figure."

"Stopping a fourteen-year-old from doing vodka shots is hardly adversarial!"

"I protect my charges from outside threats, sir, not from themselves." Sylvie kept her voice neutral, although inwardly she was scoffing.

Right. Now he objected. She hadn't seen him complaining when he sent his daughter off to 'hang out' with the nineteen-year-old son of one of his pet politicians. What did he think a nineteen-year-old would be doing at a party like the one going on downstairs? He was lucky it hadn't been anything worse.

Of course, she would have intervened if Rachel had been in danger. And she had, in fact, stopped Rachel from having a fourth drink. She just hadn't realized that three drinks would be enough to put the girl under the table. But there was no reason Chesney needed to know any of that.

"Ha," Chesney snorted. He turned to Ty Barton, the leader of the security team, and said, "From now on, Lydia's on party duty. Get Rachel home. We'll discuss this again later." He took a quick glance in the mirror, smoothed his hand over his balding head, and tweaked his black bow tie before turning and stalking out of the room.

"Sylvie," Ty started.

"Total lightweight," she interrupted him. "Three drinks, I swear. And the guys were drinking from the same bottle, so it wasn't spiked."

Ty sighed. In his mid-forties, he was tall, blond, and handsome, in impeccable physical condition, and the perfect image of a professional security expert. But he was also damn good at his job and an old friend. "He's going to want me to fire you, you know."

Sylvie shrugged. "You can if you have to."

She wasn't worried about losing her job. Working for Chesney was lucrative, but she could always find more work. Plus, Ty wouldn't want to let her go: not only because of their shared history, but because he was one of the few people in the world who knew how uniquely qualified she was to be a bodyguard. Close protection security consultant, she corrected herself wryly. Ty really preferred it when she used the fancy name.

Besides, Rachel Chesney was a spoiled brat. If Sylvie never had to listen to her whine again, she wouldn't exactly be sad.

"You didn't do this on purpose, did you? To get out of going to parties for the next month?"

"Absolutely not," Sylvie protested. And then the corner of her mouth tilted up, as she added, "Not that I mind."

She hated working parties. The advance detail work could be interesting. She liked conducting threat assessments. But crowds gave her headaches and the biggest risk at the actual event—at least here in DC—was that she'd die of boredom while wearing high heels. And if she was going to die of boredom, she really wanted it to be in comfortable shoes.

"All right." Ty rubbed his face. "We're short-staffed tonight."

Sylvie nodded. One of the three drivers on the team had quit a few weeks ago and his position was still open. Normally that wouldn't matter, but two other members of the team were out with the flu.

"If I send James with you—no, that won't work." Ty was thinking out loud.

"I can drive," Sylvie suggested. "I've done the training."

Ty considered the idea. It was irregular, but moving a charge on the spur of the moment was less risky than a regular outing. He'd never agree to let her drive Rachel to school, Sylvie knew, but there was minimal risk of ambush on an unscheduled trip.

Ty nodded. "If she hurls in the car, you get to clean it up," he added, with a spark of humor.

Just then the sound of renewed vomiting came from the bathroom. Sylvie glanced toward the sound and said with a grimace, "I'll give it a little longer before we head out."

*****

The girl ate like a bird, Sylvie thought, baffled. Well, not like a bird—didn't they supposedly eat their body weight in food every day? Rachel ate like whatever it was that ate almost nothing, which meant that logically there couldn't be anything left in her system.

But she looked like shit, her lipstick smeared, her black eyeliner running down her face, and her skin tone vaguely off-color. Girls her age shouldn't be wearing eye make-up anyway, Sylvie thought. It was no wonder those boys didn't realize she was out of her league.

"Roll the window down if you think you need to throw up again."

They were on the GW Parkway, on their way to the house in McLean. Sylvie had waited an hour, and then gotten a helpful bellhop to half-drag, half-carry Rachel to the black Mercedes via the parking garage.

"Not allowed," Rachel mumbled, head against the headrest, eyes closed.

"Just this once," Sylvie said with a pang of sympathy. Poor kid. Still following the rules, even when plastered. "Just if you feel sick."

Rachel didn't answer, and Sylvie stepped on the gas a little harder. She was breaking the ten-miles-over-the-speed-limit rule by a good fifteen miles, but she wanted to get Rachel home. Would she get pulled over? Automatically, she started planning her approach to the cops if she did: hands on the wheel, friendly, but not too friendly. Should she admit to the various weapons in the car? Mention her employer?

Her strategizing kept her busy until they were almost home. The gates swung open as the car neared them, and as Sylvie pulled into the long driveway, she couldn't help a sigh of relief and another glance at Rachel. Sylvie really wanted to get her inside, and not only because she didn't want to clean the car. All the alcohol ought to be out of Rachel's system, but the girl didn't look good. She'd feel better after a shower and something to eat.

But as she reached the house, instead of pulling around to the garage, Sylvie hit the brakes, a trickle of adrenaline quickening her pulse. Someone was in the house—she could feel it.

She looked up at the imposing brick façade with its Italian limestone trim. The floodlights had gone on automatically, spreading their warm and welcoming light over the double staircase that led to the front terrace, and the windows were dark, as they should be. It didn't matter. Sylvie knew someone was there.

She closed her eyes, the better to let her sixth sense work. This was the reason Ty would never let her go. Sight, sound, touch, feel, taste, and for Sylvie, something else: something that let her detect the presence of people and understand what they were feeling.

For a bodyguard, it was a valuable gift.

For a Marine, it had been priceless.

Sylvie froze, hands tightening on the steering wheel. Damn it. She recognized that feel-flavor-sound. What the hell was he doing here?

She licked her lips and glanced at Rachel, who was leaning against the car door, her head propped against the window, her eyes closed. She could back out, turn the car around, and run. But that would get complicated. What would she do with Rachel? And it was probably too late. If Lucas had found her here, he wouldn't walk away.

Reluctantly, her foot light on the gas pedal, Sylvie pulled the car around to the garage. He was in the second floor study, the one right next to the master bedroom suite. She'd get Rachel tucked away in her own bedroom and then go see what he wanted.

Knowing that it was Lucas waiting, not a burglar or a kidnapper, didn't slow Sylvie's heart rate. If anything, a combination of dread and anticipation had it racing. How long had it been? A decade at least, she realized.

That time in Milan was the last. She'd been just out of the corps, angry, bitter. He'd been . . . rich. Her lips quirked as she helped Rachel up the back staircase, her hands gently guiding the girl's wavering steps. He'd always been rich, of course, and wasn't that half the problem?

She would have been what, twenty-seven? Her thoughts continued inexorably on. They'd been in the galleria, that street with the huge glass ceiling by the cathedral. She'd been drinking espresso at some café, wondering what she was going to do with her life, and he'd been walking by with that woman, the one with the honey-colored hair and the little black dress that probably cost more than a Marine earned in a month. Walking and laughing until he saw her, and then his face froze.

Sylvie felt almost nauseated. Milan hadn't ended well. She pushed away the memories of Lucas's lips on her skin, his hands caressing her, the bedroom in his posh hotel that they didn't leave for two days, the bitter words that she'd thrown at him when she stormed away.

Had he looked for her then? She hated to admit it, even privately, but she probably owed him an apology. Maybe more than one.

Or maybe her sick feeling was caused by the smell of vomit that lingered around Rachel.

She wondered what had happened to the blonde.

"Do you want to take a shower?" she asked the girl as they entered her bedroom. Instinctively, Sylvie assessed the room. Ugh. She'd seen the house blueprints for security drills, so she knew where Rachel's room was, but this was the first time she'd ever been inside it. It was pretty but cold. White furniture, mauve walls, and the only personal touches were the crowded bookshelves.

"Uh-uh." Rachel shook her head.

"You should brush your teeth and change your clothes."

"Don't wanna," Rachel mumbled, dropping onto the bed, and letting her eyes close.

Sylvie eyed her, not quite sure, and then made a decision. "On your feet," she ordered, using the voice that in a different life had made recruits cower.

Rachel's eyes opened and her head rose. "Wha—" she started.

"Come on," Sylvie said, taking her arm and tugging her up, off the bed, toward the bathroom. The bathroom was as bad as the bedroom, both ostentatious and somehow austere. Marble, glass, gold-plated fixtures, but none of the mess that would say a teenager actually worried about pimples in front of the multiple mirrors. "You can get in the shower on your own, or I can put you there. Which is it going to be?"

Rachel batted Sylvie's hands away, then spotted her bedraggled self in the mirror. She winced. "All right," she said. "Okay."

Sylvie gave her a considering look. Satisfied, she said, "I'll be back to check on you."

Closing the door to the bedroom behind her, Sylvie took a deep breath. Why was Lucas here, she wondered, as she headed to the study. Why had he come looking for her? And why hadn't he turned on the lights, she thought irritably, flipping the switch by the door.

The look of surprise on his face as he looked up from an open desk drawer was an answer of sorts to her questions. Without pause, without thought, she took two steps sideways, putting her back to the wall instead of the open doorway as she slid her hand smoothly into the carefully disguised slit in her little black cocktail dress and pulled out the semi-automatic that had been holstered at her waist. She flowed naturally into a comfortable shooter's stance, both arms up, gun aimed at him, as her brain finally caught up with her actions: he hadn't known. He wasn't here for her.

She concentrated, reaching out with her sixth sense, searching for other intruders. Was he alone? The only other presence she felt was Rachel, so she let the tension drop out of her shoulders as she frowned at him.

"Beth?" He looked older, she noted. The black hair had a few touches of silver, and there were new lines around his eyes. It looked good on him. *What did you do to your hair?'* he thought. *'And—ruffles? Really?'*

She resisted the urge to touch her hair, tightening her grip on the gun. The color, a demure brown, was much less noticeable than her natural ginger and much better suited for the invisible companion she aspired to be. As for the ruffles, *'Tough to hide a gun under a skin-tight dress,'* she answered the thought. "What the hell are you doing here, Lucas?"

The flood of feeling she got back from him didn't answer the question, but she tried to sort out the emotions. He was angry, frustrated, searching for something.

But not searching for her.

And not searching for Rachel.

She straightened, letting her gun drop to her side. If her charge wasn't in danger, she shouldn't be holding a weapon on Lucas. Yeah, she wanted to know what he thought he was doing, but not enough to risk hurting him.

"Same question goes," Lucas answered. "What's your involvement with Chesney?" Sylvie felt him thinking but the thoughts were moving too quickly for her to catch. The emotions, though— suspicion, hostility, a wary anger—those were as clear as if he were acting them out in semaphores.

Sylvie looked down, busying herself with putting her gun back into its concealed holster, as she debated her response. Then, with a one-shouldered shrug, she told him the truth. "I work for him. Part of his security team." Looking up, she added with a wry twist to her mouth, "You know, the ones tasked with stopping people from breaking into his house and ransacking his desk?"

The sense of hostility she felt from him lessened, but only slightly. "Hardly ransacked," he said, pushing the drawer closed and standing. "No one was supposed to be here tonight."

'*True*,' she thought to him, '*but how do you know that?*' Aloud, she said, "Rachel wasn't feeling well. I brought her home early. And you're the one who's not supposed to be here. I should call the police, you know."

'*Yeah, right,*' his thought came quickly. '*And let the whole DC area know your security wasn't good enough to keep me out?*' His words, though, were more conciliatory. "We should talk."

Talk? Inadvertently, her gaze dropped to his lips. That's what he'd said the last time they met, but that wasn't what they'd done. Wasn't what she'd done. He was giving her the perfect opportunity to apologize. She might never stop feeling guilty, but at least she could be honest about her faults. "About Milan," she said. "I'm sorry."

He looked startled. "No," he replied, shaking his head. He paused, then continued, looking troubled, "You weren't wrong. But that's not . . . ."

She wondered what word he was searching for. Important? Relevant? Meaningful? She didn't want him to say any of them, so she spoke first. "Rachel might come looking for me any minute. You need to get out of here."

Lucas's eyes flickered around the room, a glance that tried to take it all in and store every detail, and then he stepped away from the desk.

"Looking for a safe?" she asked him, lips tight. She might be letting him go, but he needn't think he was coming back. Chesney didn't need to know about this, but she had to tell Ty. They'd find Lucas's entry point and close the hole in their security immediately. '*How did you get in?*'

He grinned at her, and she knew he'd read the underlying thought, not only the surface words. She narrowed her eyes at him, not quite a glare, and he put his hands up, in open-handed innocence. "I couldn't miss that. You know how it goes."

She did know. The two of them together reinforced each other's abilities. Sylvie hadn't even had—or known she had—her sixth sense until she started spending time with Lucas in high school. When he wasn't around, she never got clear thoughts, just flavors, sensations. Together, though, it was as if their two abilities created a feedback loop, making both of them stronger. She could understand thoughts and he started seeing below the surface, feeling people's emotional responses as well as hearing their superficial thoughts.

'*Did you take the security cameras down?*' she asked him mentally, as she gestured him out the door ahead of her. She heard the sound of the shower in Rachel's bathroom, but she put a finger over her lips to indicate the need for silence anyway. '*I don't want to get recorded with you.*'

'*In the back,*' he conceded, so she led him that way, treading as quietly as possible. Her mind was racing, trying to decide what to say, what to ask. She had so many questions. At the back door, they paused and she turned to face him.

She might not see him again, so she had to ask the most important question first.

"How's Dillon?" She tried to muster a smile. "He ought to be in college now, right? Did he follow you into the Ivy Leagues?"

"Beth . . ." he started and then stopped.

"Sylvie, now," she said into the silence. Why couldn't she read him? His emotions weren't making sense to her, as if they were a scent she couldn't identify, a taste she didn't recognize.

"You went back to your own name?"

She nodded, as if it wasn't important, as if reclaiming her name hadn't caused her months of mixed emotions, a complex twist of anger, pain, relief, satisfaction, grief, happiness, even fear. She was still trying to understand what she was sensing from him. "Lucas, what aren't you saying?"

"It's complicated." The words on the surface were meaningless. It was the words below that mattered. '*He's dead.*'

"He—what?" The words felt strange in her mouth, as if her face had suddenly gone numb and her lips couldn't shape the letters.

"It's complicated," he said again.

'*You were supposed to keep him safe!*' Her thoughts were a scream. She brought her fist to her mouth, biting down so the sound couldn't escape.

"Sylvie." Lucas reached for her, putting his hands on her shoulders, but Sylvie brought her arms up, knocking his away. Stepping back, she glared at him.

"Get out." She reinforced the words with mental fury, '*Get out or I will call the police.*'

CHAPTER TWO

At the sound of the woman's name, fascination overcame Dillon's anxiety. He let his father disappear into the darkness outside the house without a second thought.

Sylvie?

Really?

Holy crap.

She didn't look anything like her picture. He'd only seen the one, taken shortly after he was born. In that image she was a pretty teenager, gazing down at the dark-haired bundle in her arms with an awed smile. Lucas, standing next to her, was looking at her face instead of the baby, his expression almost dazed.

But she'd had a cloud of red-gold hair, completely different from the brown hair that was tied up in some kind of fancy braid now. And she'd been . . . well, round. Curvy. Okay, he could admit it: she'd been chubby. Maybe it was because she'd just had a baby? But he'd thought it was what she was like.

When he'd imagined her, it was as an older version of the same girl, the mom version. Like Mrs. Weasley from the *Harry Potter* books.

Instead, she was Alice from *Resident Evil*. Except with a stupid-looking black dress with layers of puffy ruffles that Alice wouldn't be caught dead in. But still, the way she pulled out that gun? That was seriously cool.

Dillon frowned as he thought about the conversation he'd overheard. His dad recognized her right away, but he'd called her Beth. And then she'd said something about Milan. What was that about? Dillon felt a stab of annoyance as he realized what it must mean: his dad had seen her since she'd disappeared.

She'd been standing motionless by the door, but when she finally moved and Dillon got a better look at her, his frown deepened. She was paler and she was moving slowly, without the grace and speed of her earlier actions, almost stumbling as she made her way through the house until she reached the foyer. At the base of the wide, sweeping staircase, she stopped, resting one hand on the carved wooden banister, swaying a little, eyes closed.

19

What did his dad do to her?

She'd asked about him, about college, and Lucas didn't answer, not really. But then she'd snapped at him and kicked him out. Why?

Damn. Only one answer made sense. His mom read minds, too. Dillon wasn't sure whether to be pleased or annoyed: here was further proof that he should have had a psychic gift of his own.

But that meant . . . oh.

Her weird behavior was because she knew he was dead.

Dillon felt guilty. Watching people be sad about his death wasn't the worst part of being a ghost but it was close. But even as he had the thought, Sylvie pulled herself together. She shook her head, straightened her back, and took a deep breath before starting up the stairs.

Dillon trailed behind her, not sure how he felt about her quick recovery. Didn't he deserve a little more than that? Like, really? Two minutes of sad and then she was over him? On the other hand, at least she wasn't going to cry. He would not have liked watching her cry.

At the top of the stairs, she took a left and headed down a corridor. Dillon followed, looking around curiously. He'd never been in a house this big or this ridiculously grand. The white walls were decorated with fancy trim, both along the ceiling and breaking up each chunk of wall. Lights tucked unobtrusively into the ceiling shone on paintings, mostly pastel landscapes in gold frames, spaced every few feet. The hardwood floors were smooth and shiny, with an ornate carpet running down the middle of the hallway.

Sylvie knocked on a door and waited.

Dillon wished he knew what was going on. What was his mom doing? And why had his dad come to this house? What was he looking for, if not his mom? He hadn't been able to talk to Lucas during the flight, but after they'd picked up a rental car and headed out onto the highway, he'd tried to ask Lucas what he was doing. If he had a voice, he would have said something like, "Why are you pretending to be some guy named Murray? What are you doing?" But he'd abbreviated his texted question to, *Why Murray?*

Big mistake.

His dad had answered with annoying brevity. "It's a clean identity and I don't want to leave a paper trail." Oh, like that was helpful. His dad wasn't an undercover agent. Why was he worried about leaving a trail?

Dillon had still been formulating his next question when his dad said, "Sorry, Dill, but I've got to turn the cell phone off. Can't risk it buzzing while I'm working."

Working? Was that what he called it? Dillon had tagged along, wondering the whole while. It didn't look like work to him; it looked like an impressively efficient burglary. Except for the part where he got caught before he managed to get anything, anyway.

Sylvie knocked again, a little harder this time. "Rachel?"

Dillon looked at her, looked at the door, then shrugged and pushed himself through it. Not waiting around for people to open doors was one of the few advantages of being a ghost. In the back of his mind, he imagined his grandmother scolding him for his lack of manners. But ghosts can't knock, he protested silently to the voice of his conscience, shutting it up for the moment.

Inside the room, a girl in cotton pajamas, dark hair twisted in wet tangles down her back, hurriedly slid a book onto a shelf. Dillon frowned. Something about her hurry was furtive, as if she was trying to hide the book. He drifted closer.

The spine was black with a red ribbon on it. *Eclipse*, he read. Was that one of those weird vampire books?

"Rachel!" The knock was harder, the voice a demand.

"Coming." The girl glanced back at the shelf, touching the book one last time, then crossed to the door. Dillon took a look at the other books on the crowded shelves. He didn't recognize most of them, but she had a couple by Terry Pratchett. That was a good sign.

As the girl opened the door, Dillon wondered who she was. But he supposed if he was going to be haunting her house, he'd find out soon enough.

*****

Dillon was dead.

Had been dead for a while, judging by the flavor of Lucas's emotions.

Sylvie knew that if she let it, the pain would overwhelm her. Every morning when she woke up and thought of Dillon, wondered what he was doing, where he was, every morning he'd already been gone. Every night before she fell asleep, when she'd wished him a silent good night and God bless, he'd already been gone.

Was this what drowning felt like? This choking sensation closing off her throat?

But she had a job to do.

Rachel.

She needed to check on Rachel, make sure she was okay, then test the security system, find out how Lucas had gotten in, get the cameras back online . . . yes, she needed to work. To make her charge safe.

She stuffed the pain down, burying it deep inside her. Later, she promised herself. Later.

Rachel was fine. A little forlorn-looking still, but going straight to bed and to sleep. Twenty minutes ago Sylvie might have insisted she eat something or at the very least rehydrate, preferably using a drink with electrolytes. Instead, Sylvie just nodded and walked away, heading straight to the security room on the lowest level of the house.

She and Rachel had come in that way, through the garage, and up the back stairs to the third level where the bedrooms and Chesney's private office were located. Lucas, though, exited on the mid-level, through the French doors that opened from the large family room onto the back terrace. But how did he bypass the security system?

The room that the security team used as their base of operations was tucked between the caterer's kitchen and a staff work room. A wide-screen monitor displayed multiple camera feeds. Lucas had said that the ones in back were down, but they all appeared to be running. Sylvie ran a quick system check. Managing the technology wasn't her job, and apart from turning the system off and on, the system check was all she knew how to do. But the lights were green and it seemed to be working the way it was supposed to.

She tapped her fingers on the desk, debating, and then, with a twist of her mouth, she picked up a phone and called Ty.

"Clear?" He didn't bother with hello when he answered, jumping straight to the information he wanted.

"Not exactly," Sylvie answered reluctantly. She glanced at the monitors again. Everything looked as if it was running properly, but it couldn't be.

"Not exactly? You're on the house phone."

"Confirmed. The house is currently clear." Sylvie put a little extra emphasis on the second to last word.

"Currently?" Sylvie could hear the shock in Ty's voice.

"Confirmed." She waited. In the background, she heard the noise of the party; the faint formal music, the dull clamor of conversations, the clinking of silverware against fine china. Rachel's 'friends' had made an early start to the evening, but the diners must be on dessert by now. Or maybe that was wishful thinking; she wanted Ty back at the house sooner, not later.

Finally the noise quieted, and Ty's voice came back, "Report."

Sylvie paused. She didn't know how to explain what had happened. At least not where she couldn't be sure who could overhear. "We had a visitor," she finally said. "I don't know how he got inside. The security system is up and running but he was in Chesney's office."

"What? What the hell were you—"

"It was fine." Sylvie interrupted Ty. She knew he was questioning her decision to enter the house, especially with Rachel in tow. If she hadn't recognized Lucas, it would have been a terrible decision. Maybe it had been anyway. "But I don't know how he got past the system. It's still online and it looks like it's working the way it's supposed to. Can you send a tech?"

"Fine?" There was a sarcastic edge to Ty's voice.

Sylvie pinched the bridge of her nose, trying to hold back a hasty retort. She couldn't do this, not right now.

She wanted to get home. She needed to get home, to the safety of her small apartment, the comfort of her solitude. She wanted to close the door behind her and shut the world out. "Ty, do you really want to have this conversation while you're on duty at a party? Or do you want to send me a damn tech?"

This time the silence was on his end. "Was anything stolen?"

"No." And then Sylvie added, "Not that I'm aware of." Could Lucas have stuffed something in a pocket before she'd gotten there? Damn, it hadn't even occurred to her to check.

"All right, I'll tell—"

"No."

"No?"

"Chesney, right?"

"Mr. Chesney," Ty corrected her dryly.

Sylvie tried to restrain her sigh. "Yeah, whatever. Don't tell him."

"Are you sure?"

"Yeah."

"Is this . . . ." Ty paused. They didn't often speak about her sixth sense. Ty knew about it, had for years. But for both of them, not talking about it had become habit.

After Sylvie ran away from Tassamara, she'd joined the Marines. Her first duty station was Somalia. Peace-keeping forces, that's what they called them.

Right. Peace-keeping. Sure.

In a world dominated by strong men, Sylvie kept her head down, but on a terrible October day Ty listened when she told him what she could do. For the next decade, they'd stayed close. And when the detailed background checks required for intelligence jobs killed their chances of career advancement, they'd joined forces.

In Sylvie's case, she'd gotten out of the Marines barely ahead of her dishonorable discharge. It turned out that stealing the identity of a dead girl to join the service was frowned upon. Sylvie would have loved to protest—she'd been seventeen, too young to join. She hadn't had a high school diploma and they would have rejected her. Hadn't her decade of service proved her worth? But there wasn't any arguing with the system.

And in Ty's case, 'don't ask, don't tell' hadn't been enough. He hadn't told, but he hadn't been as careful as he needed to be either. He'd never get the position as intelligence specialist that he'd been up for, and now that the service knew . . . well, his military career was dead.

Sylvie had been bitter, too bitter to move forward, but Ty had been more practical. Fortunately for her, he'd dragged her along. As he built his own security business, her skill as a bodyguard and a reader of people had been a cornerstone of his success. Enough so that he paused now, willing to listen to her reservations.

"I don't know," she said. Everything was churning inside of her. She couldn't make sense of the way she felt. But she knew she didn't want to tell Chesney that Lucas had been in his office. Not now, not yet.

"All right," Ty said slowly. "Can we talk tomorrow?"

"Yes." The words felt like a lifeline to Sylvie. Tomorrow. She'd let everything happen tomorrow.

CHAPTER THREE

She did cry.

And she had pictures. Way more of them than she should have had.

She shook them out of an envelope, and then laid them out, one by one, across her bed. Dillon perched on the nightstand next to the bed and looked over her shoulder. There he was as a baby, and that was okay, she'd been around when those pictures were taken. But then he was a little dark-haired toddler, and how did she get those? She had three of them, all different, all dog-eared and worn. Then that picture, that was him on his first day of school. He'd seen it before. And then that was his first soccer photo, followed by a couple snapshots from a Christmas. He might have been eight or nine when those were taken, he wasn't sure.

How had she gotten all those photographs? Dillon couldn't help feeling annoyed. His dad must have been in touch with her. Why hadn't he known? What was the big secret?

"You could have come and visited, you know," he told her. She didn't respond, of course, just reached through him for the box of the tissues that stood behind him. "Or called, maybe. Like on my birthday?"

She cried quietly, no gulping sobs, just a steady stream of tears rolling down her face as she touched the photographs with gentle fingers and piled up the tissues on the bed next to her.

It was weird. When Dillon had taken those pills, he'd known he might be risking his life, but he hadn't really cared. He'd been so tired of being ordinary. He wanted to be like his dad and his uncle and his grandpa and his Aunt Nat. Oh, sure, Grace and his gran were fine without being psychic, but that was different. They were girls. He could almost feel his gran smacking the back of his head for thinking that, but that didn't make it feel less true.

If he'd thought about dying, really dying, he still might not have cared. Okay, he wouldn't have done it if he'd known it was going to kill him, but if he'd imagined his own death, he would have thought that it wouldn't matter to him. After all, he'd be dead. And the people he left behind? Sure, they'd cry a little, be sad. But then they'd have a funeral and life would go back to normal. Instead his gran died. His dad stopped smiling entirely. And now this total stranger was using up an entire box of tissues on him.

Dillon felt helpless. He hated it.

Her phone rang and she reached for it, answering it without looking. "Yeah?"

"We have to talk."

Dillon was sitting close enough that he could hear the voice on the other end of the line. His dad.

"Go to hell, Lucas." Sylvie disconnected and set the phone back down. But the call seemed to have motivated her. She gathered the photographs together, and slid them back into the envelope, and then uncrossed her legs and stood.

She went over to the black dress lying on the floor of the room and picked it up.

When they'd gotten here, she'd unlocked the door, walked into the apartment, straight into the bedroom, and straight out of the dress. Dillon had closed his eyes quickly—yeah, being invisible meant that he could be as much of a voyeur as he liked, but wow, it was totally creepy to think of watching your mom like that—while she pulled on a t-shirt and yoga pants. Now, though, she shook out the dress and held it close, looking it over as if checking it for stains or smells, then with a shake of her head, tossed it over the back of the chair in front of a small desk.

"That's a really ugly dress," Dillon said conversationally. He knew she couldn't hear him, but he liked talking anyway. And maybe she'd be a sensitive, one of those people who got vague impressions of what spirits were saying. That'd be cool. Maybe she'd decide to go shopping for a new dress. It had been a long time since Dillon had been in a mall.

He supposed he could text her, but what would he say? Hi, Mom? That might be awkward, but he started considering his options as she disappeared into the bathroom and he pushed himself off the nightstand. This night had been the most exciting of his ghostly life, but she was probably going to bed now. Time for him to explore.

As the water started in the bathroom, he checked out the apartment. It was tiny. A short hallway from the front door opened onto a little kitchen, with barely room for one person to stand in it. The living room, next to the kitchen, held a couch, a small table with a couple of chairs, and several bookcases, with a door that opened straight into an overcrowded bedroom that held a double bed, a dresser and a desk and chair.

Security jobs must not pay much money, Dillon thought. Or maybe this was a really nice neighborhood? He hadn't been able to tell much from the outside because it was so dark, except that it was a tall apartment building. He'd have to take another look in the morning. It was a quick drive from the fancy house, though, so that might be why she lived here.

Still, if he had to guess much about her from her apartment, he'd mostly guess that she was camping. This wasn't a home. Except for the bookcases, there wasn't any evidence that she really lived here. The couch could have been a Salvation Army reject, the table and chairs were plastic. He would bet that she could walk away from everything in the apartment without a single regret.

Maybe that's who she was? What she was like? She'd left her kid without much regret, it seemed.

But then he thought about her tears and knew that he wasn't being fair. He didn't understand her, that was for sure. But he wasn't stupid: it was obvious that she cared about him.

And he'd had a pretty good life. He looked around the tiny apartment and tried to imagine what it would have been like to live in it. Then he thought back to his earliest memories. His aunts and uncle had been more like big sisters and a big brother. The house was crowded and noisy, but in a good way. Someone was always around to read him a story or get him a snack or play a game with him.

His gran and grandpa might not have planned on raising another kid, but they'd made it fun. They'd definitely taken him to Disney World often enough: with annual passes, sometimes he'd felt like the Magic Kingdom was the playground down the street. Not that he needed another playground—his backyard had been enough.

His grandpa had hired an architect to design his tree house. Remembering the window boxes made him smile. Gran kept planting flowers in them, but the flowers always died. Either he watered them too much or not enough, never in-between. It was a great tree house. In fact, he thought, looking around again, this entire apartment might be smaller than his tree house.

Truth was, he'd never spent a lot of time missing his mom. He wasn't some kid who felt forever betrayed by her absence so he wasn't going to dump that on her now. He'd had a good life. It was a shame he'd screwed it up, but that was on him, not her.

In the other room, her phone rang. Dillon peeked in as she crossed to the bed, her toothbrush in one hand.

"How did you get this number?"

Must be his dad again, Dillon thought, and hurried to the bed so that he could hear both sides of the conversation.

"Sylvie—"

"This is an unlisted number," she snapped at him. "How did you get it?"

"That is not important," Lucas snapped back. "I have to talk to you."

"What the fuck do you think there is to say? You—he—I trusted you. Asshole!" Sylvie spit out the last word, then hit the disconnect button on the phone, and dropped it on the bed.

Hmm, thought Dillon. He felt a smile tugging at his lips. His mom was kind of a bitch. She was definitely not the Mrs. Weasley of his imaginings.

Hanging out with her was going to be fun.

*****

Sylvie felt hung over.

She wished she was. She hated crying.

That damn therapist that Ty made her go to a few years back said that crying was healthy. Cortisol and stress hormones were released in the salty tears, she'd said. Sylvie would rather get rid of her stress through good old-fashioned sweat.

She glanced at her watch. She was sitting on a bench in Marion Park in DC, waiting for Ty. The day was crisp, the sky a pristine blue, and the small playground was already populated with well-bundled toddlers.

She didn't want to be here.

As soon as Ty got here and they discussed yesterday's events, she'd head to the gym. With any luck, she could beat the Saturday afternoon crowds. And then maybe later she'd have time for a run on the Capital Crescent trail. She probably wouldn't run the twenty-two mile Rock Creek Park loop, but five or six miles, maybe even eight, might clear her head and help her shake off the way she felt.

Her phone vibrated in the pocket of her leather jacket, and she pulled it out and looked at it. Lucas. Again. She stuffed it back in the pocket. She wasn't talking to him.

"But it's not fair." The words were a whine, and Sylvie tried to hide her wince as an adult man led a little girl in a pink jacket by the hand to her bench. Great. Company. Just what she was not in the mood for.

"Five minute time-out," responded the man firmly. "You sit right there." He glanced at Sylvie, apology in his eyes, and she nodded, a slight tip of her head, to let him know that it was fine. She wasn't enthusiastic, but she was sitting on the bench closest to the playground, inside the wrought iron fence that surrounded the park. It was the best spot for keeping an eye on a kid.

"You're so mean, Daddy." The little girl sniffled as her father turned and crossed back to the climbing structure. A littler one over there must be his, too, Sylvie realized, as he helped a toddler climb the steps to the short, curving slide. "But I want some." The girl kicked her feet sulkily. "I want some."

Sylvie glanced at her. She was maybe four or five, Sylvie thought, probably cute when she wasn't pouting.

"I want some," the girl whined again, even though her father clearly couldn't hear her.

"Kid," Sylvie said. "If you want something, you need to choose a better way to get it."

The girl looked at her warily, and Sylvie continued. "You're using a whiny voice. It's only good for two uses." She held up her hand, and extended her index finger. "One, annoying grownups. If that's your goal, you're doing great, and you should keep going."

The little girl's lower lip slid out, just a little, and Sylvie quickly added, holding up a second finger, "And two, telling grownups you're tired and need a nap. It's a good voice for that, too." She could sense the girl's doubt turning into curiosity. "But if you want to get a grownup to give you something, you need to find your sweet voice. Do you have a sweet voice?"

She waited. The expressions on the girl's face were easy enough to read, but the flavor of her feelings was even easier—mystified by this adult talking to her, but also intrigued.

"Yes, I have a sweet voice," the little girl finally said.

"Let's hear it," Sylvie prompted, then let her eyes go wide as the girl tried out an over-the-top saccharine voice. "Wow, that's sweet. Maybe we should practice?"

She and the girl spent the next few minutes solemnly discussing voices and ways to get what she wanted, until finally the father called out, "Time's up, Maria."

The girl hopped off the bench and then paused, as she said, "I'll try right now," and gave Sylvie a little nod good-bye.

"Wait." Sylvie stopped her as she turned to go. She had one more question. "What did you want to get?"

"Ice cream," Maria answered. "Sometimes on the way home, we get ice cream from the corner store," she said, pointing across the street to the Capitol Supreme market with its neon grocery sign. Concrete flower pots and a single umbrella table on the sidewalk suggested that in warmer weather it might be a pleasant place to pick up a sandwich or quick meal. "But Daddy said no."

Sylvie bit back her smile. "One last idea, then. When you're wearing your winter coat, maybe aim for hot chocolate?"

The little girl grinned at her and ran off as Ty finally appeared, pushing a stroller. He greeted her, saying hello and handing her a white coffee cup, as the toddler in the stroller chortled, "Silly, silly, silly!" and reached with extended arms for Sylvie.

"Sorry we're late," Ty said. "The line at Peregrine was out the door."

"No worries." Sylvie set the coffee down on the bench next to her and reached to unbuckle Ty's son, saying, "Joshua, Joshua, Joshua," to the excited boy, and trying not to let her feelings show.

But Ty saw something anyway. "You look like shit. What happened last night?"

"Little ears, Ty, little ears," Sylvie reprimanded him as she finally got Joshua free.

"Oh, right." He looked sheepish as he glanced at his son, who was all wrapped up in winter clothes, a hat on his head, mittens on his hands.

"Jeremy's not gonna like it when Josh starts greeting people that way." Sylvie lifted the little boy out and tried not to flinch as he hugged her, wrapping his arms around her neck and kissing her cheek wetly. She stroked his dark head and said, "Hey, baby."

"Me big boy," he protested, already kicking to get down.

"That's right," she confirmed for him. "You're huge."

She set him on the ground. "Me play," he announced, as he turned and marched toward the slides. Sylvie watched him go.

Her eyes felt hot again. Damn it, she was not going to cry.

"The security system checked out clear," Ty told her, voice neutral. She threw a quick sideways glance in his direction. He was watching his son, eyes on the playground, but he'd seen her expression. He was looking away from her out of tact, not worry for Joshua's safety.

"Dillon's dead," she told him flatly. Ty was her best friend, the only one who knew her story.

For a moment, he looked blank, and then, "Oh, Sylvie." He sat down on the bench and put his arm around her shoulders. "I'm so sorry."

For a second, two, she leaned into him, feeling the strength of his chest next to her, and then she straightened, and took a deep breath. "Not like I knew him, right?" She tried to make the words casual, but a sniffle escaped. His arm tightened around her and she pressed her lips together.

They sat in silence, watching the children, until Ty started. "So . . . ?"

She could feel his questions. "Why does Chesney need such good security?" she asked. The question seemed random, but it was the thought that had been bothering her underneath her sorrow last night. She had no idea what Lucas had been up to, but she knew he wasn't a common criminal. Why had he been in Chesney's house?

"What?" Startled, Ty glanced away from the climbing structure, where Joshua was pulling himself up the steps to the slide, to look at her face. She guessed he'd been expecting answers, not questions.

"Chesney. His security. Us. Why does he need round-the-clock guards in Washington DC? And on his kid?" Sylvie picked up the coffee cup by her side and took a gulp, ignoring the bitterness of the warm liquid.

Ty shrugged, letting his arm drop. "Can't say I've thought about it. Politics? Business? Family issues? His divorce was a long time ago, but he's got sole custody of Rachel. Maybe he's worried about the ex. Or maybe he's just paranoid."

"Maybe," Sylvie said. "Why us instead of AlecCorp?"

"Because we're better," Ty answered. "I know he's got a financial interest in AlecCorp, but they're mercenaries. Would you want them around your kid?"

Sylvie tried to keep her expression blank, but knew a flicker of pain escaped.

"Sorry," Ty apologized. "I didn't mean . . . I wasn't thinking."

She shook her head. She understood it had been a rhetorical question. And Ty was right. AlecCorp employees were the type who gave private security contractors a bad name all around the world, the ones who believed they could get away with murder and usually did.

"Maybe he wants to keep his business interests and his personal life separate?" Ty suggested.

"It just seems strange."

"He can afford us." Ty's tone was pragmatic. "That's good enough for me. Tell me what happened last night."

Sylvie took another sip, then set her cup down on the bench next to her. She stuffed her hands in the pockets of her jacket, feeling the cool chill of her phone, wishing she'd worn gloves. She'd been sitting for long enough that the day was starting to feel cold. "As we drove in, I realized someone was inside the house and I recognized him. I thought he was looking for me, so I was surprised but not worried. Turned out he didn't know I was there. He was in Chesney's office, searching the desk."

"This was someone who knew you before?" Before, Sylvie knew, meant before the Marines, before she'd run away, before she'd changed identities. Before. It was an eternity ago.

She nodded, her mouth twisting. "Dillon's dad."

"Ah, the kid." Ty's eyebrows rose, a gleam of humor in his voice.

Sylvie grimaced. "Twenty years ago, a kid," she pointed out. Lucas. She shook her head. It was hard to remember that Lucas had ever been a kid.

Sylvie moved to Tassamara with her mom in her junior year of high school. It was the smallest town they'd ever lived in and Sylvie wasn't happy to be there. But she and her mom, they moved a lot, and Sylvie had learned not to ask too many questions.

She'd also learned how to quickly size up a new school: she could peg the bullies, the cliques, the leaders and the losers by the end of a first day. But in Tassamara the usual rigid social structure of a public high school had been much more fluid. The head cheerleader was dating the editor of the yearbook, instead of the quarterback. That was just plain weird. Maybe it was because the school was so small, with less than 300 students.

And Lucas had already been six feet tall and damn cute. How was she supposed to know he was a freshman? By the time she'd found out, it had been too late. Hell, maybe it had always been too late, she thought, trying not to feel bitter.

From the moment she met him, it had been magic.

"So what was he doing? Doesn't he work for some company in Florida?" Ty sounded curious, as well as worried about the break in security. "And how did he get inside? The system tested clean. We couldn't find anything wrong with it."

Sylvie shrugged. "I don't know," she said. "He worked for his parents' company the last time I saw him, but that was years ago."

"Syl, if we've got a hole in our security, we've got to fix it."

She shook her head. "It's unfixable," she said, realizing the truth of the statement as she said it. "If the system was fine, Lucas must have gotten the code."

"We have a leak?" Ty reacted immediately. He stood, the shock in his voice showing his sense of betrayal, although Sylvie could also feel it radiating from him. The codes were changed every few days, which meant only current staff knew them. And every employee was personally screened by Ty; if someone had sold the codes, it was someone they knew.

Sylvie didn't let Ty's emotion faze her. She was watching Joshua, who seemed to have gotten distracted from his usual pattern of up-the-steps, down-the-slide, over and over and over again. "It's tough to prevent leaking information to a telepath," she said. "I wouldn't worry about it."

"Oh, he's . . . ." Ty paused, and Sylvie could almost hear the unspoken, "like you."

"Not exactly, but the same general idea," she told him. "But yeah. And, um, I think you need to . . . ." She gestured with her elbow, not taking her hands out of her pockets, at the steps to the slide, where Joshua was attempting to wrestle a toy shovel out of another boy's hand. The other boy was starting to scream in protest and a worried mom was turning their way.

"Damn." Ty hurried the short distance over to the climbing structure and started negotiating with Joshua while Sylvie buried her neck a little deeper in her jacket, hunching her shoulders.

What had Lucas been up to? Why had he been in Chesney's house? The phone in her pocket vibrated again.

Maybe she should talk to him.

But Lucas . . . he was like a drug. It had taken her years to get over the last time.

Unresolved conflict, that damn therapist had said. But some conflicts were unresolvable.

Her phone vibrated again and Sylvie pulled it out, reluctantly. She glanced at the display. It was a text, not a call this time. She touched the button to display the message.

Her heart froze.

You would have been a good mom.

That bastard.

Sylvie stood, feeling as if her face had gone numb as Ty headed back, carrying a squirming, protesting Joshua.

"You okay?" he asked sharply, seeing something in her expression.

"Yeah." She nodded, just once. "His name's Lucas Latimer. You should run a background check. We should try to discover what he wants with Chesney. And we should up the rotation so someone's at the house 24/7. But don't worry about the security system, I'm sure it's fine." Her voice sounded strange to her, cold and tinny over the ringing in her ears.

"All right." Ty nodded, shifting the complaining Joshua around in his arms.

"I've got to get to the gym," Sylvie said to Ty. "I'll see you Monday."

He nodded again, still looking doubtful.

"Silly," Joshua howled, reaching for Sylvie.

She ignored him. As she turned and walked away, she passed a trash can. Without pausing, she dropped her phone into it.

She'd get a new one with a new number after she ran the twenty-two miles of the Capital Crescent trail and Rock Creek Park loop.

CHAPTER FOUR

Oops, thought Dillon. He'd intended his text message as a compliment. He'd realized while watching Sylvie with the little girl and the toddler that maybe he'd missed out on more than he knew. Yeah, his life had been good, but he might have liked having Sylvie as his mom. But maybe she hadn't taken it that way?

"I'm sorry," he said to her back, following her out of the park. "I wasn't trying to be mean."

She didn't pay any attention, of course. But he hadn't meant to hurt her. He resolved to apologize to her as soon as she got a new phone.

Later that evening, they pulled into the parking lot of a giant mall in her sporty blue Subaru. Sylvie headed directly to the T-Mobile stand in the middle of the mall. As she shopped, Dillon watched the crowds, enjoying his freedom. He missed Rose and Akira, but this was the most excitement he'd had, maybe ever. Now all he had to do was explain that he was here to his mom.

Of course, that might be easier said than done. Maybe he should start by telling her who he was? Or that he was a ghost? No, that'd be bad. But he had time. He'd be able to convince her eventually.

As soon as she walked away from the stand, new phone in hand, Dillon starting texting her, and before she made it to the door of the mall, he'd managed a simple apology. As her phone buzzed, she paused. He stood next to her, watching for her reaction, bouncing on his toes a little. Would she understand?

Her eyes flickered from side to side, and she tilted her head slightly as if she was listening. Then she turned, eyes scanning the crowded mall as she rotated in a slow circle.

Uh-oh.

The slight expression changes on her face, the twitch of a muscle in her cheek, the crease that had appeared in her forehead: it looked as if she was silently talking.

Or trying to.

And then she walked straight back to the guy who'd just sold her the phone and said to him, with a sweet smile that didn't disguise an underlying tension, "I'm so sorry. This isn't going to work for me after all."

"I—you—what?" he stuttered, startled.

"I need to return this phone."

Dillon sighed. His mom was going to be difficult. If only Akira was around to translate for him. But Sylvie would have to get another phone soon. He'd just be persistent. Eventually she'd have to listen, right?

Monday morning, her alarm went off well before daylight. Dillon had been sitting at the window, watching the night, and when she emerged from the bedroom, dressed in lightweight gray sweat pants and a white jacket, he grimaced. He hoped this wasn't going to be another interminable run. Yesterday, he'd chased her down a sunny wooded trail that went on for what felt like forever. If he hadn't been dead, he could never have kept up.

A couple of hours later, she drove up to the fancy house and parked around back. It was close to dark, but there were glimmers of light on the horizon. Dillon didn't have a watch, of course, but if he had to guess, he'd say that it was almost seven.

Sylvie headed straight to the room with the monitors, and Dillon tagged along, wondering what the day would be like. Did she sit in the room watching the screens? That'd be boring. Okay, not as boring as sitting in a parking lot for years. But not exciting. Still, if he knew for sure that she wasn't going anywhere and he wouldn't lose her, he could explore some, check out the house, maybe visit the girl upstairs.

The guy from the park was sitting at a small desk, head down, using two fingers to type. Next to him sat a younger black guy in a dark suit. He was leaning back in his chair, with sneaker-clad feet perched casually on the edge of the desk. They were talking about football but as Sylvie walked into the room, they broke off their conversation.

"Good, you're here," said the park guy.

Sylvie's eyebrows rose. "Where else would I be?"

"I've been trying to reach you. You haven't answered your phone."

"Ah, right." Sylvie glanced over at the monitors, not meeting his eyes. "Phone problems. I need to pick up a new one."

"Well, we've got some schedule changes this week. Here, come take a look." As Sylvie peered over the park guy's shoulder, Dillon's attention was caught by sounds from the next room. He wandered over to see what was going on. Two uniformed maids were chatting as they folded laundry in a big room lined with cupboards. His basic Spanish wasn't good enough to understand what they were saying, but they seemed cheerful.

After glancing back over his shoulder to make sure Sylvie wasn't going anywhere, Dillon explored further down the stone-tiled hallway. A huge kitchen held multiple appliances, including two ovens and three sinks. He wondered how many people lived here and how big their Thanksgiving dinner had been. As he continued down the corridor, he passed an exercise room, lined with mirrors, holding stationary bikes, elliptical trainers, and weight machines, then a living room with couches and chairs. Glass doors opened onto a patio with what looked like a swimming pool. Next up was a room that looked like a mini-theater, with a giant screen on one wall and tiers for seats. Wow, Dillon thought. This house was insane. He wondered what kind of movies they liked. Maybe he'd take up haunting the theater room.

"It's not a problem." That was his mom, and it sounded like she was going somewhere. She stood in the doorway to the security room, back still turned to the hallway, but Dillon hurried back. Maybe he'd hang out at the mansion later but he wanted to stay with Sylvie for a while longer.

The girl, Rachel, who he'd seen the other night, clattered down the stairs. She was wearing a school uniform: a blue blazer over a white shirt, a short gray and blue plaid skirt, gray knee high socks, shiny black shoes.

"Ready?" Sylvie asked, turning to face her.

"Obviously." Rachel didn't look at Sylvie, just pushed past her and out the door to the garage.

Sylvie pressed her lips together as if to hold back her words, then turned and raised an eyebrow at the men in the room behind her. "Coming?"

The black guy swiveled in his chair, dropping his legs to the floor and bounced to his feet. He wasn't big, but he moved like an athlete, Dillon realized, like he knew exactly where his body was in relation to the other objects in the crowded room. "Sounds like Her Highness is in a snit."

"Watch it," Ty said, voice mild, not looking up from his keyboard. "If you screw up and call her that where she can hear you and I have to fire you when we're short-staffed, I'll be pissed."

The other guy tapped his forehead, a casual salute. "You got it, boss man." Putting the emphasis on the name, he added, "Miss Chesney sounds like she's in a snit."

Ty sighed as Sylvie chuckled. "Not much better," he muttered.

"Come on, James," Sylvie said. "Time to get the client to school."

The car was a black Mercedes with dark windows. Rachel was already sitting in the back seat, head up, staring straight ahead of her. James was the driver, Dillon realized, watching as he crossed in front of the car, while Sylvie went around the other way to get into the back with Rachel. Quickly, Dillon pushed himself through the door and took the front passenger seat.

"So, this must be the morning routine, huh?" he asked, feeling cheerful. He wondered what grade Rachel was in. She looked like she was about his age. Maybe he'd start hanging out at her school. He was just as glad that he never had to take another math test, but he'd always liked history and English. He wouldn't mind sitting through a few classes. He peered over the seat, trying to see if she had any books out, but her backpack was tucked neatly at her feet.

"We need to go over your schedule." Sylvie pulled an iPhone out of her pocket.

Score, thought Dillon. Ty must have lent her the phone. He wouldn't text her right away. Maybe he'd wait until tonight, so that she wasn't at work. And so that it wasn't so easy for her to throw the phone away. He stayed turned in his seat, watching Sylvie and Rachel. It wasn't as if he needed to wear his seat belt, after all.

"If we have to." Rachel's voice was flat, expressionless, and she didn't look at Sylvie.

Sylvie glanced at her, but didn't otherwise respond to her attitude. Scrolling through the calendar, she began calmly reciting a list of activities: piano lessons, dance rehearsal, SAT prep, soccer practice, a dentist appointment. It seemed endless. Rachel didn't answer to any of it with more than a sigh, until Sylvie said, "Friday at 3:30, you have an appointment with Dr. Oshuda."

"What? Why?" Rachel's head snapped toward Sylvie so quickly that Dillon winced. That looked like it hurt.

"I don't make the schedule, I just keep it." Sylvie's tone was matter-of-fact, but her glance at Rachel was sympathetic.

"I hate her," Rachel whined. "I really hate her."

Wow, Dillon thought. That was a serious whine, high-pitched and nasal and annoying. He could tell from the flicker of Sylvie's eyes that it annoyed her, too, and a muscle in the driver's jaw jumped as James clenched his teeth.

But then Rachel turned away, staring out the window fixedly, and Dillon saw the gleam of light in her brown eyes that said they'd filled with tears.

Sylvie didn't sigh, but her mouth tightened. "Just tell her about your dreams. Therapists love that."

Rachel didn't look back at Sylvie, but Dillon could see her swallow. James, though, flicked his gaze up to the rearview mirror and raised his eyebrows at Sylvie. She shrugged one shoulder.

"Do you have third period free today?" Sylvie asked.

Rachel nodded silently, sullenly, still staring out the window.

"Do you want us to bring you a Frappuccino?"

Rachel looked back at her, one corner of her lips turning up. "Can I sit in the car?"

Sylvie smiled at her, and held out a hand. Rachel reached for her backpack and pulled it up to her lap, unzipping the front pocket, and reaching inside.

"You're supposed to be wearing it," Sylvie said, as the car joined a line of slow-moving cars trickling through a circular driveway.

"It's not like I ever go anywhere without my pack," Rachel replied, pulling out a small circular device. She handed it to Sylvie who adeptly popped it open.

"Not the point. It needs to be on your person at all times."

"Except when you've turned it off?" Rachel's tears were gone now, and her tone almost mischievous.

Sylvie's lips twitched. "Even then. Which is only when you're absolutely safe," she added, before saying to James, "Alarm or just dead?"

He looked disapproving, but answered. "Just dead. That noise is fu—is annoying." He caught himself before he swore and Sylvie grinned at him as she did something that Dillon couldn't see to the device, and then handed it back to Rachel.

"Put it in your pocket," Sylvie ordered. "And you do not leave the school building."

Rachel nodded, a reluctant smile tugging at her lips.

As the car reached the front of the line, Sylvie looked out the window, seeming to scan the environment. Dillon looked out the

39

window too. Was this a girls' school? There were teenage girls everywhere, pouring into the front doors of the brick building, but not a boy in sight. Wow.

"We'll be back within the hour," Sylvie told Rachel. "I'll come get you for the security check, and you can stay with us while I 'repair' your alarm."

Rachel nodded.

"Clear?" Sylvie said to James. He, too, was scanning the scenery, looking carefully in every direction.

He nodded. "Clear."

"I think so, too." Sylvie nodded at Rachel. "Go ahead. We'll see you soon."

Hmm, thought Dillon. His mom was only going to Starbucks. She might even be going to a drive-through. He could spend the next hour with her in the car, probably almost silently, or with Rachel in a school filled with girls.

The choice wasn't hard.

*****

Sylvie watched Rachel until she disappeared into the school, then leaned back against the car seat.

"To Starbucks, James," she said in a mock posh accent.

"Yeah, yeah, yeah," he replied, shifting into gear and pulling out. "You're going to get us into trouble if you keep that up. That's the third time this year."

"I know. Ty would flip." She grimaced, thinking about how Ty would react. Ballistic wasn't the word. She'd just disabled Rachel's alarm and GPS tracker, the one that would alert the security team if Rachel moved outside a prescribed area. When they got back from Starbucks, she'd go into the school and notify the principal that she needed to investigate the equipment failure during Rachel's free period. The principal might frown at her, but in McLean, Virginia, home of the CIA, private schools took security seriously. Rachel would be allowed to join them.

"I don't get why you do it. The kid's a brat," James complained.

Sylvie smiled at him. She loved James. He didn't understand and it didn't matter: he backed her up 100%, anyway. "Then there came the color green," she quoted to him, reciting a chant that she knew he knew.

"Yeah, right," James scoffed. "She's mean, all right. But she ain't no Marine."

"No." Sylvie looked out the window. "But she reminds me of what it felt like."

"Boot camp? She's a spoiled rich kid at the fanciest school in northern Virginia," he protested. "They're not doing ten mile marches between classes."

"Might be easier," Sylvie answered, still staring at the passing scenery. She didn't like Rachel. It was almost impossible to like Rachel. But she'd never sensed anyone unhappier. The girl was living in a world of despair, and if a Frappuccino and a chance to escape from school for forty minutes lightened that darkness for a minute or two, Sylvie was willing to take a few chances.

James turned into the parking lot of Starbucks. Every space was full. "You're buying the coffee."

"No problem," she agreed, reaching for the door handle. "You want some frou-frou drink?"

"Damn straight. I'll take one of those peppermint things."

"Ick. You're such a girl, James."

As she entered the coffee shop, his call of 'sexist pig' still ringing in her ears, Sylvie was smiling. But then her smile faded. From outside, the textures of the people in the crowded café blended together like the multiple instruments in an orchestra playing a single tune. But now that she was inside, she could hear the individual notes.

'What the hell are you doing here?'

'Closest coffee shop to Rachel's school,' Lucas answered.

Sylvie joined the line at the counter, refusing to look around her. He might be here but she didn't have to acknowledge him.

'You were bound to show up eventually,' he continued.

Sylvie gritted her teeth. Ty would scream himself hoarse if he heard that. And damn it, he'd be right. She'd gotten careless if she was so predictable.

'We have to talk.' His feelings were a mess, she realized dispassionately. The calm, practical Lucas on the surface was barely holding his chaotic emotions under control.

"A peppermint mocha, a Frappuccino, and a black coffee, just straight coffee," she told the clerk. It was always easy to get the weird drinks at Starbucks, hard to get the simple ones. *'No, we fucking don't,'* she thought at Lucas. *'You didn't want to talk at the mall the other night. Why now?'*

'What are you talking about?' he thought back at her. *'What mall? No, never mind, that's not important. Have you seen Dillon? Heard from him? Akira's freaking out. She wants to come up here but Zane doesn't want her flying when she's pregnant.'*

Sylvie frowned. Had Lucas made any sense at all? Or was he talking pure nonsense? She moved down the counter to the space where drinks were served. *'Zane?'*

'Gone insane. Protective's not the word. Paranoid. Obsessed with the idea that since she's already died once, they're living on borrowed time.'

Okay, Sylvie had no idea what Lucas was thinking about. Without moving away from the counter, she did a slow turn, as if she was casually shifting positions. The blur of feeling from the crowd was hard to separate into individual pieces, but she spotted Lucas immediately. He stood in the corridor that led to the bathrooms, placed where no one coming in the front door could spot him. He hadn't shaved, and maybe he hadn't slept either. It didn't matter; just the sight of him sent a melting shiver down Sylvie's spine. Damn him.

He looked like a Floridian still, she thought. A little too tan, his leather jacket a little too lightweight for the wintery DC weather. But hot as hell. The easy charm of the privileged teenager had become much more compelling on the man who looked as if he rarely smiled.

She hated the way he could make her feel, truly she did. "Could I get a tray, please?" she asked the barista, already planning.

'No idea what you're talking about,' she thought at Lucas.

'Right, of course not. Sorry, I should . . .' The thought came through clearly, but then the emotion around it made it blurry, as if it was all feeling, no words.

Sylvie frowned. What the hell was going on? What was Lucas doing? This wasn't like him. He sounded almost desperate. And Lucas didn't do desperate.

'It's Dillon,' Lucas continued. *'He's not talking. Is he with you?'*

'You told me he was dead!' Confused wasn't the word. Sylvie's fury must have shown on her face because the boy behind the counter took a step backward before pushing her drinks toward her.

She picked up the tray, her hands clenching white-knuckled on the cardboard, and took the two steps to the condiment bar. Should she? Shouldn't she? Oh, God, this was petty of her. But her back to

Lucas, she took the top off the plain coffee cup, trying hard not to think about what she was doing.

'*No, no, I mean, yes. I mean—we have to talk. I can't explain this way.*'

'*Is he dead or isn't he?*' Sylvie tried to think the words as clearly as she could. She could sense Lucas approaching, moving past the counter, closing in on her.

'*Yes, but—*'

'*Then there's nothing to say,*' she interrupted his thought, turning quickly, and letting the tray jerk upward, as if accidentally. Coffee spewed out of her open cup, splashing onto Lucas. As the hot liquid hit, he reeled backward in surprise and she slid her foot forward to catch his heel and tug his foot toward her.

It worked beautifully, as precisely as if she'd choreographed it. As he stumbled backward, crashing into the man behind him, she straightened the tray, catching her still half-full coffee cup before it tipped completely over, and turned to the side, avoiding Lucas's forward rebound as he tried to recover from being tripped. The man behind him was protesting as Sylvie murmured, "So sorry, so sorry, let me get you a towel," and kept moving. The barista was leaning over the counter to see what was happening, the woman at the nearest table standing, exclaiming, as Lucas tried to avoid falling onto her.

The scene inside the Starbucks was still crazy as Sylvie slipped into the front seat of the car with a sigh of satisfaction. Okay, it was petty, but it had felt damn good. And maybe Lucas would think twice the next time he tried to text her any back-handed compliments.

"What happened in there?" asked James, glancing over at Sylvie as he pulled out of the parking lot and onto the roadway. "You're as revved as if you just robbed a bank."

"You say that as if you know what it looks like. Were you a getaway driver during your mysterious past?" Sylvie said the words lightly, but her heart was racing, she was breathing a little too fast, her cheeks were flushed. Yes, she was revved. What had Lucas meant? Did this have something to do with why he was searching Chesney's study?

"Don't you wish you knew," James retorted. "I'd be a good one, though."

Sylvie smiled at him. "You can be my getaway driver any time."

Could Zane be in trouble? Sylvie knew who he was, of course. He'd been a gap-toothed little kid back in the day, but a lanky adolescent when he and Lucas showed up on her doorstep a few years later. It was just like Lucas's luck that his little brother had a gift for finding the lost. Not that Sylvie had been lost, of course.

"I prefer to stay on the right side of the law." One hand on the steering wheel, James reached over and grabbed his peppermint mocha. He took a gulp. "Ahhh, delicious."

"Girl," Sylvie drawled her response to their running joke, but it was automatic, most of her brain still obsessing on Lucas's words. He'd been making no sense at all.

And why did he want to talk to her now? Okay, she'd ignored his phone messages, but that text he'd sent was hardly urgent. And he must have been in the mall the other night: the only way he could have gotten that new phone number was if he'd been close enough to hear the thoughts of the sales clerk assigning it to her. Why hadn't he approached her then? Why hadn't he answered her when she tried to talk to him?

"Seriously, though," James said, shooting her another glance as they paused at a stop light. "What's got you so wired?"

She shook her head, but answered without thinking. "Just this guy."

"Oho!" James responded with delight. "What guy? Tell me more. All the deets. Leave nothing out."

Sylvie gave a puff of laughter. "No, not like that," she said, waving off his words. Well, not really like that. It was strange to look at Lucas and realize that he still did it for her. Weren't people supposed to outgrow their high school loves? Shouldn't she be able to see him and think, wow, he's gotten old, instead of feeling breathless?

James pressed for more, but Sylvie ignored him, still trying to puzzle out Lucas's behavior. Someone was pregnant, she'd caught that much. But that couldn't possibly have anything to do with Chesney. Or she supposed it could, but ew. If that was the connection, she didn't admire the unknown woman's taste.

As James pulled up in front of the school, Sylvie finally let go of her preoccupation. Maybe Ty's background check on Lucas would turn up something interesting. And if not, she'd probably see him again soon. She doubted that pouring coffee on him was going to deter him for long.

Exactly as Sylvie expected, the principal looked disapproving at the idea of letting Rachel out of the school building but didn't resist Sylvie's calm persistence. Sylvie waited for Rachel outside her classroom door. As the bell rang and uniformed girls streamed through the hallway, though, Sylvie frowned.

The girls coming out of Rachel's classroom felt wrong: too bright, too excited, too giggly. Something must have happened. And then Rachel emerged and Sylvie's eyebrows rose in surprise. Rachel also felt bright, much more so than the promised Starbuck's treat deserved.

"Rachel, I need you to come with me for a security check," Sylvie said, using a formal voice for the sake of any nearby teachers. She tried not to let her curiosity show as they walked together through the hallway, but Rachel was close to skipping. And the feeling . . . was it joy?

She wanted to ask, but not with others around. And outside, of course, they walked silently. Rachel knew better than to speak to her bodyguard when they were in the open. Even though they were on the school grounds, Sylvie continually scanned for potential threats.

As she opened the car door for Rachel to slide inside, though, Sylvie couldn't resist any longer. "So anything interesting happen this morning?"

"Oh, yes," Rachel replied. "It was the best."

Sylvie slid in next to her. Reaching over the seat, she grabbed the drink from the front and passed it to Rachel, then held out her hand for Rachel's alarm. "Yeah?" she prompted, when Rachel didn't seem inclined to continue.

Rachel was almost shivering with glee, her cheeks pink, as she took a long slurp on her Frappuccino. "Marlie Eversoll got in trouble."

Sylvie's eyes met those of James in the rearview mirror. She could feel that he was as taken aback as she was. She'd never seen Rachel happier and it was because another girl had gotten in trouble?

"You don't like her?" she asked, as she popped open the back of Rachel's alarm and re-set the battery. Then she winced as Rachel's feelings flooded over her. 'Not like' was much too gentle a way to describe Rachel's opinion of Marlie Eversoll. Sylvie's hand tightened on the GPS tracker in automatic reaction.

"She's okay," Rachel said, a belated caution entering her voice. "It was just funny."

"What happened?" James asked from the front seat.

Rachel looked at him, a little doubtful, but then let the story spill out in a rush of words. "Her phone kept ringing. We're not allowed to have phones in class. She didn't get in trouble the first time, but then she told Mrs. Walden she'd turned it off. It rang again, and Mrs. Walden got real mad at her for lying. Then it rang again, and Mrs. Walden gave her detention for a week. She talked back. She talked back to Mrs. Walden! And then she got sent to the office."

Hatred and happiness made for a strange and not particularly pleasant mix of emotion. But on top of Rachel's feelings, Sylvie almost caught words. *'Pathetic? Facebook? Slut?'* What was this?

Wait, words? Sylvie turned her gaze to the window. Lucas had to be out there somewhere, close enough to be affecting her. She didn't get words when he wasn't nearby, just sensations. Her eyes scanned the road, looking for a car that might be parked, a pedestrian that she might recognize.

'Lucas?' It was a call, not simply a thought. But no answer came.

Her eyes narrowed as she passed the GPS tracker back to Rachel, her attention still focused outside the car.

James picked up on her uneasiness. "What are you looking at?"

She shook her head. The words were gone. If Lucas had been nearby, he'd moved on. She let Rachel take her time with the drink, but then insisted on walking her inside. As she returned to the car, her eyes swept the surroundings, looking for anything out of place.

'Lucas?' She tried again, but got no response.

But she paused, car door open, one hand resting on the roof, as a nondescript beige car parked across the street caught her attention. The distance was too great for her to feel the emotions of the occupants, but it looked as if two men were sitting in the front seats. She glanced back at the door of the school. Could Rachel be in danger?

And then she shook her head and got into the car. Whatever this was, it didn't have anything to do with Rachel.

"What's all that about?" James asked.

"I don't know," Sylvie answered, not trying to hide her uncertainty. "I think I need to call Ty." She pulled out the phone he'd given her.

"Ah, you're not planning on telling him we let the kid play hooky, are you? 'Cause it's almost Christmas and I don't much want to get fired today." At the exit to the parking lot, James checked both directions.

"Go left. Left," Sylvie ordered, looking up from the phone.

"What? Why?" James turned to the left without waiting for an answer.

"I want to go past that . . . ah," Sylvie said with satisfaction. They'd driven alongside the beige car which was pointed in the opposite direction, and she'd caught a burst of frustration from the men inside. "That car's going to follow us," she told James. "You might want to lose them."

She found the number for the security room in the house and tapped it, as James accelerated away. The phone rang once, twice, then Ty picked up.

"What's up?" he asked, not bothering with a greeting.

"I'm not sure," Sylvie answered. "Did you find out anything about Lucas?"

Ty chuckled. "More or less."

"What does that mean?" Sylvie asked. The amusement in Ty's voice didn't make any sense.

"I found out that he has higher-placed friends than we do," Ty answered. "Fortunately, Gibbs is cool with it. Apparently getting dragged out of bed in the middle of the night impressed his girlfriend. And one of the guys who did the dragging told him to apply for a job with them, that he did good work."

"What the hell?"

Ty must have taken pity on the shock in her voice. "Gibbs tried to do a background check on the guy," he explained. "He wound up in a basement somewhere. He thinks Arlington."

"The Pentagon?" Sylvie blinked rapidly. That didn't make sense. Lucas wasn't—he didn't—how could he . . .

"Oh, shit," she said as the sirens started behind them.

"No, he thinks maybe DEA," Ty answered, not realizing what she was swearing about.

"Ah, Sylvie?" James said, voice tentative.

"Awesome," said Sylvie. "That's just peachy. I gotta go, Ty. Talk to ya' soon."

With a sigh, she added, "Pull over," to James as she disconnected.

The cops used their loudspeaker to order them out of the car, but Sylvie didn't hesitate, even as James obediently put his hands on the roof of the car. She marched straight back, past the police officer who ordered her to halt, glaring at him in passing as he reached for his weapon.

"Stand down," ordered a man in a lousy suit from the car behind the police car. The beige car was nowhere to be seen, Sylvie noticed. They must have called it in when James got away from them. Instead, there was a police car with two uniformed officers, one of whom was currently patting James down, the other who was staring after her, looking annoyed, and a blue Toyota, with Lucas stepping out of one side, brown suit guy on the other.

As she reached Lucas, she cocked her head to one side. "Really? For a cup of coffee?" she said, voice dangerous. "Should I tell these guys what you were up to Friday night?"

He sighed. He looked tired, she noticed with a pang, his blue eyes shadowed. "I'm sorry," he said. "You wouldn't believe the favors I called in for this."

Sylvie turned to the guy in the brown suit. "This is Raymond Chesney's car," she said. "You know that, right?"

He grimaced, closing his eyes and shuddering with exaggerated dismay. Then he opened them and said cheerfully, "Five jobs, right?" to Lucas.

"Yep."

Brown-suit-guy tapped his forehead and said, "I'll leave you to it, then." Grinning at Sylvie, he headed away, up to where the uniformed police officer was putting his gun away.

"But not Zane," Lucas called after him. "Not for another six months, anyway."

The guy waved over his shoulder as Sylvie said, keeping her voice low despite her fury, "What the hell is this, Lucas?"

"I'm sorry." He put his hand on her upper arm. Despite her anger, Sylvie didn't resist, didn't step away. "I know you don't understand. I need—I want to explain to you. But it's not—"

A buzzing from his pocket interrupted him and he reached for his phone. "Oh, thank God," he muttered as he looked at the screen. He put the hand that wasn't holding the phone across his eyes, pressing as if to hide his expression or his tears.

Sylvie saw him swallow hard and she felt the tidal wave of relief that washed over him. "Lucas?" she asked. What was going on? She was lost.

"I know you must have questions. I know you must be angry. I'm sorry I didn't tell you everything. But it's complicated and—" He paused as his phone buzzed again.

"What are you talking about, Lucas?" Sylvie asked as he looked at his phone. "What's complicated?"

He half smiled. And then he rubbed his face again and took a deep breath. *'It's okay,'* he thought to Sylvie.

'What's okay?' she thought back, frustrated.

'You're cool.' His thought was flavored with joy and Sylvie shook her head.

"Lucas," she said carefully, speaking out loud again. "Do you need help?" She hated therapists. But maybe Lucas needed medical attention. A psychiatrist, perhaps?

"No," he answered. "But I do need to talk to you. Will you meet me?"

Sylvie sighed. She looked back at James, who was no longer leaning against the car. He was talking to the police officer and brown-suit guy, and although their conversation looked friendly enough, he was going to be pissed. She thought about her schedule. She was working long hours and would be until the flu finished beating up their team and Ty managed to find a new employee, but . . . .

"Wednesday night. I'm off at 8." It was two days away. Would he be willing to wait that long?

"I can do that." He nodded.

Sylvie's eyes narrowed. The desperation she'd sensed earlier was gone. He seemed close to relaxed. Still intent, still focused, still Lucas, but the chaotic emotions she'd felt at Starbucks had settled into a peaceful exhaustion.

"I'll be on duty at a holiday party at the Fairmont. Do you want to meet me there?" The words were straightforward but the thought asked for more. *'Do you want to tell me what this is about?'*

'Wednesday,' he promised. He slid his hand up her arm to her shoulder and grinned at her.

'Lucas,' she thought a warning, feeling the dangerous heat spark in her belly. They were not, not, not going to repeat past patterns.

"It's okay," he told her, then leaned forward and brushed a fleeting kiss across her lips.

It was worse than static electricity, less than lightning. Sylvie took a hasty step back, and glared at him. *'Damn it,'* she thought.

'Sorry.' His thought felt both contrite and happy. *'Wednesday?'*

'Fine. Wednesday.' She turned and stomped away. Damn it. What had just happened? But the curling heat was its own answer. How was it that Lucas could always do this to her?

CHAPTER FIVE

"Whoa!" Dillon protested. "What's up with that?"

His dad had grinned at his mom. And then he'd kissed her. Oh, not a serious kiss, not like a kiss with tongue or anything. But lips had definitely touched lips.

"She left us, remember?" he pointed out to the oblivious Lucas, who gazed after Sylvie's departing back with a half-smile still tugging at his mouth. "Shouldn't you be mad at her?"

"You still here, Dill?" Lucas asked, his voice quiet.

Dillon tried to answer, but all he could manage to send was a "Y."

Damn.

Ghostly exhaustion didn't feel like physical exhaustion. He had no sore muscles or itchy eyes telling him he needed sleep, but he didn't have enough energy left to send the signals that would generate letters on Lucas's phone. Spelling out "she's cool" had finished him off.

Trying to make that bitch of a girl's phone ring in Rachel's English class had been tricky. He knew how to send messages but powering on a phone was more challenging. It was totally worth the effort, though. Wow, Dillon was glad he hadn't gone to an all-girls school. Rachel's classmates were flat-out mean.

His dad looked at his phone. "Why?" he asked. "Why what?" He frowned, looking puzzled and then said, "Oh, you mean yes?"

Dillon groaned. Texting could be so annoying. "Yes, Dad," he said, knowing that Lucas couldn't hear him. "And you'd better answer some of my questions, too."

"I've been so worried about you," Lucas said, looking at the display on the phone. "If I'd known, if I'd had any idea—"

"Who ya' talking to, Latimer?" The guy who'd been driving the car was back, his conversation with the police officers over.

"Long story," Lucas answered, tucking his phone into his pocket and opening the car door. He waited, hand on the door. Sylvie was already seated in the black Mercedes and the police officers were getting back into their squad car.

Dillon felt torn between his choices. Did he want to stay with his dad or did he want to hurry and catch up to his mom? He definitely wanted more time with Sylvie—not to mention that haunting Rachel's high school might be fun—but he wanted to talk to his dad, too.

And his dad might give him answers. Yeah, he could either spend the next two days trying to convince Sylvie he was real and hoping she didn't throw her phone away again, or he could hang out with his dad until Wednesday night and maybe find out what had happened between his parents and why his dad had never told him about seeing his mom.

His dad it was. With one last glance at Sylvie, Dillon entered the car through the open door, then shifted through the seat and into the back. Being sat on didn't hurt, but it made it tough to see.

The driver slid behind the wheel, saying, "Chesney's an awfully big fish to be messing with, you know. Are you sure you want to show up on his radar?"

Dillon eyed him curiously. He was on the skinny side, with a receding hairline, a wrinkly forehead and ears that stuck out, but his face was friendly. Dillon knew he must be some kind of a cop, but he sure didn't look it.

Lucas grimaced. "Call him what he is," he suggested. "A shark."

"Ha." The other man grunted in agreement. "An octopus, maybe. Tentacles everywhere."

"Don't insult the octopi," Lucas muttered. Dillon smiled. His dad always claimed that the octopus was the smartest animal in the ocean.

"Seriously, man, I was willing to do this one for you. No ticket, no record, everybody's cool. But Chesney's got half the senate in his back pocket. You mess with him and you're going to find yourself legislated into a black hole. Or worse." The cop started the car and pulled out onto the road.

"Worse?"

"The IRS. The SEC. OSHA. Chesney's got connections everywhere. If he decides to destroy you, you're already dead. He could probably get the CDC to investigate you for potential zombie outbreaks if he wanted to."

Dillon's smile disappeared. That didn't sound good. Not the zombies, he was cool with them, but all those other initials. Was his dad in trouble? Was that why he'd been using a fake name?

Lucas shook his head. "The guy is corrupt as hell."

"Not the point, my friend."

"I'm serious. He's selling guns to the Mexican drug cartels. I know he is. God knows how many deaths he's responsible for."

The driver sighed. "Proof?" he asked, as he turned onto the highway.

Lucas let his head fall back against the head rest of his seat. From the back seat, Dillon winced. He recognized that look. His dad was not a happy camper.

"Look, you know I believe in you and what you can do. You guys at GD have been invaluable for me. That little blonde—"

"She'd probably kill you if she heard you call her that," Lucas interrupted.

"Yeah, whatever," the driver said. "Tell me she's not married yet."

Lucas chuckled. "Still engaged."

Dillon frowned, trying to think of who his dad meant, then said, "Oh, you're talking about Serena!"

He'd met Serena a couple of times. She was a clairvoyant. She could touch an object and tell you its entire history: the last place it had been, who had held it, what it had been used for. None of the information was admissible in court, of course, but he could see that a cop might like working with her. And yeah, she might murder a guy who called her a little blonde, even if it was technically true. Despite her name, Serena was not the serene type.

"Is she ever gonna dump him?" The cop's voice was plaintive.

"Nope." Lucas sounded sympathetic.

The cop heaved a sigh, tapping his fingers on the steering wheel before returning to the subject. "Still, compared to Chesney, you're small potatoes. The dude has an inside track on everything that happens in DC."

"Yeah," Lucas replied, sympathy gone and voice grim. "And he's selling guns to the cartels, Andy."

"But why?" protested Andy. "He's got more money than God, more power than the devil. Why would he take that sort of risk?"

Dillon didn't care about that. He wanted to know the important stuff, like why was his mom working for a bad guy?

Lucas shook his head. "Zane did a job last year. With Maia out of the Orlando office, you remember her?"

"Yeah, yeah." Andy nodded, taking one hand off the wheel and gesturing as if trying to hurry Lucas's story along.

"It was a local job. He found a stash of drugs, guns and cash. No big deal. Completely unimportant. But they'd built a tunnel."

Dillon remembered that tunnel. It had been right after Akira moved to Florida. His Uncle Zane had taken her with him that day and she'd come back muttering things about quantum entanglement and paradoxes.

"A tunnel in Florida?" Andy glanced at Lucas. "What were they gonna try? Digging under the Gulf?"

Lucas chuckled. "Exactly. Total overkill for the location. Florida's not prime territory for border crossings. So why a tunnel?"

The cop scowled as he smoothly navigated the heavy traffic on the roadway. "The Sinaloas do the tunnels. They're West Coast."

"Yeah. So two possibilities—"

Andy shook his head. "One," he said, voice grim. "The Sinaloas shouldn't be challenging the Zetas. Not after the BLO in 2008 and the AFO situation. It's gotta be the Zetas, planning to expand their operations into Sinaloa territory."

Dillon scowled. He had no idea what Andy was talking about. He'd never heard any of those names before. But the tone in Andy's voice made it clear that it was not good.

"Maybe, maybe not," Lucas answered. "One way or another, though, Maia figured this was trouble. And the guy they caught was a Mexican national. She sent him up here and I sat in on the interrogations."

"And the guy tagged Chesney?" Andy raised an eyebrow, voice skeptical.

Lucas rubbed his hand across his forehead, looking tired. "Of course not. That would be too easy."

"Not that it would matter. Even if the guy swore on a stack of Bibles and his mother's grave, no way would anyone believe him."

"He didn't. He didn't talk. Didn't say a word." Lucas looked out the window of the car.

"Uh-oh," Andy said. "I'm detecting guilt, my friend. Let me guess—murdered in prison?"

Lucas shrugged. Dillon tried to see his dad's face and find out what he was feeling but Lucas had his head turned away, still looking out the window.

"You didn't kill him."

Lucas rocked his hand back and forth in a gesture of equivocation.

"You didn't kill him," Andy repeated, enunciating each word. "The Zetas killed him. Hell, he was dealing drugs for them. He had to know the risks."

"During the interrogation, I caught a name. It was a guy who worked at the Mexican embassy. We arranged surveillance. He spotted it, but not before he'd met with Chesney." Lucas's sentences were short and clipped.

"It's a long way from a casual meet to selling guns."

Lucas shook his head again. "I was there. The conversation was innocuous but the thoughts weren't."

"Ahh," Andy said. "And he made you?"

"Not Chesney. But the Mexican, yeah. Enough to be suspicious, anyway."

"And you think he put a hit on the dealer because he thought the dealer identified him to us?"

Lucas shrugged. Dillon sat back in his seat, scowling. He knew his dad did jobs for the government, sometimes dangerous jobs. Lucas had already been shot twice, once in Oregon with Zane and another time somewhere overseas. He'd been home for two whole months the summer Dillon was twelve because of it. But listening to them talk about hits and dealers and cartels made it more real. And scarier.

"He was a drug dealer, Latimer."

"He was twenty-four years old with two kids and a third on the way. Yeah, he screwed up. But he didn't do anything that deserved a death sentence."

"You didn't kill him," Andy repeated.

"No," Lucas agreed, but he was back to staring out the window.

"Is that why you're after Chesney? Guilt?"

"No." Lucas shook his head immediately, and then looked at Andy and smiled, a little rueful. "I have easier ways to soothe my guilt. A good immigration lawyer and a trust fund for the kids worked wonders."

"Ha. Must be nice."

Lucas sobered. "It has its pros."

There was a silence. Dillon wondered what his dad was thinking. Andy must have been wondering as well because he shot Lucas a pointed look before prompting, "So, Chesney?"

55

"A nice, clear thinker. When he met up with the guy from the embassy, he was trying to figure out if he could offload a bunch of Calico M960s on him."

"Huh." Andy looked intrigued. "Submachine guns? Old, though. They stopped making those in the 90s, right?"

"Most of Chesney's money comes from AlecCorp, a private military contractor. They did great in Iraq for the first few years of the war, but by 2008 the money over there was drying up. And then the market crashed. Not everyone recovered. Chesney was rich, but I'm not sure he's rich anymore."

"Dude still has money."

"Yeah, but maybe not money like he used to have. Or maybe he panicked when the market tanked and got into something that there's no way out of. Or he sees it as a profitable line of business and doesn't care about the human costs. I don't know what his motives are. But he's working with the cartels."

Andy shook his head. "And all you've got is what you heard?"

Lucas grimaced. "I know, I know. Not admissible. Not enough for a wiretap, not enough for a search warrant, not enough for anything. But selling guns to drug dealers is about as low as a human being can go these days."

"The Zetas deserve their reputation."

"Only thing worse would be dumping guns into Somalia. And I wouldn't put that past him."

Andy sighed as he turned onto the bridge into downtown DC.

Dillon sighed, too. He desperately wanted to ask his dad questions, starting with the first one that had occurred to him: why was his mom working for a bad guy?

*****

Sylvie stumbled over the box on her way out the door for her morning run on Wednesday.

Lucas.

It had to be. Who else would find a way to get a box into a secure building and then leave it lying in the hallway?

Not that it mattered. She wasn't going to let him get to her.

Bending over, she picked up the box. It was silver, light cardboard, a gift box from a department store if she had to guess. An envelope taped to the outside had her name on it. With a sigh, Sylvie tossed the box, Frisbee-style, into her apartment before closing and locking the door.

She'd look at it after her run.

Maybe.

If she felt like it.

Or maybe she'd just ignore it, try to stuff it out of her mind the way she'd been trying to stuff Lucas out for the past forty-some hours, ever since Monday morning.

Running, though, didn't work the way it should have. She couldn't find the sweet spot, the place where her brain went quiet and all that mattered was the thud of her feet against the ground, the burn of her breath in her lungs, the pleasant stretch of the muscles down the back of her legs. Instead her mind kept churning.

Lucas.

The first time she'd met him, she hadn't known it was him. She'd been panicking during a math final. It was the end of her junior year; she'd been in Tassamara for about six weeks; and she was about to fail geometry for the second time. And she'd studied, she had, but the classroom was so noisy, she couldn't concentrate, and the more she stared at the paper and thought about how bad it was going to be if she failed again, the less she could remember. Then suddenly the answer to the first question was in her head. *'42. Write it down.'*

One after another, the answers came to her. She didn't ask questions, she just wrote them down. And that was that. End of the school year, she'd passed geometry. She was thankful for the miracle, but she tried not to think too hard about it. Because if she questioned it—well, who could she ask? Her mom had enough to worry about without thinking that her daughter might be going crazy.

But then she met Lucas. Really met him. She'd gotten a summer job at the concession stand at the state park. She'd been storing a kayak, lifting it above her head to slot it into the storage rack, when suddenly he was helping her.

"Thanks, but I had it," she'd said.

"I like helping you," he'd answered.

Great. Another tourist looking for a vacation fling, she'd thought. "I don't need help." The words were dismissive, and she'd turned her back on him without waiting for a response.

"Ouch," he'd said. *'I cheated on a test for you,'* he'd thought, and she'd whirled around at the words.

He'd grinned at her, and that was it. The dark hair, the bright blue eyes, the even features—sure, they added up to handsome, but Sylvie didn't trust handsome. Yet when Lucas smiled it was like the sun breaking through the clouds on an overcast day.

Never once, never, had he told her he was fifteen. And he'd been in her math class.

Not that it would have mattered if he had. Lucas didn't look at her like she was insane. He had his own gift and understood hers and together they were stronger; thoughts flowed back and forth between them like water running downhill.

Feelings, too.

She was pregnant before summer's end.

Her mom was great about it. A little disappointed, a little worried, but she'd been a sixteen-year-old mother herself. His parents were not quite so calm, but by the time Dillon was born, they'd been excited to have a grandson. They were nice people, Lucas's parents.

What could have happened?

How had Dillon died?

And why was Lucas in Chesney's study?

And what was in the box?

Six miles and not once had Sylvie hit the zone.

She glared at the box lying on the floor and walked around it as if it were dangerous on her way to shower.

Dressed, hair dried, she ate a bowl of granola while standing in the kitchen, eyes on the box. What if the note said something important? That he couldn't make it tonight? What if the box held . . . but she couldn't think of anything that fit the box's shape and light weight. Papers? Information? Answers?

No, she knew what the box held.

Putting her bowl in the sink with a clatter of spoon against ceramic, she crossed to the box and picked it up. Setting it on the table, she plucked the envelope off, slid a finger deftly under the flap, and slipped out the card inside.

Ruffles don't suit you.

She bit back her smile. It was so Lucas.

But then she sobered. Dillon was still dead. That wasn't something that she was going to get over easily. Not after Milan.

Reaching for the box, she broke the tape and shook off the top. The dress inside was wrapped in tissue paper, neatly folded. She took it out gently, lifting it by the shoulders and held it up in front of her.

It was a cocktail dress made of black chiffon and black leather. The bodice was leather, with a sweetheart neckline, the kind that shaped to the body, and chiffon straps. From a high empire-style waist, layers of chiffon draped to mid-calf length. She looked a little closer, then dropped the dress over one arm, pushing the layers of chiffon aside. Underneath the fluttery, flowing cloth, the black leather continued for several inches. It would hug her body all the way down to her thighs before it flared out into more layers of chiffon. But more than that, it would hug her gun. There were pockets tucked into either side of the leather. It was a concealed carry dress. She'd never even heard of such a thing.

She glanced at the clock.

Not enough time to try it on.

She scowled. What did she want to do?

*****

'*You didn't wear it.*' It was a thought, not a sound.

Sylvie didn't flinch, just finished her low-voiced conversation with Ty. As he stepped out into the garden, she turned away from the French doors, letting her eyes scan the room in front of her but trying to seem casual. Should she tell Lucas? But the thought slipped out before she could stop it. '*Not working the party.*'

'*You liked it then?*'

'*Smug, much?*' He'd be able to feel the acerbic tone to her thought, before she relented and conceded. '*It's beautiful.*'

Where was he? Sylvie's location in the loggia, adjacent to the hotel lobby, gave her a good view of her surroundings. She let her eyes drift over the wide chairs, the white and black marble floor, the plants, the piano, the well-dressed people populating the elegant environs.

December in DC was party season. Chesney, with his connections, his wealth, and his political acumen, would be attending holiday events almost daily leading up to New Year's. Tonight's was relatively low-key, although exclusive—a political action committee's celebration for its biggest donors, to be held in the Fairmont's Colonnade Room. Fortunately, Rachel wasn't attending. Sylvie had dropped her off at the house after her afternoon activities and then come to the hotel to run the advance screening and risk assessment.

'*Dillon will—*' Lucas started, before breaking off the thought.

Sylvie stilled. Dillon would what? Why was Lucas talking about Dillon in the present tense? She'd thought from the feel of his emotions that Lucas had recovered, that he was over his grief. That feeling had only made her angrier. But was Lucas in denial instead?

She swallowed, mouth suddenly dry, and kept looking. Lucas must be close by, but she couldn't see him.

'*Look up,*' he answered her unspoken question.

A curved staircase led down into the lobby. He was standing on the platform, wearing a dark suit.

'*Holy—*' It was Sylvie's turn to bite back a thought. But she'd never seen him in a suit before. He looked . . . debonair. Dangerous. Not that he hadn't always been dangerous to her, but she hadn't ever seen him looking so formal. She couldn't help the amused appreciation that slipped through to him.

'*What? You object to the suit?*' His thought radiated amusement back at her.

'*Not in the least,*' she assured him, not looking away as he made his way down the stairs to her. And then she sobered. Damn it, this was so typical. One sight of him and she forgot all her reservations.

Three times.

She'd seen him three times in the past twenty years. And every time, they fell into bed together as if it was as easy as breathing. But it never was, not really.

"Dinner?" he asked, when he reached her. "I'm told the Juniper has an excellent mushroom casserole."

She quirked an eyebrow at him, skepticism clear.

"Ah," he answered the expression. "Still a meat and potatoes girl? Woman?"

"Mushrooms are fungus. Athlete's foot is fungus. Would you eat athlete's foot?" she asked. "Yeah, didn't think so," she added, answering his wince.

"I'm sure they have something that would suit your tastes," he said. '*Probably no MREs, though.*'

'*Hey, that beef stew's not bad,*' Sylvie answered the thought, unable to hold back her smile. But then she sobered. "We need to talk, Lucas."

"Garden?" he asked her, gesturing toward the French doors. The loggia was entirely walled in glass but opened onto an enclosed courtyard garden with a stone fountain and carefully tended plants. Even at the end of November, it was verdant and beautiful.

Sylvie nodded and preceded him through the door. It was cold outside, and she shivered instinctively. She was wearing a dark suit of her own with a sleek silk top underneath the jacket. It wasn't really appropriate for this weather. But the hotel had space heaters positioned around the courtyard to encourage guests to take advantage of the outdoor tables, and she headed straight to one of them.

Under the light of the heater, she turned to face him. "Dillon first," she said. "When was it?" She pressed her lips together and swallowed hard.

"Five years."

Five years. She would have been in Iraq. Zane couldn't have found her from that far away. But five years? And Lucas hadn't yet accepted his death?

"What happened?"

"He wanted to be psychic."

"Ha." Sylvie couldn't contain her instinctive objection. Sure, her sixth sense came in handy sometimes, but it caused a lot more problems than it solved. Her life would have been easier—if possibly shorter—without her ability.

"I know," Lucas said. "He didn't understand. I think he only saw the positive side. But he found a website that claimed hallucinations could start psychic powers so he took some medication of my mom's. The prescription said that hallucinations could be a possible side effect."

Sylvie closed her eyes and took a deep breath. That was almost worse than she'd imagined. She'd pictured car accident or long slow illness. At least Lucas hadn't known that time was short and not tried to find her. One of her fears was wrong. It would have been quick.

"But that's not . . ." Lucas started and then paused again. "Let's talk about Chesney first."

Sylvie frowned. She didn't want to talk about Chesney. But she did need to know why Lucas had broken into Chesney's office and she also knew that talking about Dillon was likely to end the same way every conversation between them about him had ended in the past twenty years: with her stomping off in fury.

"What about Chesney?" The words were reluctant. They were both being careful, she could tell. She was trying to hold her emotions in rein and he was controlling his own. But what she got from him with the mention of Chesney was like a bad taste showing up in her mouth, a bitterness that made her grimace. "He's highly respected in DC," she protested.

'Have you read him?' It was a thought, not spoken aloud.

Sylvie shrugged. The answer was no, not really. She didn't work around Chesney. He'd wanted female protection on his daughter and she was Ty's best female op. Most of her time was spent accompanying Rachel to school or after-school activities. "I guard his daughter."

"He's mixed up with the Mexican drug cartels."

Sylvie laughed. "No way."

But Lucas's expression was serious. She took a step closer to him, looking up into his face, trying to read his emotions, to feel the flavor of his thoughts.

"He's Raymond Chesney," she said, pointing out the obvious. "He's the ultimate DC power broker. Hell, his company probably raked in millions from their Iraq contracts. Maybe billions."

"AlecCorp?"

"They were everywhere in Iraq," Sylvie confirmed.

"You were there?"

Sylvie nodded. "Private contractor. I wanted to re-enlist using my real name, but I couldn't." She gave a half-chuckle, not really amused, but no longer bitter, either. "No high school diploma. So I served my country for money instead of honor."

Lucas paused. Sylvie could feel the questions he wanted to ask, but she forestalled him by saying, "Not the point. Chesney has no reason to be in business with the cartels."

"He's selling them weapons," Lucas answered.

Weapons? Sylvie frowned, searching Lucas's face. He believed he was telling the truth, she could see. And the idea of Chesney selling weapons illegally didn't cause the same instinctive recoil on her part as the thought of drugs did. It felt unlikely, but not impossible. "Someone at AlecCorp would have to be involved."

"Yeah," he agreed. "But I don't know who."

Sylvie didn't answer. He'd just told her what he was looking for in Chesney's office, she knew. But what was she supposed to do with that information? "I work for him," she finally said. "I'm not going to spy on him. And I'm definitely not helping you break into his office."

"I didn't ask you to," Lucas answered.

"I think you're crazy to believe he'd get mixed up with drug dealers. He's Raymond Chesney. He supports the tough-on-crime, pro-drug-war politicians. Pro-every-war actually, but that's not the point."

"It might be," Lucas answered, but Sylvie ignored him.

An idea had just occurred to her. Was it terrible? Possibly. Spending time with Lucas was dangerous and she needed to remember that. But he was also persistent and unlikely to give up this ridiculous notion easily. "Next Friday night . . ."

Lucas waited before prompting her. "Yes?"

She looked away from him, shaking her head, already regretting her own insanity. "AlecCorp has a big holiday party. We were all invited, some kind of collegial courtesy thing because of Chesney. I wasn't going to go, but all the bigwigs will be there, including Chesney. If you wanted to peek into a few minds . . ."

Lucas was starting to smile. "Are you inviting me to a party, Sylvie?"

She rolled her eyes. "I have no intention of spying on my employer. If reading a few minds will reassure you, I'll help you. But only with this. I'm not doing anything else."

"I don't want you to," Lucas said quickly. "It's too dangerous for you. I don't want you involved."

"Dangerous?" Did he forget which one of them was an ex-Marine? "I can take care of myself, Lucas."

"I know you, Sylvie. If you find out—"

"You know me." Sylvie interrupted him, scoffing. "Lucas, you don't know me. You haven't seen me in years and I work for Chesney. I could know all about his questionable business practices."

"You could be working for the Zetas?" Lucas offered. It was his turn to step closer, close enough that he was almost touching her, and she could feel his warmth on her front, gentler than the warmth of the heater at her back. "You're not."

"Ha." She tried to laugh. "We haven't met in a decade. Life happens. People change. We're not the same. For all you know, I'm married. With kids. You could be married." She wasn't asking a question. Really, she wasn't.

"I'm not."

"Lucas . . ." It was almost a whisper, and then Sylvie shook her head and took a decisive step backward, out of the circle of light cast by the heat lamp and into a shade lit by the tiny holiday lights decorating the garden. "Ty investigated you. You're still working for your dad's company, but people in DC think it's some sort of psychic think tank, instead of a research lab and investment firm. No one wants to talk about you officially, unless it's to laugh at the idea, but the people who don't want to talk are way more interesting than those who do."

'Changing the subject?'

Sylvie's chin went up. She wasn't blocking him, she couldn't, but she wasn't thinking in words. "You've met other telepaths by now. You've had this . . ." She let the sentence trail off. She didn't know the word that could describe what they had.

"I've met other telepaths, yes," he answered. *'It's not the same.'* He took a step closer to her and Sylvie automatically took another step back, until her legs hit the wood of a planter.

"You don't know me," she insisted.

"You'd work for the Zetas?" he asked her, voice mild, as if the question was casual, even as he moved closer.

When did he get so big, she wondered? The wide chest, the muscular arms? The Lucas she'd known had still been boyish. "Of course not," she snapped back, finally answering his question, but feeling pressured by his intrusion into her space.

'Then I do know you,' he thought, bending his head to hers.

Her murmur was protest, truly it was, but her lips parted under his as if she had words to say instead of just breath to give him. The fire started at her toes and soared up through her veins, turning her muscles into molten lava, her brain into mush.

'Damn it, Lucas,' she thought, even as she melted into him, even as her lips greedily took his and she felt the warmth of his hands sliding up her back as her own hands slid under his jacket and tugged at his shirt, pulling it loose from his pants. Closer, closer, that was always the way with him. As if they could find a place where the two of them became one, not only metaphorically but literally.

Her hands were burning against his skin, her lips teasing his, their tongues tangling, when she felt the faint buzz of a vibrating phone against her waist.

She ignored it. He did, too. But it kept buzzing, pausing momentarily and then starting up again, until finally Sylvie pulled away from Lucas and, breathless, said, "Your phone?"

He stroked his hand up her arm, and even through her suit jacket, she shivered at his touch.

She could hear the regret in his voice as he said, "I know."

She frowned. What was that about?

"She's going to be pissed," Lucas said, conversationally, as he pulled his phone out and looked at it. Sylvie's frown deepened. She? Who was Lucas talking to? Her?

He turned the phone to her. The text read, *Tell her.*

Sylvie scowled. "Tell who?"

"You."

"What?" she snapped. Damn it, Lucas was confusing her. Again.

"Dillon," Lucas answered.

Sylvie had no place left to retreat. The wood of the planter was solid against the back of her legs. But she straightened her back automatically, chin firming. "What are you talking about?"

"Dillon," he repeated.

"What about him?"

"He's a ghost."

CHAPTER SIX

His mom laughed.

His dad didn't.

"Lucas, have you gone insane? First you think Chesney— Raymond Chesney—is dealing with the drug cartels and now you think Dillon is a ghost?"

Dillon made a face. His dad had warned him that his mom would be difficult. Lucas smiled though, as if Sylvie had said something encouraging instead of dismissive.

"I know it sounds unlikely."

"Unlikely? It sounds certifiable."

"I understand how you feel. I wasn't too happy when Max started claiming that Dillon was haunting his car. But he was right." Lucas sounded more amused than convincing and Dillon scowled.

He wanted his mom to know that he was here, that he was thinking of her, that he was interested. He wanted to talk to her, and he wanted her to believe his messages when he sent them. His dad needed to help him make that happen, which meant persuading her that ghosts were real, not letting her think he was crazy.

"Your father thinks he can see the future. He's not exactly a voice of sanity," Sylvie snapped, and then her tone softened and she put her hand on Lucas's sleeve. "I can't believe I'm saying this, but I know a therapist. She's good at her job. She can get you help."

Lucas laughed and put his hand over Sylvie's, stroking her fingers as she continued. "I'm serious, Lucas. Paranoia and delusions are dangerous. You need real help. Probably, I don't know, medication. Something!"

"I'm touched by your concern," Lucas answered, his voice husky, before running his hand all the way up Sylvie's arm and over her shoulder until he cupped her cheek. "If our ghostly son wasn't watching, I'd—oh, hell, I will anyway." Bending his head, he started kissing her again.

"Damn it. That is so not cool, Dad." Dillon turned his back to them. He didn't mind if his parents got together. In fact, haunting them would be a lot more convenient if they'd spend more time in the same place. But they were his parents. He shouldn't have to watch them fool around.

He concentrated hard, closing his eyes. When he'd first started manipulating energy to send messages, he'd had to touch the device as if he was using static energy discharge to make a connection, but his technique had gotten better with practice. Now his energy made him more like a walking cell phone himself, one that could send a message to any nearby phone. He heard the sound of his father's phone buzzing and then Lucas's low chuckle.

"How are you doing that?" Sylvie asked. "Do you have someone watching us?"

"Yes, Mom," Dillon said. "I'm watching you." He turned back. She'd taken a step away from Lucas, moving her hand from his sleeve to his chest, as if to hold him off.

Lucas was smiling at the phone, where Dillon's text said, *STOP THAT*, in all caps.

"I know perfectly well that your grandparents used to kiss in front of you," Lucas responded to Dillon's text before saying to Sylvie, "Not unless you count Dillon. He's here."

Sylvie opened her mouth as if to say something and then closed it before she let the words out. Then she opened it again. Then she sighed and closed it. She sat down, hard, on the edge of the planter at her back and put her hands up over her eyes as Dillon finished sending another text to Lucas.

As Lucas's phone buzzed again, Sylvie put her hand out. "Let me see that," she ordered.

Lucas handed her the phone and she read the text aloud. *Not the same.* She looked around the garden's shadowy corners, as if searching for a hidden watcher, but between the twinkling holiday decorations, the heat lamps and the light spilling out from the glass hotel windows, the garden wasn't truly dark.

Dillon looked around too, following her gaze. No one seemed to be watching them. "It's just me, Mom," he said, feeling more cheerful. Maybe between them, he and his dad would convince her after all.

Sylvie looked up at Lucas. "You're saying that ghosts are real?"

He nodded. "As real as telepathy, precognition, finding, and whatever you're calling your gift these days."

Sylvie shook her head in seeming disbelief. "Please tell me that crazy lady with the auras wasn't telling the truth."

"Mrs. Swanson?" Lucas chuckled. "No idea. Not sure there's a way to prove auras."

"But you've proved—to your satisfaction—that ghosts exist?" Sylvie's eyes were intent upon Lucas.

"Yep."

"And that Dillon is a ghost?"

"Yep." Lucas nodded, still smiling.

"And it's not a fake? It's not some spiritualist conning you?"

"Conning me how? You see the message. It's coming from my phone. But I didn't type it in. I was busy."

Sylvie looked skeptical. "A bug? Like the listening device kind of bug? And then some kind of cell phone virus, like those thingamies that take over your computer remotely, only for a phone instead?"

Lucas's smile grew wider. "That sounds plausible," he said. "I bet someone could do that. But no. Dillon is a ghost and he's with us now."

"Then why haven't you helped him?" Sylvie demanded, abruptly standing up again. "What are you thinking? You're just letting him follow you around and send you text messages? What kind of existence is that?"

"Ah, help him how?" Lucas asked, taking a seemingly involuntary step back as his smile disappeared. Sylvie looked irate, Dillon noticed. Ha. It was fun to see his dad—his always confident, always in charge, always certain dad—looking abashed.

"Help him move on, of course. Find a white light, go into it, do what spirits do. Don't you ever watch television?" Sylvie's fair cheeks were flushing with vehemence.

"We tried something like that this summer," Lucas told her. "He doesn't want to move on."

Dillon frowned. That wasn't exactly right. It was true that he hadn't gone with his gran when she disappeared into a ghostly passageway, but he'd never seen a door of his own. Unlike other ghosts he'd met, no passageway had opened up for him. Rose said that meant it wasn't time yet. And since Rose was the only ghost he'd ever met who'd moved on and then come back, he was taking her word for it.

"He's a child," Sylvie protested. "Why are you giving him a choice?"

"Child?" Dillon objected. "I am not." He wasn't even a typical teenager, he knew. If he'd been alive, he'd be twenty by now. Okay, so maybe he was stuck in the form of a fifteen-year old, but he'd still existed those entire twenty years. And maybe his last five had been less stimulating than those of the average teenager—being trapped in a car meant a lot of time spent staring at garage walls and parking lots, and not a lot of time going to school or parties—but he'd had plenty of hours to think.

Plus, no body meant no hormones. He still had feelings—he could be happy, sad, interested, excited, afraid, all of the repertoire that he'd had while alive—but the weird surges of anger and irritability and frustration that had been plaguing him in life stopped the day he died.

"He's a ghost," Lucas answered. "What do you want me to do, ground him? Send him to his room without any dinner?"

"Nice, Dad. Thanks," Dillon said dryly.

"Help him," Sylvie said. "What does he need?" Then she turned away from Lucas and for the first time addressed Dillon directly, talking to the space around her as she looked from side to side. "What do you need?"

Aw. Dillon felt touched. With the exception of his Uncle Zane, who had always talked as if he could see Dillon, most people took a while to get used to the idea. But unfortunately, he had no idea what to tell her. What did he need?

He wouldn't mind answers to his questions.

After he'd met up with his dad again, Lucas told him the story of how he'd found Sylvie after she'd run away. She'd been gone three years. He'd been eighteen, about to go to college, and Zane had just discovered his ability to find missing objects. Lucas made Zane look at Sylvie's picture every day to see if he could find her, but with no luck. Then one day, Zane said yes, that she was somewhere to the north. They'd told their parents they were going on a brother-bonding camping trip and then drove north until Zane found her.

Lucas wouldn't tell him what had happened then, but he admitted that he'd seen her twice since. Once as he was graduating from college, the second time in Milan a few years later. He'd refused to talk about why she'd left and why she'd never come back. Those answers were hers, he'd said, looking grim.

Still, Dillon didn't think knowing the details would open a door to a different type of afterlife.

"It's more complicated than that," Lucas said. "He can't move on."

Dillon glanced over his shoulder, just to check. Yep, no cloudy passageway waiting behind him.

"Why not?"

Lucas raised his eyebrows. "Maybe he has something left to do?" he offered, sounding doubtful. "But I don't think it's that easy."

"Lucas . . ." Sylvie paused and rubbed her forehead, then said, in a tone that started with long-suffering patience and ended with annoyance, "You're being haunted by our dead son and you're not putting every possible effort into fixing that?"

"Ah, no." Lucas folded his hands together and then seemed to think better of that and stuffed them into his pants pockets.

"Why not?" Sylvie snapped.

"I think we're headed back into Milan territory," Lucas replied, words sounding almost light. Dillon, who had been watching Sylvie, sent a sharp look his way. What did that mean? There was an undercurrent in his tone that Dillon didn't understand.

Sylvie paused. "Let's not go there, then."

"I'd prefer it that way, yeah."

His parents had fought in Milan, Dillon knew. Lucas had told him that they'd argued about whether Sylvie should come back and about what was best for Dillon.

"So this is what you wanted to tell me?" Sylvie asked. "My employer is a criminal and Dillon is haunting you?"

"Well, ah . . ." Lucas looked reluctant to say any more before he finally added, "More that I think he might be haunting you for a while."

"What? What the—" Sylvie's lips were forming words but no sound was coming out.

Dillon wasn't good enough at lip-reading to be sure, but it looked to him like most of the words were bad ones. Well, she'd get used to the idea. It might take a while, but it wasn't like she could send him home. Or leave him with his grandparents.

Lucas slid his hands up her arms and rested them on her shoulders. "It'll be okay."

"I'm not a mean ghost," Dillon offered. "I promise not to do anything creepy."

Sylvie shook her head and then tugged away from Lucas. "I need to think about this. I need to—" She turned away from him and started down the path toward the door, then turned and called over her shoulder. "AlecCorp party. Next Friday. I'll see you then."

"Wear the dress," Lucas replied, his voice light, but his eyes shaded.

71

Dillon glanced at him. He hated the look on his dad's face, the sadness he could see there. But he wanted to learn more about his mom and he couldn't do that unless he followed her so he hurried after her.

She might need to think, but he intended to get to know her, whether she was happy about it or not.

*****

Sylvie headed straight to the gym.

Lucas was insane.

Or Dillon was a ghost and Chesney was a criminal.

No, no, far more likely that Lucas was insane.

But somewhere along the way, in their half verbal, half unspoken conversation, he'd denied sending her any texts. And it hadn't felt as if he were lying.

So was Lucas so insane that he had delusions, hallucinations, and blackouts where he didn't remember later what he had done? That seemed pretty damn crazy for a guy who was walking around looking debonair, not to mention doing the type of top-secret government jobs that got the person investigating him dragged out of bed in the middle of the night.

So Dillon was a ghost. And Chesney a villain.

No. Lucas was insane. Definitely, Lucas was insane.

And damn, it was after 9 already, and Sylvie had forgotten how much she hated her gym in the late evening.

"Jealous boyfriend. Better luck next time," Sylvie tossed off her standard reply to the third guy to approach her, including a quick smile before turning her head away. The first two had accepted her answer gracefully. Maybe they recognized it for the lie it was, but she found most guys appreciated its face-saving quality. But number three wasn't as bright.

"Hey, I'm just being friendly," he claimed, leaning over the front bar of the elliptical and into her space.

Sylvie bumped up the resistance level on the keypad before looking back up and responding. "Jealous boyfriend. Lots of guns. Have a nice life." She stared directly into his eyes, no smile, her gaze steady and unflinching. It took only a few seconds before he backed away, hands up.

She heard him mutter, "Bitch," under his breath as he moved off to try his luck elsewhere and she promptly forgot him.

Lucas: insane. Or Dillon: a ghost. Both choices sucked.

But that text. "You would have been a good mom." From Lucas, it would have been callous and mean-spirited. From a fifteen-year old? He might not have understood how his words would affect Sylvie. From him, the words might be sweet.

So Lucas: insane, callous, and mean.

Or Dillon: a ghost. A sweet ghost.

Damn it.

She pushed the elliptical up to its highest level, pushed her heart rate to its highest level, and tried to stop thinking.

In the shower, the realization suddenly hit her. The ghost of a teenage boy might be watching her every move as she stretched to shampoo her hair, ran the soap over her body. She froze, instinctively reaching out with her sixth sense to feel the presences in her vicinity. She brushed against the active minds—most distracted, busy, a couple in the mindful flow state of a good workout, one with an unpleasant seething excitement that caused her to recoil. Then she remembered that she wouldn't be able to feel Dillon even if he was there. She hadn't felt him before, back at the hotel, so however her sixth sense worked, it didn't read ghostly emotions.

Definitely, Lucas was crazy. She liked that option so much better. Except . . . sitting on the bench in the dressing room, pulling on her shoes, Sylvie took a long deep breath before exhaling slowly. Lucas wasn't insane. He didn't feel insane. Which meant that she and Dillon needed to have a long talk as soon as possible.

Lucas might not care if Dillon moved on, but Sylvie had always wanted what was best for Dillon, and being a ghost did not fit that description as far she was concerned. She was going to find out what he needed and get her boy a damn white light.

On the other hand, it might be nice to have a chance to get to know him a little. As she walked toward the exit, she tried to imagine what it would be like to live with a ghost. He wouldn't eat much. She wondered what he liked to watch on television. Or what music he enjoyed. Would he want to go places with her? DC had lots of museums. She could take him to the Smithsonian. Or maybe the Iwo Jima Marine Corps Memorial. It offered a good view of the city on a clear day, and maybe he'd be interested in the Marine Corps history on the placards.

Her distraction made her a little slower than usual, but not so slow that she didn't realize the unpleasant mind she'd felt earlier was waiting for her as she pushed open the door. Ugh. Like she needed this tonight.

It had to be guy number three.

Did she care? He'd backed down easily enough and a broken finger might serve to dissuade him. And maybe teach him better manners. She swung her bag lightly by her side, whistling softly between her teeth. She didn't have a gun on her: she didn't trust the fancy digital locks on the lockers at the gym, so she always left her weapon secure in her car. It wasn't as if she expected danger when off-duty.

The parking lot had cleared out while she was inside. Only a few cars were left, scattered around the rectangular space. Of course, she'd gotten there at exactly the wrong time, right when the gym was busiest, so hers was at the far end of the lot. She glanced over her left shoulder. The front desk, through the glass doors and already twenty paces behind her, was empty. Figured.

He was on her right, not moving as she left him behind. Maybe she was wrong. Maybe he'd simply been answering a phone call in his car. Maybe that ugly taste was directed at someone else.

She could feel the adrenaline starting, the tension charging through her muscles, so she slowed her breath, filling her lungs as deeply and patiently as she could as she strode toward her car, head high, letting her body language radiate confidence.

Or maybe he'd been leaning against the side of the building, watching. She felt the spike in his emotions as if they were her own. Damn. Yeah, he was targeting her and he'd started to move, too quickly, too eagerly.

Decision time. Could she get to her car and inside before he reached her? Probably not, so she veered to the left, approaching a car that wasn't hers, and pulling her bag around her as if she were reaching inside it for her keys as she planned her line of attack.

Time started to stretch, slowing as her brain moved into a clear-headed lightness that encompassed everything around her: the crisp chill of the air, the smells from the vegetarian restaurant two doors down the street, the glow of light from the streetlamp, the darkness of the shadows under the trees that edged the lot, the metal glint on the handle of the car door, and the bitter tang of her pursuer's emotions . . . and then as he reached her, she swiveled, swinging her bag out and up, hoping to hit his face. There was nothing heavy in the bag, only gym clothes, so it wouldn't hurt him, just confuse and disorient him long enough for her to put him in a wrist lock.

But, oh, shit. This guy wasn't the guy she'd brushed off earlier, she realized.

Her bag had missed his face, tangling instead in his already raised right arm. She took two steps forward, making a rapid adjustment to her plan, and grabbed his left arm, twisting and spinning. Leaning into her hammerlock, she shoved him forward into the car door. His surprise let her get a decent grip on him, but it wasn't going to do a damn bit of good in the long run.

Bodybuilder, she thought, fatalistically. Or steroids. Or both.

Definitely both, she decided, as he roared with fury and tried to push back off of the car. "You fucking bitch!"

Her bag had fallen to the ground, along with whatever he'd been holding in his hand. She'd heard the clunk, but hadn't seen what it was. If it was a gun . . . .

She forced all of her weight against him, but her feet were already slipping on the smooth asphalt. "You shouldn't get near strange women in parking lots," she said. "You never know what they might do." The words came out more breathless than she liked, and she tried to steal a glance at the ground. If she let him go, could she get the bag and retrieve whatever he'd been holding?

No, she decided regretfully. He was too close, she wouldn't have enough time. Choke hold? No, the bastard was too big. And too tough.

She felt the snap more than heard it, but his scream of rage could have been heard halfway down the street if there'd been anyone around. Damn. She dropped his arm and then kicked her bag and whatever was beneath it under the car as she danced backwards and dropped into a combat stance.

Had the break even registered with him? He turned to face her, his arm dangling at his side. Pale skin, hair in a buzz cut so short it was almost shaved, probably 280 pounds of muscle. She noted the details automatically, hoping she'd need them for a police report later.

This guy was huge, fast, and too hopped up on steroids or something else to care about the pain of his broken arm. Her best bet was to get help. And quickly.

Ty would kill her for being so over-confident.

"Now I'm gonna kill ya', bitch."

Okay, Ty would have to get in line.

The car alarm on the car they'd been leaning against finally started sounding, a "hoo-wa, hoo-wa" klaxon that blared through the darkness. Sylvie ignored it, aware that everyone else who heard it was likely to do the same.

She smiled tightly at her assailant, a tense baring of her teeth with no real humor, as she said, "You can't kill me. I'm too pretty for God to let me die. Check out my chiseled jaw."

A look of confusion crossed his face, his eyes narrowing in puzzlement.

"Malcolm Reynolds?" Sylvie offered. "No? *Firefly*?" When he still looked lost, she couldn't resist rolling her eyes. "Great, I'm being attacked by a cultural illiterate."

He glared at her and she felt the flicker of doubt that entered his mind. He growled, "Not gonna to be too pretty when I'm done with you."

Behind Sylvie another car alarm went off, from a car closer to the door of the gym. She resisted the temptation to glance backwards as he looked past her, over her shoulder, his scowl deepening.

And then farther down the parking lot, in the other direction, a third car alarm started. And then a fourth. It was a chorus of annoyance, a clashing mass of sirens and klaxons. But the parking lot was empty. Sylvie tried not to let her reaction show as she realized what must be happening but her smile went from fake to real.

"Dillon," she said, as loudly and clearly as she could, not sure how far away he might be. Did he have to be next to the car to make the alarm go off? "Call 911. My phone's in my pocket."

The situation had changed, and her foe recognized it, too, but he wasn't smart enough to cut his losses and run. Sylvie felt his fury grow as he decided to attack.

He charged forward, but instead of retreating, she waited, hands up, body evenly balanced on her feet. When she felt him start to swing, she ducked instead of blocking, diving under his arm and heading straight for his center. She'd never done this move before, not for real. Simulated, sure, in LINE training, the Marine close combat techniques that she'd learned much too long ago, but not with genuine intent.

Fortunately, he was wearing sweats, not blue jeans. She turned her head to the right to shield her face and neck, raising her left arm to protect her exposed side from his flailing fist, as she reached with her right hand, searching, grabbing, and squeezing as hard as she could, then pulling down the same way.

Wow.

It worked just as advertised.

He reeled backward and his sound this time wasn't so much a scream as a high-pitched wail. Then he toppled, falling to the ground and curling around his groin as he wheezed with pain.

From her pocket, Sylvie heard the voice of the 911 dispatcher. "911, what's your emergency?"

*****

Much, much later, Sylvie leaned her head back and closed her eyes. Bodyguards and Marines were good at waiting patiently, but the post-adrenaline downward spiral had her securely in its grip, and she was so tired that her bones felt as if they were melting. If the cops didn't make a decision soon, she might beg them to throw her in a cell, just so she could lie down without fear of being stepped on.

"What the hell is going on?" Sylvie would recognize that voice anywhere.

She didn't open her eyes, but the corners of her lips pulled up. "What are you doing here?"

"I got a text. Mom's in jail, it said. Has our past finally caught up with you? "

"Ha." She opened an eye in protest and then pulled the other one open as well at the sight of Lucas. He'd obviously slept. He looked well-rested, freshly shaved and showered, dressed in business casual slacks and a gray button-down shirt. "The statute of limitations is long past and you know it."

Her senses had been dulled by exhaustion, hunger, and the sheer overload of sitting in a crowded police station for hours, or she would have felt Lucas come in, but now that she was paying attention, she could feel his worry.

What did you do, Syl?

"Won." She grinned at him and rubbed her hands over her face, trying to force herself awake. Ouch. She grimaced as her action reminded her of the one hit her attacker had gotten in. It was probably accidental, but he'd managed to bang her right cheekbone at the edge of her eye on his way down.

Lucas reached out and touched her cheek with a gentle finger. She let him turn her head, tilting her eye to the light. "Does he look worse?"

"Oh, much. That's why I'm still here. They're a little confused about who to charge with assault." Sylvie yawned and stretched, locking her fingers together and pushing, palms out, toward the ceiling.

The balding cop seated at the desk across from the bench where Sylvie had been waiting hung up his phone. "Statute of limitations?" he asked. Sylvie just looked at him. Hastily, he waved his hand in the air as if erasing the question. "Never mind, I don't want to know. Is this your lawyer?"

Sylvie's eyes narrowed. Something had changed. She could feel it. "No," she said slowly, trying to understand the officer's emotions. He'd been annoyed at her earlier, then resigned to her refusal to talk. Now he was excited. Or was it happy? Jubilant? His feelings didn't make sense. But maybe they had nothing to do with her. Had he gotten good news from home? She concentrated. With Lucas here, maybe she'd be able to pick up his thoughts.

"Does she need a lawyer?" Lucas pulled a phone out of his pocket. "I can have one here within the hour." He started to tap.

"No," said the cop and Sylvie simultaneously.

"I left a message for a friend. He'll be here when he gets it." Sylvie's response sounded abrupt, even to her ears, but she didn't need Lucas to rescue her.

"She doesn't need a lawyer." The cop stood, scooping up a pile of papers from his desk. "If you insist on immunity in writing, you'll have to wait until someone from the Commonwealth Attorney's office can get here, but I'll put it in on record in the interview room if you're willing to talk now."

"I don't understand." Sylvie frowned, unsure of herself. The police and ambulance had arrived with efficient dispatch after her conversation with the 911 operator, but events had gone downhill from there. "Is the surgery done?"

"I don't give a shit about the surgery." The cop gestured with his head for her to follow and Sylvie stood uncertainly. She glanced at Lucas.

'Can you read him?'

'No words. He's happy, though. It's like he's humming.' Lucas joined her as she followed the police officer into an interview room. The room looked suspiciously warm and friendly for Sylvie's taste; the walls

painted a cheerful yellow, the table and chairs standard office furniture. Something closer to the stereotypes she'd drawn from too many ancient episodes of *Law & Order* would have made it easier to stay on her guard.

The officer gestured Sylvie to a chair, looked at Lucas, shrugged and pointed him to a chair against the wall, saying, "Eh, we'll call it moral support. Sit over there and keep quiet."

"Did you find the weapon?" Sylvie asked the cop. Whether or not her attacker had been armed had been the source of most of the night's doubt. She said yes, but he'd claimed no, and by the time he'd started accusing her of attacking him without provocation, everyone had left the scene: the goon in an ambulance, Sylvie to give her statement at the police station. Sylvie knew that he'd been holding something in his hand, but she'd kicked whatever it was under a car. They'd sent a crime scene team to search, but no one had retrieved it yet. That, plus the results of her attacker's surgery for a ruptured testicle, had been what everyone was waiting for.

"Doesn't matter," he told her.

"Oh, yeah?" Her skepticism must have showed, but instead of scowling at her, the way he had for most of the eight hours she'd been sitting next to his desk, he smiled, a smile that looked genuine, not forced. A smile that even looked happy.

"You can rest assured, ma'am, that we'll find the object you mentioned. However, during the course of our investigation, we obtained a search warrant for the vehicle of the suspected perpetrator and while I cannot, at this time, provide you with further information about the nature of our discoveries, I can assure you that we are no longer in any doubt but that you made a good call earlier this evening."

Sylvie scrunched up her face involuntarily while she tried to weave her way through the police officer's long words and complex phrases. What had he said?

He leaned forward a little and said softly, "Ya' done good. Let me just get your statement and you can go home."

She glanced at Lucas. He nodded at her. She wavered, uncertain, doubtful.

'It's okay, go ahead and talk to him,' Lucas reassured her.

Sighing, Sylvie sat down and did as she was told.

CHAPTER SEVEN

Dillon watched his father silently reading a paperback, flipping through the pages at a speed that suggested Lucas barely saw them. They were sitting at Sylvie's table, Lucas in one of the plastic chairs, Dillon cross-legged on top of the table.

After leaving the police station, Lucas brought them straight to Sylvie's apartment. She'd complained, saying that she wanted to get her car, but she'd been falling asleep on her feet, and Lucas hadn't bothered to argue with her. She'd walked straight into her bedroom, dropped onto the bed, and mumbled something that sounded like, "See yourself out." Then she was asleep.

Lucas hadn't left, though. Dillon had watched as his father looked around Sylvie's apartment, checking out the refrigerator, the bookshelves, even the space under the television, before finally plucking a book off a shelf and settling down at the table. Every so often, he answered a phone call or responded to a text message, but they mostly sat in silence with only the brush of paper from the turning pages to disturb the quiet.

Dillon wished he could talk to Lucas. Really talk, not just text. His exertions of the evening and night had exhausted his ability but even if he could send another message, what could he say? How could he describe what it was like? The confusion, the fear, the frustration at his own helplessness. The speed at which Sylvie moved, the smile on her face that didn't meet her eyes. The exhilaration he felt when he realized he could set off the car alarms, the relief when the mugger was curled up on the ground.

And then the police station. That had almost been worse. Sylvie had been giving her statement to one officer, as calmly as if she did this kind of thing every day, when another officer hung up his phone and said, "He's claiming you attacked him, that he was just walking by."

The police officers had been smiling as if it was a joke but Sylvie had stilled and said, "Oh, did he?" She'd leaned back in her chair. Dillon had been annoyed. He'd been there, he'd seen the whole thing. The guy was lying! Why didn't his mom defend herself?

Instead, at the officer's next question, Sylvie smiled, looking regretful, and responded, "I'm afraid I'm unable to answer any more questions without a lawyer present. Or immunity from prosecution." The words sounded rehearsed. She'd said them often enough over the next several hours that maybe they were.

Dillon had been frustrated beyond belief. Why didn't she just talk? Why didn't she just tell them what had happened? When he finally had enough energy to send a text, though, he knew better than to send it to her. He'd always thought his grandpa was stubborn, but he bet Sylvie could teach Max lessons. He texted his dad instead. Lucas could fix it, he knew.

And maybe he had. Dillon didn't really understand what had happened after Lucas had arrived, but it didn't matter. They were home and safe. At least for now.

Was his dad ever really safe, though? His job seemed even more dangerous than Dillon had realized. And if his mom was working for a guy who was mixed up with drug dealers, well, she wasn't really safe either. Dillon didn't know anything about the cartels his dad had been talking about, but he knew his mom must be in danger.

He didn't like it.

He wished Akira were here. She could talk to them for him, tell them to stop doing scary shit. He was definitely not going to stop haunting them until they did. Maybe he could use one of his parents' phones to text her when he got enough energy back and ask her to come to DC? But then he remembered what his dad had said about Zane not wanting her to travel and sighed. It didn't surprise him that Zane was being over-protective; his uncle had gone a little goofy over Akira. Still, it was awfully inconvenient.

Being a ghost had never been harder. Somehow he had to get his parents—both of his parents—back to Florida so that he could get Akira's help to communicate with them. But how? He rested his elbows on his knees, cradling his chin in his hands as he stared at his dad and tried to think of a plan.

From the next room came the sound of the shower starting. Lucas looked up from his book as Dillon looked toward the closed door. Good, his mom was up. Now maybe something would happen.

Several minutes later, Sylvie emerged dressed in casual clothes with her hair wet and dangling loose around her shoulders. She paused in the doorway, seeing Lucas at the table.

Lucas dropped the paperback he'd been reading, a shiny-coated thriller, on the table before him. "That book sucks."

Sylvie glanced at it as she crossed into her tiny kitchen. "I haven't read it."

"Gaping plot holes, bad characterization," Lucas continued and then paused. "Oh. Why is it so beat-up?"

"Bought it at a garage sale for a quarter," she answered, pulling a mug out of her cabinet. "What are you still doing here, Lucas?"

She pulled the coffee pot out of the machine and poured the final dregs into her mug.

"That's cold," Lucas pointed out, standing up and moving to where he could watch her.

"I'm not picky." She took a sip, looking at him over the top of the mug. Her expression showed no reaction to the taste of the bitter beverage, but she put the mug down on the counter. "Why are you still here?"

He leaned against the wall, and for a moment, there was silence. Damn it, Dillon wished he could swear at them. They were talking to one another without words again, he recognized. But he wanted to hear what they had to say.

"And did you learn anything?" Sylvie asked, turning back to the coffee maker and opening the top.

Lucas also turned away. He looked out into the Spartan living room. "No DVDs," he said. "So I don't know anything about your taste in movies. No CDs, so ditto music. Books a mix—you've got some of everything, and no way of telling which you really like."

"I like them cheap," Sylvie answered. "I buy them at garage sales, and get rid of them when I've read them."

"No photos on the walls, no mementos, no souvenirs," Lucas continued. "White walls. I'd say you didn't paint, just left the place as the landlord had it, so no idea about your taste in color. Refrigerator almost empty, so you don't cook."

Sylvie made a noncommittal sound as she dumped the old coffee grounds into the trash.

"Sherlock Holmes couldn't learn anything about you from this place, Syl. Except maybe that this is just a bed to sleep in, not a home. You might as well be living in a hotel."

"So why were you trying?" Sylvie scooped coffee grounds into a fresh filter.

"Because you were right before."

She looked at him and lifted an eyebrow. Dillon didn't know what Lucas was talking about either. From his perch on the table, he said, "Go on."

He knew his father couldn't hear him, but Lucas obeyed. "You said that people change, that we weren't the same. You were right. I'm not who I was at fifteen or even at twenty-five. You don't know who I am. And I don't know who you are either." He paused, maybe waiting for an answer.

Sylvie filled the coffee pot with water, not looking at him.

"I want to learn, though."

She still didn't answer.

Dillon would have pounded on the tabletop in frustration, except that he'd fall right through it if he did. Why couldn't his parents just talk to one another like normal people? He wanted to know what his mom was thinking.

Lucas spoke again. "We never had a chance."

Finally, Sylvie turned away from the coffeepot. "Is Dillon here?"

"I don't know," Lucas answered. "He hasn't sent me any new messages." He stuffed his hands into his pockets. "Check your phone?"

She nodded and returned to her bedroom for a moment, then came back, phone in hand. "Nothing," she said, looking troubled. She looked around the room. "Dillon?" Her voice sounded tentative. "Are you here?"

She looked down at her phone. Lucas watched. Dillon tried again to send a message. But nothing happened. The events of the previous evening and night had used up his energy. He'd have to wait.

"Where is he?" Sylvie asked.

"I don't know." Lucas shrugged. "Last time, Akira said to give it twenty-four hours before I worried. But I didn't hear from him until I found you again."

"Akira?"

Lucas didn't quite smile. "Zane's girlfriend. Soon-to-be-wife. She talks to ghosts."

Sylvie didn't smile back.

"I know. But she's not crazy. Or at least not crazier than anyone else at home."

Sylvie didn't quite sigh. Lucas's not-quite-smile turned into a grin. Dillon had to smile, too. Akira could see and talk to ghosts but she didn't much appreciate the ability.

"So we're just supposed to hope?" Sylvie asked. "Just wait and wonder?"

"Yeah."

"Holy Christ, that sucks." Sylvie grimaced. "Is he okay? Could he have gotten hurt?"

Lucas raised his hands in a gesture of uncertainty. "I don't know."

Sylvie stared down at her phone, as if wishing it could talk. "How can he be a ghost?"

"I don't know."

"What does he need?"

Lucas shook his head. "I can't answer that." His smile was gone. He looked grim, the way he'd looked most of the time since Dillon had been a ghost. If Dillon had realized that his death would screw up his dad so badly, he would have been more careful. But it was too late now.

"Does he want something?" Sylvie continued. "Is there something he has to do? Something unfinished?"

Lucas crossed his arms. "Unanswered questions, you mean?"

Sylvie scowled at him. "I made the right choice."

Lucas didn't answer her. She turned her face away from him. Then she walked back into the kitchen.

That was interesting, Dillon thought. His dad sounded almost angry. And he didn't do angry, usually. He did quiet. Cold. Not even that very often, really.

"I am not an idiot," Sylvie called from the kitchen. Uh-oh. Where Lucas had sounded almost angry, as if a hint of temper was tucked under his stoic surface, Sylvie sounded pure mad.

She returned to the living room, her fair skin flushed almost red, fingers tight around the coffee cup in her hand.

"I didn't say you were."

"You thought it."

A muscle twitched in Lucas's cheek. "Yeah, well, if you cared what I thought, maybe you should have listened back then."

"You thought everything would be fine!"

"It would have been." Lucas scowled.

"You heard the sheriff's thoughts as clearly as I did. He was waiting for my eighteenth birthday so he could try me as an adult!"

"It wouldn't have happened!" Lucas snapped.

Dillon wanted to scream. This was almost as bad as when they'd been communicating telepathically. He had no idea what they were talking about it. The sheriff wanted to arrest his mom? And his dad—his dad, who never got angry, never raised his voice—was looking at least as furious as his mom, blue eyes bright, an edge of color touching his tan cheeks.

"You can't—" Sylvie started furiously. And then she stopped. She took a deep breath. Carefully, she placed her coffee cup on the table, narrowly missing Dillon's leg. "I can't believe we're having this argument again."

Lucas's mouth twisted. He glanced at his watch. Anger still edging his voice, he offered, "Took us longer this time. We've been together for at least six hours."

"I was asleep," Sylvie protested, half smiling, half sulky.

Lucas shrugged. "Still a record."

Sylvie shook her head, expression rueful. She looked at Lucas for a long moment, then turned away and crossed to the window. She pushed the curtain aside and looked out. Dillon had already spent a long time looking out that window. He knew there was nothing to see but a parking lot and some trees.

"Is that his unfinished business?" she asked, her voice sounding muffled. "Is he a ghost because I abandoned him?"

Dillon stood, jumping off the table. He wished he could talk to her. He was sure she was wrong. He didn't know why he was a ghost, but he knew it couldn't have anything to do with his mom leaving him.

Lucas followed Sylvie to the window. "I don't think he's a ghost because of anything you did, Syl. Or anything I did."

"But you don't know."

"I do," Dillon said, annoyed. "It's nothing to do with you." Or was it? Perhaps his continued existence did have something to do with his parents. Not that he needed questions answered. And not that they'd done anything wrong. But maybe the reason he was stuck—he paused and glanced over his shoulder, but nope, there was still no sign of a passageway to another plane of existence—was that they needed something from him.

Forgiveness? Absolution?

Or better yet, lives.

Both of his parents lived like campers. No real homes, no real belongings, no real relationships. He knew his dad had girlfriends, but he'd never had one important enough to bring home, and his mom clearly didn't have anyone significant in her life.

"It's not your fault," Lucas said gently.

Sylvie turned toward him. "This is how this story goes," she said, voice bleak. "We make up, we fall into bed together, we fight again, we don't see one another for years. Right?"

No, Dillon thought. He didn't like that story. It was time for a new one. Time for a story where his parents stopped doing scary shit and started living instead. Now that he'd met his mom, it was like he finally understood his dad.

"We could skip the second fight this time around," Lucas suggested. He reached out and touched Sylvie's hair where it fell across her shoulder. It was looking coppery, Dillon noticed, as if the fake brown color was washing away.

"Good idea, Dad," Dillon said. That was it. He needed to get his parents together. Together the way they always should have been.

*****

Sylvie stared blindly out the window.

She'd tried to do her best for her son. Leaving him had been the hardest moment of her life. A hundred times, a thousand times, she'd thought about turning around and going back for him.

Joining the military had been a way of tying her hands, a self-imposed prison sentence to limit her own freedom. She hadn't expected to like it. But she had. She definitely hadn't expected to be good at it. But she was.

Was that why Dillon was a ghost? Because she'd moved on to other things? Because she'd left him to spend his life wondering why his mother had rejected him?

But Lucas had promised her that Dillon was fine. Happy, healthy, thriving. She'd seen the pictures. She'd believed him.

"It's not your fault." Lucas's answer should have been comforting.

She could feel him behind her. He'd gone from angry to soothing and gentle in no time, the way he could, but she still felt the lingering burn of insult.

She turned toward him, searching his eyes for traces of the boy she'd once loved beyond reason. That boy was still there, she realized, as he reached out and touched her hair. But it was too late for them.

And besides, their ghostly son could be watching even now.

"Ha." She tugged her hair away from Lucas. "Not this time. Not when an invisible teenage boy could be watching every move we make. No, this story ends here."

"He's not malicious," Lucas protested. "He's not some angry poltergeist."

"Not the point," Sylvie answered. "He's a ghost. He shouldn't be!"

"Come back to Tassamara with me. We can talk to Akira. Maybe she'll have some way you can help him move on."

"Not a chance." Sylvie glared.

Lucas sighed. Sylvie could feel him restraining his impatience. "It's not—"

"Don't even go there," she interrupted him. "I'm never going back there. Never."

"Sylvie," he started.

"Don't patronize me," she snapped, before taking a deep breath and turning away again. Oh, God, wasn't this always the way it went? "Shut up," she added. He hadn't said a word but she could hear the rush of thought flowing through his brain and he was feeling just as annoyed as she.

She pressed her hands together in front of her face, trying to find some patience. "Let's just do it."

"Do what?"

"Tell him. Talk to him."

"Tell him what?"

"Whatever." Sylvie turned again, letting her hands drop, still folded together, to her waist. "If he needs to know why I left, fine, I can tell him that."

She stepped forward, brushing past Lucas, and looked out into the room. She took a breath, and then let it go. Hell. This would be harder than she imagined. Would she really have to revisit their whole past?

"I moved to Tassamara when I was seventeen," she started, feeling stupid, even as tears sprang to her eyes. She blinked furiously. She was not going to cry, damn it. It was a long time ago. She was so over this.

"My mom was a waitress," she continued. "Some guy had offered her a job there, and she liked the idea of a small town. We'd been living in Orlando, and it was . . ." She paused. Could she explain what it had been like? Would it mean anything to Dillon? Fifteen years old, all of them spent in Tassamara. He wouldn't understand. ". . . rough," she finally finished.

"So we moved to Tassamara. Frickin' weird place."

She swallowed hard. March of her junior year. What had she been like to them? She'd been used to working hard at being invisible, good at the skill of disappearing in the sea of trouble, but Tassamara wasn't big enough. Instead, she'd been the new kid.

"I met your dad. Without him, I'm, maybe, empathic. I know how people feel. I don't need to see them or hear them, I just know. But with him . . ."

She tried, so hard, not to glance at Lucas, standing behind her, but she couldn't help herself. The sympathy she felt from him didn't make her words come any easier, but she took another deep breath.

"With him, I can read minds. I can't believe you wanted that. It's really not much fun. People—even nice people—their thoughts don't always match their words. And being a pregnant teenager . . ." She paused. Did this matter? Of course it did.

"Some people thought I was a slut. Some people felt sorry for me and even sorrier for you. And the sheriff wanted to arrest me." Her laugh was bitter. Ignorance was no excuse under the law, but she hadn't known how old Lucas was. And maybe it wouldn't have mattered. What she and Lucas had was hard to resist.

"He would have been a laughingstock," Lucas muttered.

Sylvie clenched her teeth. She hadn't told Lucas she was leaving, but he'd known why. He'd overheard the sheriff's thoughts, too, and he'd found her for the first time after he turned eighteen. But even if she could have, she wouldn't have come back. The statute of limitations didn't run out until five years after his eighteenth birthday.

"The law's changed now," Lucas continued. She glanced back at him, startled. "In Florida, anyway," he added, mouth twisting in a wry smile. "It's called the Romeo and Juliet law. Consenting teenagers are now allowed a four year age difference."

"Ha." She gave a puff of laughter, then turned back to the empty room. "Back then it was two, and the age of consent was sixteen. I was seventeen and your dad was fifteen. That made us, me, our—" Sylvie couldn't believe she was explaining her sex life to her invisible child. Could this get more awkward? "I could have gone to jail. And then I would have been a registered sex offender. I didn't want that."

She paused and licked her lips. This part would be harder to say aloud, harder to say in front of Lucas, who took so much for granted.

"I could have taken you with me. I thought about it. My mom would have helped. She'd been a teenage mom herself and she'd raised me on her own. That meant, though, that I knew how hard it was." She stopped. She could leave it there. It would be easier. But it wasn't the whole story.

"And I knew what your life would be like," she continued, voice steady. "I didn't want that for you."

She thought back to her childhood, the tiny apartments, the cold cereal dinners, the thrift store clothing, the regular moves for a better life always just out of reach. It hadn't truly been unhappy. Her mom had loved her. Maybe she'd made a mistake.

"I wanted you to have your dad's life. I wanted you to live in the big house, with a bicycle. And your own bedroom. A safe place. And Santa Claus. I wanted you to play soccer and have neighbors who knew your name." The words were coming faster, even though her throat felt like she was choking and her face felt hot and flushed. "I wanted you to take the SATs and go to college."

She felt Lucas's hands come up behind her and rest on her shoulders, warm and strong, and she shivered. The room felt cool, colder with his hands on her. "I made a mistake, I guess. I was wrong. I'm sorry."

"Sylvie." She could feel the rush of feeling from Lucas, the guilt and the grief and the sorrow.

But she waited for something more.

Nothing.

And then her phone buzzed.

It's OK.

That was all the message said, but Sylvie took a deep breath. That was it, then.

That was what he'd needed.

Now he could move on.

CHAPTER EIGHT

Dillon had no intention of going anywhere.

If St. Peter had appeared, beckoning him toward the pearly gates with flights of angels playing trumpets—or would it be harps?—floating on fluffy white clouds above him, Dillon would have ignored them.

He had to agree with his dad: his mom's reason for leaving was stupid. His grandparents would never have let her go to jail. Except . . . well, now that he thought about it, he wasn't one hundred percent sure of that. His gran had been strict with him, always treating him like a little kid. He'd figured it was because he was so much younger than his aunts and uncles, but maybe it had something to do with his dad growing up too fast?

While he would never have said so—not to anyone—his gran's overprotectiveness probably had a lot more to do with his death than his mom's abandonment. Being psychic had felt like a much-needed ticket to adulthood. Still, maybe those pieces were all connected.

But none of this mattered anyway. No door had appeared, so just as he'd anticipated, learning why his mom left had nothing to do with why he was a ghost.

Did he want his parents to know that, though?

He frowned, tuning Sylvie and Lucas out as they started yet another low-voiced argument about whether or not he was still around. His mom didn't seem to like the idea of him haunting her. Even once she was over the shock, her first thought had been how to get rid of him. She hadn't been mean about it, but if he let her know he was still here, would he have to spend all his time fending off mediums and exorcisms?

Maybe he should just keep quiet for now. At least until he figured out how he was going to fix his parents' lives.

It'd be simplest if Akira could help him talk to them. But he'd seen Sylvie's reaction to that idea, and he'd seen how stubborn she could be. The direct approach was probably out. If she wouldn't willingly come to Tassamara, though, he was going to have to get her there by stealth.

Yeah, he needed subtlety. He needed strategy.

He needed a plan.

And until he had one, he'd keep quiet. He'd talk to his parents when he was ready. Meanwhile, let them argue. Which they would. Apparently, it was what they did best. He sat back down on the table to watch them debate, but it was almost over.

"Fine." Lucas raked his hand through his hair, scowling with frustration. "Next Friday, then. But don't count on this being the end, Sylvie."

"Never." She sounded resigned.

"And will you wear the . . ." he began, stepping closer to her and starting to slide his hand around her waist. Dillon rolled his eyes. It was like being back with Akira and Zane again without the advantage of being able to retreat to hang out with Rose.

"Lucas!" It was half-laugh, half-command, as she put her hand flat on his chest and began pushing him toward the door. "I'm tired. And whether or not Dillon is gone or Chesney is working for the cartels, I've got to call Ty, deal with work, talk to my lawyer, and find out what that mess last night was all about. I'm not letting you sidetrack me."

"Ah, I've got part of that puzzle solved for you."

Sylvie stopped. "Yeah?"

"It hasn't hit the news yet, but I texted a friend and asked him to find out what the police thought they had."

Sylvie's eyes narrowed. "The same friend who gets the cops to pull over perfectly innocent, law-abiding drivers?"

Lucas's smile flashed. "I've got plenty of friends in law enforcement, but yeah, Andy's the one I called. He knows the locals."

"And so?"

Lucas sobered. "They're waiting on forensics from the guy's car, but they think he's a serial rapist, probably a murderer. They're looking at him for a couple of disappearances from last summer. Apparently one of the missing women was abducted from a gym parking lot in Alexandria."

Holy shit.

If Dillon had blood, it would have all drained from his face as he realized what could have happened.

His mom could have been murdered.

Abducted, tortured, killed.

And he wouldn't have been able to do anything but watch.

He would have been helpless to save her.

"Oh?" Sylvie let her hand drop from Lucas's chest, and then tucked both hands behind her back, almost as if she was falling into a parade rest. "Oh." The first word was surprised, the second thoughtful.

"You had to have known he was there. What were you thinking?"

"He wasn't wearing a sign labeled murderer." But then she shrugged. "I figured I could take him."

"Jeez, Mom," Dillon protested. Had she seen the size of that guy? Was she insane?

Lucas, though, just quirked a brow at her.

"Hey, I won," Sylvie said, before adding, "Okay, I might have been a little over-confident."

Lucas didn't comment, at least not in a way that Dillon could hear, but Sylvie's smile flickered on and off like a lightning strike.

"You'll need to testify at his trial." Lucas sounded calmer than Dillon liked. Why wasn't his dad telling his mom not to take crazy risks? That guy could have killed her!

Sylvie shrugged again. "Not a problem. It might be good for business."

"How very pragmatic." Lucas's voice was dry.

Dillon shook his head. Okay, he was definitely getting his mom a new life. A nice, safe life. A happy life, too. But more importantly, a life where dealing with serial killers didn't have a positive side.

"Hey, I don't work for some mysterious company that no one wants to talk about. 'Close protection security consultants' get jobs from word-of-mouth and recommendations," Sylvie said, putting mocking air quotes around the title.

"If you need work—"

"Stop," Sylvie interrupted him. "Don't even go there."

Ooh, that was a good idea. If his mom went to work for his family's company, she wouldn't be in danger from any Mexican drug cartels. Maybe his grandpa ought to have a bodyguard?

"We'll talk about it later."

"Lucas." Sylvie's voice held a warning.

Lucas grinned at her, but didn't answer. Turning, he said to the air as he moved toward the doorway, "Dillon? I'm sure you want to stay with your mom for a while. Thanks for the message this morning."

"See you later, Dad," Dillon answered absently, thinking about jobs at GD. It might be tough to convince his mom to stay in

Tassamara. But he knew GD sometimes did work for insurance companies: maybe she'd be willing to do that?

"He's not still here," Sylvie protested. "Why would he be?"

"Notice how cold it is in here?" Lucas said.

"Yeah." Sylvie sounded doubtful. "The heat must be off."

"Ghost sign," Lucas said, sounding cheerful. "When a ghost gets upset—and I'm guessing Dillon didn't like hearing about the serial killer—they pull in energy from the atmosphere. It makes the room cold."

"Don't tell her that," Dillon complained, paying attention again. "She'll start trying to exorcise me."

"You have got to be kidding me."

Lucas's grin grew a little wider but he didn't say anything.

"No way. He's moved on. He must have."

"We could argue about this forever," Lucas answered her. "I'm not going to. We'll find out eventually."

"Damn it, Lucas, if Dillon needs help moving on—" Sylvie started.

"If Dillon needs help—any kind of help—I'll do my best to give it to him," Lucas interrupted, speaking directly to her. "But I'm not making his choices for him. If he wants help, I'm here. He knows how to find me." Turning away again, he added to the air, one hand on the door, "Text me if you need me, bud."

"That's—you're—that's—" Sylvie almost spluttered a response and then stopped and simply glared at Lucas. Dillon could tell that she was speaking to him telepathically again.

"I'm not being unfair," Lucas answered her aloud. "For twenty years, you've made the choices for all of us. Not anymore." He smiled at her, the expression wry, and added, "I'll see you next week. Wear the dress."

As he pulled the door closed behind him, Sylvie seemed torn between kicking the door and yelling. And then she sighed, bending her neck and pressing her forehead with the base of her palm as if her head hurt. "Dillon?" she asked, voice muffled slightly by her position, before lifting her head, moving her hand, and repeating the name. "Dillon?"

She looked around the room, eyes intent, as if she could see him if she looked hard enough. "Are you here?" she asked. She looked down at the phone that she'd been clutching all along, but Dillon didn't send her a text. He felt sorry for her, but not so sorry that he wanted to get pushed into leaving before he was ready.

"I tried to do what was best," she said. "Really I did."

He believed she had. But Dillon agreed with his dad. He didn't want Sylvie making the decisions anymore.

*****

It was like waiting for the sword to fall.

Sylvie couldn't remember whose sword it was, or why it was hanging by a single thread, or what it had to do with anticipation. But checking her phone for text messages had become a nervous habit over the past couple of days.

She glanced at it again now.

Nothing.

No texts from a sweet boy ghost nor any word from his aggravating father. For the hundredth time, she wondered if she should call Lucas. Just to ask him if he'd heard from Dillon, of course.

Lucas had thought Dillon was staying with her, but maybe Dillon had heard enough. Maybe he wanted to be with his father. Or maybe he really had moved on.

She slipped her phone back into the bag at her feet, then turned to look at the monitors. It was Sunday morning and she was sitting in the security room at the Chesney mansion. She didn't usually work on Sundays, but Ty had reshuffled the schedule to deal with her unexpected Thursday absence and she'd picked up the Sunday shift for her replacement.

A gentle knock on the doorframe interrupted her and Sylvie swiveled her chair. Rachel stood in the doorway, still wearing her going-to-church clothes: a navy blue button-down dress with white piping and matching navy blue flats.

Sylvie let a polite smile curve her lips, covering her surprise, as she said hello. Rachel didn't seek out her bodyguards. In fact, as far as Sylvie could tell, when at home, Rachel usually emerged from her bedroom only for meals.

"I have an art project due for school. Do you—I need you—could you take me to an art gallery this afternoon?" Rachel started briskly, before trailing off uncertainly under Sylvie's gaze. "For school," she repeated, rubbing her foot against the back of her leg and dropping her eyes.

Sylvie didn't let her expression change. "Sure thing," she said. "What time do you want to leave?"

Rachel was lying. Sylvie probably didn't even need her gift to tell her so, but with it, she could feel Rachel's mix of guilt and nervous excitement even as they transformed into a burst of anticipation at Sylvie's words.

A boy? Sylvie wondered, but it didn't matter to her. She didn't need to know what the teenager was planning or why Rachel felt the need to lie about it. Her job was to keep Rachel safe. It'd be easier if Rachel trusted her, but an art gallery wasn't likely to be dangerous.

Just boring.

Sylvie tried not to let her lack of enthusiasm show as Rachel bubbled over with delight at the gallery three hours later. It was surprisingly crowded for a space dotted with the bleakest, ugliest metal structures Sylvie had ever seen. That was good news: it meant Sylvie could focus on the people instead of the equally dark paintings on the walls.

"Don't you like this one?" Rachel asked her.

Sylvie glanced at it. It looked like a dead tree. Why would anyone want to paint a dead tree? A living tree, okay, that might be pretty hanging over your sofa, but a dead tree?

"It's very nice," she answered Rachel, trying to keep her voice noncommittal. Inwardly, she was wondering. What were they doing here? Rachel had a frenetic quality to her enthusiasm that only added to Sylvie's suspicions, but as she scanned the room, Sylvie felt increasingly doubtful. Where was the teenage boy she'd expected to see? Or even a teenage girl? Rachel was the only adolescent in the gallery.

Rachel's lengthy list of activities didn't include art lessons, so despite her apparent enjoyment of the paintings, it seemed unlikely that it was the art that brought her here. But what else could it be? Automatically, Sylvie scanned the emotions of the people nearest them, looking for flavors of danger but finding none.

A nearby woman was showing a decided interest in the two of them, however. Sylvie looked in her direction, meeting her stare and assessing her quickly. The woman wasn't typical Washington or even typical Georgetown: with three inch heels on knee high boots, artfully tousled hair streaked with vibrant almost-natural color, and a gray dress with bold geometric black lines, she could have stepped off the plane from New York or Paris. Meeting Sylvie's gaze, she stepped forward and gave a bright smile.

"Ms. Blair?" she said.

"Yes?" Sylvie responded warily, glancing at Rachel but feeling nothing from the girl but mild curiosity. This meeting wasn't what Rachel was excited about.

"I thought it was you." As the woman fumbled open her black clutch purse, Sylvie tensed, but it was automatic, not instinct. She didn't feel a threat, just an eagerness almost equal to Rachel's. The woman pulled out a business card, handing it to Sylvie with a breathless laugh. "I hate to say it, but it was the black eye that convinced me."

Sylvie resisted the urge to touch her cheek—the bruise from Wednesday night had darkened to a deep purple edged with green—and glanced down at the card. Stylist? What the hell was a stylist?

"I'm sure you're going to be busy over the next few days. The offers from the morning shows must be pouring in. But if you need any fashion advice, I'd love to help. I could recommend a great concealer, for example, to help cover up that eye. And the right colors make a huge difference on television. I'm sure the all-black look works for your job, but some softer shades—maybe a forest green or even something brighter, like a royal blue that matched your eyes—would really stand out."

Television? The woman continued to talk but Sylvie, after glancing down at her black slacks and shirt, had stopped listening. She'd thrown her phone away just over a week ago. Although she'd picked up a new one on Tuesday, the number was unlisted. Half the world could be calling her and she wouldn't know about it.

"Well, congratulations again, and do keep me in mind." The woman flashed another smile at Sylvie and backed away. Sylvie nodded, hoping she'd said something polite and didn't look as horrified as she felt.

"Television, Sylvie? Are you going to be on television?" Rachel didn't sound intrigued, just curious.

"No," Sylvie said firmly. Definitely not. She looked at the girl. "Why are we here, Rachel?"

Guilt, uncertainty, defensiveness, and a flash of that same frenetic excitement all shot to the surface of Rachel's emotions, and then Rachel's chin rose as she said, "I have a school project."

Sylvie looked at her without saying a word.

"A report to write. For art class. On modern art. Um, very modern art," Rachel continued, cheeks slowly starting to pick up color as she wove her lie.

Sylvie remained silent, but crossed her arms. One more untruthful word and she'd start tapping her toe on the ground.

"Ma'am?" Sylvie had felt the worried presence approaching her, but hadn't bothered to register his intent. Still, she didn't jump at the tap on her shoulder. "I'm very sorry to interrupt you, ma'am, but I need to ask you to leave now."

"What?" Sylvie looked over her shoulder in surprise. The tapper was a security guard, dressed in the standard blue uniform, his dark face uncertain.

"No," Rachel protested. "Not yet. I haven't even—" She let her sentence break off.

"The artist asks that you and the young lady leave the premises, ma'am." Sylvie followed the direction of his doubtful gaze back through the room. A woman and a man were standing in a doorway, clearly arguing. The dark-haired woman looked on the verge of tears while the man's tense frame radiated frustration even as he awkwardly patted her shoulder. And then, as another man approached, the first man's face broke into a beaming smile and he stepped forward, away from the woman, displaying jovial enthusiasm.

What was going on here?

"Is that her? The artist?" Rachel asked the guard.

"Yes, miss," he replied, still looking uncomfortable. "I'm sorry, but I need to escort you out."

Rachel's eyes were wide and intent, fixed on the dark-haired woman, her expression blank, but the burst of desolation that flooded her was so intense that Sylvie gasped. Without thinking, Sylvie put her arm around Rachel's shoulders and pulled her closer.

"Excuse me?" she said to the guard, voice cold, Rachel stiff against her side. "Have we done something to cause a problem?"

Maybe it was her tone of voice. Maybe it was the stylist, talking with animation and many glances back at Sylvie to a small cluster of people nearby. Maybe it was the distress of the woman in the doorway, the artist. But for whatever reason, people were starting to pay attention. Like bugs crawling on her skin, Sylvie could feel them noticing her.

The security guard wasn't important, she decided. The artist was. Arm still firmly around Rachel, she started off, tugging the unwilling girl in the direction of the artist.

"No," Rachel whispered a protest.

"Hush," Sylvie ordered. Maybe she wouldn't speak to the artist, but she was definitely getting close enough to feel her emotions.

And then she did and almost staggered. If Rachel was desolate, this woman was bereaved. It was the bitter taste of overheated black coffee, a scream breaking silence, the gagging smell of death.

"Ma'am, please." The security guard's words behind her were as inconsequential as the buzzing of a fly as Sylvie pushed forward.

"Please." The woman's words were a murmur as Sylvie and Rachel reached her, but her eyes were greedy, focused entirely on the girl, completely ignoring Sylvie. "You can't be here. He'll destroy me."

Emotional overload, for Sylvie, was being in a group of eighteen-year-olds under fire for the first time. She'd done that, more than once. It wasn't pretty and this was nothing close. But the density of the emotion, the depth, the purity of the grief, was unique.

Sylvie hated it. She wanted nothing more than to leave, as quickly as possible. "You're the artist?" she heard herself saying.

The woman nodded. "You need to leave," she repeated, voice weak.

"Yes," Sylvie agreed with her. "We're going."

Rachel didn't say anything. Sylvie pulled her even closer until the girl was nestled against her, tucked up by her body, pressed next to her skin. It was barely enough. "He has custody?" Her voice sounded odd to her, as if she was talking underwater.

"He has everything," Rachel's mother answered. "Everything." She pulled her gaze away from Rachel as if fighting against a current, and looked at Sylvie. "Everything," she repeated for the third time. She shook her head. "You can't fight him. He'll always win."

Sylvie nodded. And then, without another word, she headed toward the door of the gallery, arm still tight around Rachel's shoulders.

She didn't know what Rachel understood.

If Rachel understood.

But it didn't matter.

Keeping Rachel safe meant keeping her away from her mother. At least for now.

They didn't speak in the car. The driver was new, just hired, and Sylvie didn't know him well enough to be comfortable talking to Rachel in front of him. Not that she knew what to say anyway. The girl's misery was palpable. No Frappuccino would even make a dent.

When they reached the house, Rachel fled upstairs, almost running in her haste to get away. Sylvie frowned after her, trying to decide what to do as she entered the house at a slower pace and headed toward the security room. Should she follow Rachel and try to talk to her? But what could she say? Should she confront her about her lies? Or console her for her loss? Rachel was unlikely to welcome either.

She could ask Ty, but she already knew what he'd say. He'd tell her to forget about it. It was none of her business unless Rachel was in danger, in which case she needed to report it to Chesney immediately. The thought made her feel queasy. Telling Chesney about the scene in the art gallery would be awkward as hell, made worse because how could she share the emotions she'd felt? Besides, Rachel wasn't in danger.

But following the first part of Ty's imagined orders felt equally difficult. Forget about it? Forget Rachel's misery, her mother's despair? How? It would be like trying to forget witnessing a car wreck.

Maybe if she knew more about their background, about who Rachel's mother was and what had happened to give Chesney sole custody, she'd have a better idea of what to do.

She slipped into the chair in front of the monitors, and frowned down at the keyboard. Information meant internet. Chesney was famous: maybe she could Google him?

Two hours later, her queasiness was back full-force.

She needed to go talk to Chesney.

Not because she'd found out anything useful about Rachel's mother; it would take her a lifetime to work her way through the ten million results on a search of Chesney's name. But she'd found Rachel's Facebook page and now she understood what the girl had been thinking that morning at the school when Sylvie had caught an inadvertent peek into her thoughts.

She shouldn't have let that slip by that day. She'd been distracted by knowing that Lucas was nearby, but she should have asked questions.

She rubbed her face, grimacing when she inadvertently pressed against her healing bruise. She could spend forever planning this conversation. Or she could just get it over with.

Outside the door to Chesney's home office, she paused, hearing raised voices and feeling anger and frustration from the people inside. Maybe this was a bad time. Maybe she should call Ty. Maybe he should have this conversation with Chesney.

Before she could decide whether to knock or not, the door was flung open. A woman—one of the maids, Sylvie thought—startled back at the sight of Sylvie, and then muttered something in Spanish as she brushed by, heading away down the corridor.

Chesney stood in front of his desk, face flushed, but he managed to produce a strained smile.

"Congratulations, Ms. Blair," he said.

Sylvie's hand was still upraised to knock. She dropped it, feeling awkward, and took a step into the room. "Congratulations, sir?"

"It's not every day that you catch a criminal, is it?" He was still angry, Sylvie realized, but hiding it well. She would have been unable to tell anything about his emotions without her gift. His smile seemed almost natural now, and his skin color was rapidly fading.

"Ah, no, sir," she said, frowning, not hiding her confusion.

He responded immediately, gesturing to the newspaper lying open on his desk. "You made the front section of the *Post*." He turned away from her, walking back to his chair. "I hope you'll continue to maintain your press silence," he added, as he reached his seat. "I have to imagine that too much recognition would prove distracting while on duty."

"Of course, sir," Sylvie murmured an automatic agreement. Press silence? The front section of the *Post*? Shit. She'd have to get a newspaper and take a look at the story as soon as she got the chance.

"Is that why you're here?" Chesney asked. "If you need time off to handle the repercussions, you'll have to speak with Mr. Barton. I don't get involved in his personnel management."

Sylvie blinked. Indeed. She was tempted to respond sharply, but she bit back her instinctive disdain for his lack of knowledge. As if she would ever come to him for something so mundane.

"No, sir." She kept her voice calm. "I'm here about Rachel."

"Rachel? What about her?" Chesney sat and pulled open his desk drawer. He could not have expressed his disinterest more clearly if he'd tried. Sylvie couldn't read his mind, but she knew he was barely listening.

"She's being bullied," she said, wishing she'd found some better way to phrase what she'd discovered.

"Eh?" he asked, looking up from the papers he was pulling out of a file.

"Online. On Facebook. Other students at her school are . . ." She paused, not sure how to explain what she'd discovered. She hadn't learned some of those words until she'd joined the Marines. ". . . calling her names."

Chesney didn't roll his eyes, but his glance at the ceiling asked for patience. "Children do that, Ms. Blair. I'm sure it's nothing serious."

Sylvie took another step into the room, not sure how to protest his cavalier attitude. He hadn't looked at the site. He didn't understand. "I think it may be making Rachel quite unhappy," she said, trying to be careful. She didn't want to mention the art gallery or reveal her ability to perceive emotion.

"She's a teenager. They're notoriously unhappy," Chesney replied, dismissing her concern as he took out a pen.

Sylvie felt pressure in her jaw. She was clenching her teeth, she realized. She didn't believe in Lucas's suspicions—it was too farfetched to think a man like Chesney would risk working with drug dealers. But God, he was an ass. Still, liking Chesney wasn't part of her job description. Protecting Rachel was. "Respectfully, sir, I have to disagree. I believe you should take a look at these comments."

Chesney's grunt would have been rude even without the flavor of his feelings. "As you've told me before, Ms. Blair, you're a bodyguard, not a babysitter. Rachel can handle a few names. Your job is to keep her safe from kidnappers."

Sylvie felt her cheeks heating as she swallowed an angry response. "Yes, sir." She paused but Chesney had already begun marking up the document with his pen, visibly dismissing her.

Turning away, Sylvie left without another word.

She'd review the comments, every one. She'd follow every link. She'd look at every vicious word Rachel's classmates had written. And somewhere in there, she'd find a threat. And when she did, she'd take it straight to the school principal.

Reporting bullying might not be her job, but investigating threats definitely was.

CHAPTER NINE

Dillon wished he could fry Chesney's electronics. He'd killed quite a few devices by accident while learning how to use his ghostly power to communicate: maybe he could manage a few more on purpose. And if anyone deserved to have his computer zapped, it was Chesney.

What an asshole the guy was.

The man hadn't even bothered to look at what those bitches were saying about Rachel. Not even after Sylvie left the room. He'd just gone back to his work as if what she'd told him was inconsequential.

Dillon was disgusted. He'd already had an idea of how bad things were for Rachel at school from his morning there. Those girls were nasty. And reading the things they'd written online over Sylvie's shoulder had made him even more sympathetic to Rachel. If he'd said even one of their lesser insults out loud, his gran would have grounded him for a week and made him write a note of apology to the person he'd insulted.

He said to Chesney, voice disapproving, "You're a crap dad, you know that?"

Chesney, of course, didn't respond. Shaking his head, Dillon walked through the closed door. As he headed down the hallway on his way downstairs, he paused at Rachel's room.

If he went back to his mom right now he'd be tempted to talk to her. He'd managed to resist the desire for days and he still wasn't ready to let her know he was around. Maybe he should visit Rachel instead.

Acting on his impulse, he pushed his way through the wall. It was the first time he'd visited Rachel since that first night, and she was again standing by her bookcase. She was holding the same book she'd been holding the first night, but not opened as if she'd been reading it. Instead she was using both hands, and staring down at the cover as if the red ribbon held an encoded message only she could see.

"You must like that book," Dillon said, joining her by the bookcase. He felt almost relieved, and realized that he'd been a little afraid she'd be crying. He couldn't see her face, but if she had been crying, she was over it by now.

Still holding the book in an awkward two-handed grip, Rachel carried it over to her bed and set it down. Then she disappeared into the bathroom. Dillon didn't follow her, of course, but she returned just a few seconds later with a full glass of water that she set on her nightstand next to her cell phone and iPod docking clock.

She climbed onto her bed and sat cross-legged next to her pillow, reaching for the book and sliding it over in front of her. But she didn't open it.

Dillon began to feel uneasy. Something about the way she was handling the book was wrong. She didn't hold it by its spine, the way people grabbed books. She held it like it was a plate instead. And then she flipped open the cover. He craned to see what she was looking at as she pulled out a plastic baggie.

Uh-oh.

She'd cut out the interior of the book, not all of it, just a chunk from the center of the pages, about an inch wide by two inches high and probably an inch deep. It wasn't a book, it was a hiding place.

She unrolled the baggie and held it up to the light, her eyes narrowing.

Mixed pills, Dillon realized. Some blue, some pink, some white. Different shapes, different sizes.

With a shake of her head, Rachel flipped the cover of the book closed and carefully spilled the pills out on top of it.

He recognized this from kids at his school. She'd been stealing from people's medicine cabinets. Not a lot of pills probably, just a few at a time so she wouldn't get caught. When he'd stolen the pills that killed him, he'd taken the whole bottle. He'd meant to take just enough to cause hallucinations and then put the rest back later. He'd miscalculated, though. Or maybe under the influence, he'd kept taking them? He didn't really know what had happened.

And he didn't know what Rachel was doing now. Did she take drugs to get high? His sense of unease was growing. It wasn't any of his business if Rachel took a painkiller or a sleeping pill, even if she was stealing them, he tried to tell himself. But maybe he should text his mom anyway.

She was lining the pills up, one by one, organizing by color. Her finger tapped along the line as she counted.

He looked at her face, trying to decipher her expression. She had been crying earlier, he saw. She had that look around her eyes and her skin was still almost blotchy. But she wasn't crying now. If anything, she looked determined.

Determined.

Determined was bad.

Determined wasn't taking a pill to sleep. Determined wasn't getting high.

Determined was something else, Dillon decided with a sinking feeling, just as Rachel stopped counting and nodded to herself as if making a decision.

Shit.

Dillon needed to do something. And quickly. Text Sylvie? Then his eyes fell on the cell phone on Rachel's nightstand. Would this work? Would she believe him?

Rachel pressed her lips together and for a moment she looked like maybe she'd start to cry again. And then she took a deep breath and stuck her chin out and reached for the glass of water.

Then she startled as her phone buzzed. Instead of picking up the water, she picked up the phone and glanced down at the screen. Her eyebrows drew down immediately and she stilled, before her glance flickered around the room, just her eyes moving.

She started to type a response and her frown deepened.

She must have realized that the text didn't come from an outside line but from the phone itself, Dillon thought. He waited, wondering how she'd react.

Would she throw her phone away, the way Sylvie had when he tried to talk to her?

Or would she be willing to listen to him?

Don't, he'd sent.

What? Rachel typed.

Take those, Dillon responded eagerly, feeling a glad relief. She was going to listen.

Rachel looked around the room, this time not just with her eyes, but with her entire head swiveling from side-to-side as she searched for a camera. Dillon waited. What would she say?

Why not? She typed, returning her gaze to her cell phone.

Ouch. That was a hard question. And not the one he'd expected. Why wasn't she asking who he was, how he was talking to her?

I want to die, she added, still silent, just typing one letter after another.

Or maybe this would be easy. *Bad idea,* he answered. *Dead is boring.*

She looked up again, away from the cell phone, and this time her glance around the room was slow and steady, focusing on the ceiling and then the walls. Slowly, carefully, typing with only one finger, she responded. *Boring would hurt less.*

Dillon wished he could write paragraphs in response. He wanted to tell her what it was like four days after he'd died, when his Aunt Grace had driven the car he'd died in with tears streaming down her face, barely able to contain her sobbing long enough to brake at the stop signs. Or six months after his death, when his uncle had yelled at him, not really knowing that he was there, and Dillon had no way to apologize. Or two years after he'd died when he'd seen his father for the first time in months and had to wonder if that grim man was the same cheerful weekend visitor he'd always known.

And his gran—well, he couldn't even go there.

Death didn't hurt less. It just hurt different.

No.

She would have to read into his answer what she would. If Akira was around, he could expostulate passionately but without a translator, it was just too hard. But if Akira was around . . .

That was an idea.

Who are you? Rachel wrote.

Dillon, he responded readily.

"I don't know any Dillons," she said aloud, frowning at her phone.

Dillon's mouth twisted in a crooked smile. This would be tough to explain. Impossible, probably.

No, he responded again.

"Well, who are you?" she repeated, still talking rather than typing.

Ghost, he typed into her phone.

Rachel's frown deepened. She looked around the room again, clearly wanting to find the cameras. "That makes no sense," she said. "This house is new. My father had it built just a few years ago. It can't be haunted."

Dillon liked the way Rachel thought. Of course, she was wrong, but still, the analytical way she was looking at the problem was a good sign. Maybe they could work together.

Not haunting house, he answered. *Haunting mom.*

"So what are you doing in my bedroom?" Rachel asked. She didn't look tearful anymore. She looked skeptical, wary, her dark eyes doubtful.

Dillon thought. He was surprised that she believed him. She'd looked for the camera and the computer manipulation, but not for long. He thought her acceptance was a measure of her desperation. She didn't really want to die; she just didn't want to keep on living the way she had been.

Mom worried about you, he answered her, hoping she'd ask the obvious.

She didn't. She didn't have to. "Sylvie?" Her voice was tinged with doubt, but at the same time held an absolute certainty. Dillon wasn't surprised. Rachel didn't seem to have too many people who cared about her in her life.

Y. He was running out of energy. He could feel it. It wasn't like tired, more like slow. But he knew he didn't have too many letters left in him before he'd need to regroup.

"I didn't know she had a kid," Rachel said.

Dillon didn't answer. What could he say to that?

"I guess if you're dead," Rachel started. She stopped. And then continued, the words bursting out of her, "It doesn't matter, you're wrong. Dead would be better. Would have to be better. I can't, it doesn't, I don't—" She pressed her palms to her eyes and Dillon knew she was stopping herself from crying.

NO, he quickly texted, forcing her phone to buzz. *Dead = bad. Help me instead.*

"Help you?" Rachel asked. She sounded reluctantly intrigued. "How can I help you? I can't even help me."

Run away.

Rachel stared down at her phone. She laughed, but it wasn't a real laugh, more like a breathy chuckle. "Right, like that would work. I have bodyguards. I'm never alone. They'd catch me in two minutes."

Plan.

"Plan," she scoffed. "What difference would that make? There's no place for me to go."

Tassamara. Each letter took an effort. He had to pause between them as if he was gasping for breath on the twentieth lap of a track run.

"Tassamara?" Rachel repeated. "I don't know where that is."

Dillon didn't say anything. He couldn't. He had, at most, a couple of letters left. How could he explain to Rachel that if she could get herself to his home town, Akira could talk to people on her behalf? He couldn't be sure that his family could help her, but he knew they'd try and that would be more than she had now.

"Tassamara," Rachel repeated again. Dillon wished he could plead with her, but he didn't know how. What few words could explain what it would mean to him if she could get his mom to a place where he could talk to her, really talk?

But he didn't have to explain.

Rachel pressed her lips together, looking down at her phone. Then she glanced at the book where her pills were lined up in neat rows. She tilted her head from side to side almost as if she were responding to music, to some rhythm he couldn't hear.

Then she nodded.

She picked up the baggie and carefully swept the pills into it, making sure that each one found a safe destination inside the plastic. Then she folded it up neatly and tucked it into her book, closing the cover.

"Tassamara, huh?" she said, sounding almost cheerful. She stood and carried her book back to the bookshelf and slid it into its place. Then she crossed to her desk and turned on her laptop. "Let's see how to get there."

*****

Sylvie's plans to help Rachel went awry as soon as she got back to the security room.

Ty was waiting for her, face grim. He didn't bother with a greeting, just asked, "Why aren't you answering your phone?"

"What are you doing here?" Sylvie responded. He was dressed more casually than usual, no suit jacket or tie, but his shirt was pressed, edges even, and his slacks held a crease as crisp as if he'd never left the military. But it was Sunday. He should be home with Jeremy and Josh, wearing a t-shirt and blue jeans.

"Looking for you," he answered. "I've been calling all day."

He sounded impatient and Sylvie frowned, wondering why she hadn't heard a phone ring. Then she shook her head, annoyed at herself. Impulsively throwing her phone away had been a stupid move. "Oh, right. I got a new cell this week. And we've been out, so I wouldn't have heard the phone here."

Everything had been so crazy. She'd meant to give Ty her new number, but she'd forgotten. In fact, except for her mom, who she'd called yesterday afternoon for their traditional weekly call, no one had her new number. Even Lucas, with his magical ability to find unlisted numbers, might not realize that hers had changed.

Could Dillon be with him? Sylvie glanced around for her bag. Maybe she should call Lucas. She needed to know whether her son had moved on or was still a ghost after all, she thought, trying to ignore the sense of relief she felt at the idea of talking to Lucas.

"Did you know this was going to happen?"

"What?" she asked, as she reached for her bag, digging into it for her phone. Ty couldn't be asking about Dillon; she hadn't told him anything. She would, eventually, but she hadn't had time. And Ty, although accepting of her abilities, was going to have a hard time believing in ghosts.

"The story in the *Post*."

"Oh, right." Sylvie paused. She needed to look at that story, find out what it said. "Not exactly, no."

"Have you seen it?" Ty asked.

"Yo," said James, entering the room with a wide grin on his face. "Superhero Sylvie. Hot stuff, my friend."

"James?" Sylvie blinked in surprise. He shouldn't be here either. They worked together Monday through Friday and he hadn't missed work on Thursday. "Are you working today?"

"Nope," he answered, cheerfully. "Just stopped by to visit the hero. I tried to call but couldn't get through. I figured your phone must be off the hook with reporters calling."

"Uh-oh." Sylvie dropped into the chair by the desk. She looked from James to Ty and back again. James was smiling, Ty was not. "That doesn't sound good."

"Depends on your point of view," Ty responded, voice dry. "Did you want to be famous?"

"Famous?" It took a second. "Because of the guy in the parking lot?"

"What were you thinking? How could you take that kind of risk?" The anger in Ty's voice didn't cover the worry and concern underneath.

She waved off his words. "It wasn't that much of a risk, honestly." She was grateful that he couldn't read her emotions the way she could his or he'd know she was lying. He was right. That guy had been big and tough and she could have been in real trouble. She should have been more cautious.

"Too late now." Ty's worry reached the surface, the anger in his voice disappearing. He sighed.

James was looking between them, smile fading. "What's the big deal?"

Ty shook his head. "Nothing. Except the hell it's going to play with my schedule while Sylvie takes the week off."

"Wait, what?" Sylvie protested. "I can't take a week off."

Ty rubbed his forehead, pinching his brow as if he had a headache. "We're going to have to hope it blows over in a few days. You'll have to decide how you want to deal with it, of course, whether you want to talk to the media or hide out, but either way, you can't do your job while this is going on."

"This? What this?" Sylvie protested again. She couldn't leave Rachel, not now. "I say no comment to a few reporters and ignore my phone calls. What's so hard about that?"

Ty folded his arms and just looked at her. Sylvie could feel that he was exasperated, but she didn't think she was being stupid. Reporters moved on to new stories like terriers chasing squirrels; once they realized she wasn't talking, they'd be gone.

James started whistling between his teeth, trying to suppress his smile. "That photograph is the real problem," he offered. "It makes you look . . ." He paused.

Sylvie glared at him. Why the hell was he so amused? "What photograph?"

"Hang on, it's in my car," he answered, grin breaking free, as he turned and hurried out the door.

"What photograph?" Sylvie demanded of Ty. She should have known, of course. The woman in the art gallery had recognized her, therefore her image was somehow public. But it had all happened too quickly and Rachel's situation had taken precedence.

"The *Post* ran a picture of you," he said, a half-smile tugging at his lips. "James is right, it's the problem. It's a nice picture, though."

Sylvie shook her head. How could anyone have gotten a picture of her?

"Someone must have taken it at the police station," Ty added. "Maybe with a cell phone? You're sitting, and there's a guy standing next to you, checking out your bruise."

Lucas. Sylvie hadn't noticed anyone taking a picture, but she might not have if it was a cell phone, not a camera. "And?"

Ty's half-smile turned into a real smile. "And you get to choose how to handle the media."

"I can't take the week off, Ty," she said, feeling annoyed, as James returned with a folded newspaper in hand.

"Here you go." He passed her the paper.

She took it, about to ask where to look, and then glanced down at it. Oh, hell. She didn't say the words, but she probably didn't have to. The paper was open to her image. She was seated, hair messy, head tilted up, lips slightly parted, with Lucas standing next to her, head bent to her, his finger touching her cheek.

"Oh, God." Something about the perspective, Lucas's size, the worry on his face, and the angles of hers made her look almost delicate. "I look—" she started in dismay before pausing, searching for the right word.

"Pretty?" Ty offered. "Attractive?"

"Cute?" James suggested, openly laughing. "Although sexy as hell would work, too."

She swatted at him with the paper before pulling it back to her and looking again. Any of those adjectives would do. The photograph was very flattering. She might have liked it if it wasn't running in a national newspaper.

She looked away from the image and up at Ty.

"Cute little girl takes down two-hundred pound serial killer. You can understand why the media might be interested," he said, voice sympathetic, before frowning and adding, "A week might not be long enough."

She scowled at him. "He was at least two-fifty," she said huffily. Not that that was important, but still . . .

"Oh, that makes it so much better." Ty rolled his eyes.

She grimaced and leaned back in the chair, rubbing her neck. The timing was terrible. How could she help Rachel if she wasn't even here? "I changed my phone number. They can't reach me. I'll ignore them."

"I drove by your apartment building on the way here. There are at least twenty satellite trucks in the parking lot."

"I'll stay someplace else at night," Sylvie offered.

"And if a reporter or photographer catches sight of you while you're on duty?" Ty asked, before shaking his head.

Sylvie tilted her head, staring up at the ceiling. Ty didn't need to state the obvious: a distracted bodyguard was a bad bodyguard. She couldn't do her job if she couldn't focus on Rachel. Damn it.

"Your choice is about how you want to handle it, not whether you're taking the time," Ty said, tone gentler than the words.

*****

Sylvie was bored.

Seriously, seriously bored.

And it was only the third day of her exile. Pulling aside the curtain on her hotel room window, she stared down at the busy street below. It was raining, hard, the wind whipping big drops of water that splattered and dripped down the glass, turning the scene into something out of an impressionist painting. That is, if there were any impressionist paintings that were mostly gray and bleak. Sylvie was almost bored enough to Google impressionist painters and find out, but instead she let the curtain drop with a sigh and turned back to the room.

It was lovely as hotel rooms went. Maybe a little bland for her taste, with the colors all whites and navy blues, but the four-poster bed that dominated the room was elegant and the Italian marble bathroom pure luxury. The television set into the bathroom mirror was an interesting high-tech touch. Sylvie didn't actually care to watch television while she used the bathroom, but she appreciated the concept.

Jeremy, Ty's husband, was a partner at a prestigious DC criminal defense firm and he'd taken care of the arrangements. Sylvie didn't know the details and she was sure she didn't want to see the bill, but her faint hope of heading to North Carolina to spend her enforced week of vacation with her mom, her step-dad, and her half-sibs had been shattered when her mom had called to ask why there were television news crews in the driveway.

She'd see them in a few weeks anyway. One of the nice things about being back in the States was getting to go home for Christmas. She hadn't told her mom what she was doing when she ran away, but she called about a month later, after she'd enlisted and was partway through basic training at Parris Island and desperately homesick. Her mother had promptly moved to South Carolina, picking up a job as a waitress in a nearby roadside diner, and then followed Sylvie to Camp Lejeune in North Carolina. There she'd met a staff sergeant, married him and started having babies. After her solitary childhood, Sylvie now had two half-sisters and a half-brother, all teenagers. She smiled as she thought of them, remembering how excited her brother Sam had been about the television crews.

And then she sobered. Would Dillon have been excited? She looked at her phone, sitting on the nightstand next to the four-poster bed. He hadn't texted her. And Lucas hadn't called.

And she hadn't called Lucas.

Was she being cowardly?

She thought the answer might be yes. It wasn't that she didn't want to call him. It was that she wanted it too much.

It was maddening.

She needed to do something to take her mind off him. But she'd already spent two hours in the fitness room and the weather was miserable for a run. She'd watched all the television she could stand. The hotel had a lovely little book room, but she was too restless to read.

She had her laptop with her, so she could work on researching Chesney again. But she'd spent enough hours trying to learn more about his history during the past two days to realize that she didn't have the skills to discover anything useful. Ten million Google hits were about nine million, nine hundred ninety-nine thousand more than she had the patience for. No, if she wanted to know more about Chesney, Google wouldn't work. She'd need to get help.

She touched the top of her laptop, closed where it rested on the desk next to the window, thinking about who she could ask for help while firmly pushing thoughts of Lucas out of her mind, even as a traitorous whisper in the back of her head pointed out that he must have thoroughly researched Chesney already. And then she paused.

She'd been aware of the man in the room next to hers all morning long. His anxiety level was so high that she couldn't not know of his presence, any more than she'd be able to ignore him if he were playing a violin or burning incense. But she almost thought she'd caught a wisp of thought there.

She stepped away from the window, closer to the wall between their rooms. No, nothing.

And then, suddenly, his voice was in her head talking about earned income ratios and value added. He was preparing a presentation, she realized, but she was hearing his thoughts, not spoken words.

Hurrying to the door of her room, she pulled it open and stepped out. She recognized Lucas's back, the dark hair curling at the nape of his neck, even before she felt the sense of him that was indefinably Lucas and no one else. He was halfway down the long hallway, turned away from her, talking to someone she couldn't see.

"Lucas," she called his name without thought. She didn't know why he was here, but she couldn't help but feel glad to see him. And then he whirled around and she felt the full brunt of his emotions as he saw her.

Fear.

Relief.

Fury.

Lucas's emotions washed over Sylvie as he strode down the hallway toward her, his long legs eating up the distance between them, and she felt herself responding automatically, her anger rising to meet his own. Her chin went up, her back straightened, and she braced herself, feeling hot words simmering on her tongue.

He reached her, eyes searching her face, then grabbed her shoulders, fingers tight, pressing into her muscles. "Damn you." He wanted to shake her, she could tell. He was angry. Deeply, seriously angry. And under it, hurt? But violence was close to the surface.

'Ten, nine, eight, seven . . .' She took a deep breath and started silently counting backwards. She could feel the intensity of his emotions as if he were shouting. Ten years ago, she would have shouted back first, thought later. But not now, not this time. She didn't know why he was so angry but she didn't have to let him get to her.

"Are you all right?" His words were almost mild, the question a surprise, but his thoughts tumbled over one another in a chaotic babble.

Unanswered phone calls. Unreturned messages. Dillon. Chesney. Drug dealers. Danger.

114

"Of course," she answered automatically, trying to make sense of what he was thinking.

"Counting?" he asked, voice light but with an edge to it that almost matched his emotions.

She didn't answer. Anyone else would have believed him calm, but she knew better. And putting the pieces together, she finally understood.

She'd disappeared.

He hadn't known why.

"I'm sorry," she said, breathing the words out. Her own anger, usually quick to rise but slow to fade, was gone as she realized what she'd done to him and what his past few days had been like. While she'd been sitting in a hotel room, bored and aimless, he'd been desperately searching the city for her. Or for evidence that Chesney had killed her or had her killed.

For a second, his fingers gripped a little harder, and then he released her, stepping back. "Not a problem." To someone without her senses, he would have sounded nonchalant, as if the matter were trivial.

'*Liar,*' she thought at him. The retort was instinct, but it was a little like waving a red flag at a bull. Behind him, a door opened.

"I thought I'd gotten you killed. I thought you'd looked for evidence and gotten caught. Your boss works for the Mexican—" he started, snapping out the words, no longer trying to disguise his fury. Her eyes widened fractionally and she shook her head at him, raising a hand to shush him, as the man who'd been working on a presentation stepped out of his room and glanced in their direction.

Lucas fell silent, but his thoughts continued. '*—the Mexican drug cartels and you just disappear? What was I supposed to think, Sylvie? No word from you, no word from Dillon—*'

Sylvie forced a smile at the stranger, who'd paused, looking uncertain. Grabbing Lucas by the wrist, she tugged him into her room and closed the door behind him.

"I'm sorry," she said, interrupting his mental diatribe as she turned back to face him.

"I—what?" He blinked at her, and then shook his head as if he hadn't heard what she'd just said.

"I'm sorry," she repeated herself, feeling impatient. "You're right. I should have called you. It was stupid and inconsiderate of me not to."

He blinked at her again. And then a third time. And then, blue eyes narrowing, said slowly, "What have you done with the real Sylvie Blair?"

She scowled at him, folding her arms across her chest.

"No, no, don't get mad." He put a hand up in protest and a quick grin flashed across his face before he sobered. "Do you understand—"

"Yes," she interrupted him again. "I got all of that. But my boss is not a criminal and I am perfectly safe, just hiding out from crazy television news people."

"So I see." He sighed, and ran his hands through his hair, looking tired. "And Dillon?"

She shook her head. "No word. Or text. Whatever."

He nodded. His mouth twisted. "Well." He fell silent, but his thoughts continued, flavored with sorrow, *'Maybe you were right then and that was all he needed.'*

She didn't say anything, but she felt her heart beating a little faster than usual. She'd never felt Lucas sad before. Not like this. She wanted to comfort him.

The twist of his mouth turned into a wry smile. "I don't need your sympathy, Syl. I lost him a long time ago. Knowing that he was okay was an incredible gift. And if he's moved on now, that's okay, too. I'll see him again." The words were even but his eyes were bright.

Sylvie pressed her lips together, but the thought slipped out again. *'Still lying.'* He was a good actor, but she could see the truth. She might have thought Dillon should move on, but Lucas was not so sure.

Lucas let a reluctant chuckle escape, looking away. He took four or five steps into the room and sat down on the edge of the bed, facing the wall. He shook his head then dropped it into his hands, letting his palms press against his cheekbones. "It's been a long few days," he said, voice muffled. "You did a good job of hiding."

"Found me anyway," Sylvie answered, trying to keep her voice light, as she followed him into the room. "Zane?"

"Ha." Lucas sounded disgruntled, raising his face out of his hands. "He couldn't tell me a damn thing. Without Dillon, I had nothing of yours to give him as a focus."

Sylvie frowned. "Why not use a photograph?" She was no expert on Zane's skill, but she remembered some from when they'd found her the first time. Zane had still been young enough to be bubbling over with enthusiasm for his newfound ability and she'd had to admit, it was a nifty talent. She would have happily traded her own gift for it.

"I don't have one that's current. Zane needs images that are recent," he answered, standing again.

She looked at him, wondering whether she should tell him, but the thought escaped before she could stop it. *'Every subscriber to the* Washington Post *has a recent picture of me.'*

"Oh, hell." Gently, he banged his head against the post of the four-poster bed, once, twice, three times. "Of course they do. Of course I do. Damn me."

"Stop it," she ordered him when it looked as if he would hit himself harder and harder.

He looked over at her, standing a few feet away from him. "You make me stupid, Syl."

She tried not to smile, but couldn't help herself. *'The feeling's mutual.'*

Uh-oh. She hadn't meant it teasingly, but she could see the spark she'd lit flicker in Lucas's eyes, the blue darkening with desire as thoughts of the past crowded into both of their minds. The sensations were so tangled up that she couldn't be sure whose memories were whose. Humid Florida air, a barely cool evening breeze, the buzz of the mosquitoes, the sandy grit of the ground, skin against sweaty skin, the feel of him pushing inside her or was she enveloping him? Their first time. Stupid, so stupid. And yet irresistible.

And then they were her memories, skipping ahead, North Carolina, the car where her mother had sent them to talk away from her toddler siblings and his teenage brother, the feel of the seat leather against her back, Lucas's mouth stroking down her body. And then his memories, definitely his, of that one stolen weekend leave, and then Milan, and every memory raised the temperature in the room by another two degrees until Sylvie's cheeks felt hot and flushed and the rest of her was burning and melting.

"Lucas," she murmured his name, licking her lips.

"Sylvie," he whispered hers, his voice husky.

And then he shook his head. "I've got to go. Andy's waiting down at the end of the hall."

"Okay." She swallowed. She stepped aside to let him move past her toward the door. He was careful not to brush against her, but she could feel the same ache of unfulfilled desire within him that she felt herself even without his touch.

She was trying not to think, not to put words to her emotions, not to let a thought form that she might regret.

"We still on for Friday?" he asked, as he opened the door.

"Sure," she answered, grateful to turn her attention to something other than the energy still flowing between them. AlecCorp's holiday party was being held in its corporate office building, which ought to be as secure as any military base. Certainly no news media would be able to get inside. And by Friday, she ought to be able to get in and out of her apartment building without running a gauntlet of TV crews and reporters. If not, James or Ty would bring her appropriate clothes. "You're wasting your time, though. Chesney's not a drug dealer, just an ass."

'*And a rotten father.*' The thought inadvertently formed. Poor Rachel. Sylvie hadn't been able to do anything to help her but as soon as she got back to work she was going to figure out something.

Lucas glanced at her. She could feel his curiosity but she shook her head. Maybe she'd ask him later about helping her find out more about Chesney's past, but now wasn't the time.

"Okay." He nodded and slipped out the door.

She let him go.

She let the door close behind him and with enormous self-restraint didn't kick it. She could feel him moving away down the hallway.

Damn it. Lucas just . . . he just did it for her. They hadn't even touched, apart from her brief tug on his wrist, but she was as hot and yearning as if they'd been kissing for hours.

What had he said before, about wanting the chance to learn who she was? Maybe that was what they needed. Maybe if she spent time with him—real time, not stolen moments—these feelings would burn themselves out. She'd look at him and think . . . her thoughts stopped there.

Ha. Sure, maybe she'd get so used to his presence that she'd stop looking at him, really looking, the way people did with the familiar. Maybe she'd start to take him for granted. But she was never going to look at him and not wish that his hands were on her.

She closed her eyes.

She didn't mean to concentrate her sixth sense, but she couldn't help herself. The guy in the room next door was gone, but as she reached out she brushed up against other minds, trying to catch a last touch of Lucas.

And then her lips started to tilt upward. She rested her hand on the doorknob, but waited until she heard the first knock before pulling it open.

Lucas's hand was still upraised, ready to fall again. He looked at her and she could see the question.

She stepped back, into the room, gesturing him inside and then closed the door behind him. She leaned against it. "This is a terrible idea."

He'd already turned. "I thought you were dead."

She licked her lips, her hands already undoing her top button. And then the second.

And the third.

And then he was reaching for her, pulling her to him, his hands on her hips, lifting her into him, and she went gladly, joyfully, feeling the passion spiraling between them as his mouth captured hers.

They made their way to the bed, stumbling, tugging at the clothes that were in the way, Lucas never letting go of her, until they were falling onto the softness.

"Sylvie, Sylvie," he murmured, lips moving across her skin. "I hated calling you Beth, you were never a Beth."

"What?" She arched under him, feeling his taut muscles and the warmth of his skin and wanting him closer, closer, always closer.

"Milan. You were so angry."

She didn't want to talk about Milan, she didn't want to think about Milan, she wanted his head—and all the rest of him—right here, right now.

She bit him. Hard. Not a gentle loving nip, but a clench of her teeth on his shoulder.

"Ouch!" He protested. "Shit, that hurt, Sylvie."

"Quit talking," she ordered him. She raked her nails down his back. "I can do worse than that."

He half-laughed at her, eyes hot. "Biting. Like kissing, only there's a winner."

She froze, eyes widening. "You just quoted *Doctor Who*."

He raised his eyebrows, lips curving. "Well, Neil Gaiman, anyway. Have we found something we have in common?"

She laughed and pulled him down toward her, feeling giddy. A British sci-fi TV show might not be much to base a relationship on, but it was a place to start.

119

CHAPTER TEN

Worrying about Rachel was becoming Dillon's favorite hobby. Or if not his favorite, at least what he spent most of his time doing.

Rachel had been dismayed by what she found out about Tassamara. "It's the middle of nowhere," she protested. "You want me to go there?" It had taken Dillon hours to convince her, hours made longer by his need to gather energy between texts.

And then she'd wanted to know all about him and about being a ghost and all about Sylvie. Between interruptions for sleep and meals and school and homework—which, much to Dillon's frustration, Rachel still insisted on completing—making a plan to get to Tassamara felt as if it was taking forever.

Rachel ruled out the simple approach. She'd scoffed at Dillon's suggestion that she sneak out of school and hop on the nearest bus. "My father is rich and famous," she told him, not sounding happy about it. "If they think I've run away, every police officer in five states will be looking for me. My picture will be everywhere. I bet I wouldn't make it ten miles. No, if I'm going to get all the way to Florida, we've got to distract them. They have to think I've been kidnapped."

Dillon had reluctantly agreed. He didn't like it, but to get Rachel away from here, they were going to have to trick a whole bunch of people, starting with her security guards.

At least his mom wouldn't be one of them. He'd been freaked out when she hadn't shown up for work on Monday, but some easy eavesdropping on the other bodyguards revealed why she was missing. It was perfect, really. He'd get Rachel to Florida, then text Sylvie and tell her he could help find Rachel if she'd come to Tassamara. She wouldn't want to tell anyone that she was getting messages from a ghost, so she'd have to fly down there and talk to him.

Perfect.

If only the rest of it went smoothly.

Escaping from the house was out. Apart from the security system, there were too many people and too many cameras. Escaping from the school was just as bad. Strangers weren't allowed on the grounds and students weren't allowed off them. Plus, more cameras.

No way could Rachel convincingly pretend to be kidnapped from the school.

A field trip would have been a good opportunity, but it was early December. Rachel didn't know when the next school trip would be, but she was sure it wouldn't be until after Christmas and they both agreed that was too long to wait.

That left her after-school activities. They'd been using Google Maps to trace out the distance between each of Rachel's activities and the bus station. When Rachel paused, Dillon peered over her shoulder to see what she was looking at. "I know that address," she'd said, pointing at a location two blocks away from the train station.

Train? he texted. No train tracks passed through Tassamara, only a bus line. If she took a train, she'd have to stop somewhere along the way and switch to a bus.

She didn't answer him, just quickly switched websites and started searching the Amtrak schedules. "Look at that," she said. She leaned back in her chair.

Dillon looked, but he didn't know what she wanted him to notice, so he turned to see her face instead. She looked pale and pinched, almost scared.

Bad? he texted. She didn't look at his message right away, still staring at the computer screen, but then she visibly shook off her reverie and picked up the phone.

"No, no." She shook her head. "It's just—it's real." The volume of her voice dropped until she was almost whispering. "I can do this." Her eyes grew bright with excitement. "I can do this," she repeated.

"Tell me," Dillon demanded. He started texting but before he'd even gotten the first few letters out, Rachel started talking.

"That address is where AlecCorp has its offices," she told him. "I've been there before. I didn't pay much attention, but it's right near the train station. And look, a train leaves for Florida at 9:40 on Friday night."

"So?" Dillon asked when Rachel paused.

"Somehow I have to get him to let me go to the party." Rachel pushed back her chair. Standing, she began pacing around her room, head down, staring at the floor. She was still talking, but the words were mumbled and Dillon could only understand a word here and there.

"If I—no, that won't work. Maybe I—no. But if he thinks . . ."

Dillon wanted to yell in exasperation. Instead, he flopped onto Rachel's bed and waited. Being a ghost had taught him far too many lessons in patience.

Finally, Rachel stopped moving and looked up. "AlecCorp is having their holiday party on Friday. If I can get to the party, I can catch a train to Florida. Look." She crossed back to the computer and pointed at the screen. "I could get one of these little rooms. I wouldn't have to worry about people seeing me. If we timed it right, I could be on the train before anyone even knew I was gone. I'd take the train to this place, Palatka, and get there before lunchtime. And then find a bus."

She sat down again and her fingers flew over the keyboard as she pulled up bus schedules. "Look," she said with delight. "The bus station is right at the Amtrak station. I wouldn't even have to look for it; it's right there."

She turned around again and looked at the empty room. "What do you think?" she asked, sounding tentative, and reached to pick up her phone. She stared at its blank screen and waited.

It's perfect, Dillon texted her. A party was even better than an after-school activity—noise, confusion, crowds, maybe even dim lighting if they were lucky. He'd cause a distraction and Rachel would sneak away. The only problem would be her bodyguard.

Well, probably not her only problem. Maybe just the biggest. Rachel smiled.

"We can do this," she said. "I can get you home." Her voice held a mix of determination and excitement as she turned back to her computer.

"And I can get you away from here," he told her. He didn't know how he'd help her once they got to Florida, but he'd find a way.

*****

By Friday afternoon, almost all their problems had been solved, but Dillon couldn't help worrying.

U sr? he texted her, as he watched her trying to carefully grind a pill into dust. She glanced at her phone when it buzzed, then frowned and tilted it up.

"Sr?" she said aloud. "Serious?"

123

Dillon rolled his eyes. He was trying to be careful how he used his energy. *Sure*, he sent, feeling impatient.

"Oh!" She frowned. "Yes, of course. I'm serious, too, though. Lydia always carries around her own drink, this weird red tea from Africa. She keeps it in the refrigerator in the staff kitchen, the big one downstairs. I can sneak in there and put this in the tea right before we leave for the party."

Dillon hated this part of the plan.

"Or almost right before we leave," Rachel said. She paused in her grinding. "If I put it in too soon, she might start feeling funny before we get to the party. But if I leave it too long, she might have already refilled her bottle." She stuck her pinky in her mouth and started chewing on the fingernail.

Dillon would have loved to point out the other risks. What if Rachel misjudged the amount and gave her bodyguard only enough to make her sick? If Lydia called someone for help, Rachel could wind up with an alert and now paranoid guard watching her. Or what if Rachel put too much in? What if she didn't just knock Lydia out, but killed her?

"No, this idea is still the best." Rachel pulled her finger out of her mouth and returned to work. "It'll be okay."

Dillon thought she was reassuring herself as much as him. Gloomily, he wondered whether he'd have to keep her company if she wound up in jail after this.

She'd already stolen money and a credit card from her father. She'd bought a plane ticket online with the credit card. It would serve as a distraction, she told Dillon. They'd realize she'd run away eventually, maybe within a couple of hours depending on how long it took them to trace her GPS tracker. With any luck, the plane ticket would send them to the airport first. The extra time that would give her might be enough to get her to Florida. With her own savings and the cash she'd stolen, she'd have enough money to buy the train ticket without leaving a paper trail.

But first they had to get out of AlecCorp. She'd managed to convince Chesney to let her accompany him to the party. He'd been doubtful, but she'd told him she wanted the opportunity to make him proud, to erase the shame of throwing up at the last party. Dillon had been awed and a little worried at what a good liar she was.

She wasn't going to be able to bring much with her. They'd tried to figure out how she could sneak her backpack into the car, but even if she could manage that, how would she get it into the party? Instead, she was wearing a shirt and rolled-up leggings under her long-sleeved dress. Fortunately, she was so skinny that the extra layer wasn't too noticeable.

"All right," she finally said, looking down at the powder she'd made. Carefully, she scraped it into a plastic bag. Looking up, she said, "You'll stay with me the whole time, right?"

She was going to have to leave her phone behind. If she didn't, the GPS in the phone would give her away as soon as someone called the phone company. That meant no way to communicate with her.

The whole time, he promised her, texting the words as he said them. But what good would he be? If she got into trouble, how could he help her?

She nodded. "Here we go then."

Dillon grimaced. Here they went. And if this went badly, it would be all his fault.

*****

Sylvie swiveled. Layers of black chiffon floated slightly up, then slowly settled down.

She spun. The dress spun, too.

"You look amazing."

Sylvie stopped spinning so quickly she almost tripped. Smoothing the layers of skirt, she turned toward Lucas. He was leaning against the wall, dressed in formal evening attire, his hair still wet from his shower.

"That was fast," she said, feeling a slight burn of embarrassment climbing to her cheeks at having been caught playing like a little girl.

"No, don't," he said, straightening and taking a step closer. *'Don't?'*

"I like seeing you happy," he answered her thought.

The color rose higher. They'd spent the past two days in her hotel room, eating room service meals, occasionally watching the latest movies on television, leaving only for brief interludes in the exercise room, and he'd definitely seen her happy. Very happy.

He grinned. "Not what I meant, but that's nice too." He reached for her and she came willingly, flowing into his arms as if she was meant to be there. She lifted her face for his kiss, but before his lips touched hers, a thought slipped free.

'How much longer?'

He paused, arms tight against her. *'Ever the optimist.'*

"I'm sorry," she said, pulling back. "That wasn't meant for you to hear." She tried to smile at him.

"Most things people think aren't," he answered, a twist to his mouth. "Why are you afraid, Syl?"

"I'm not afraid," she answered, heat in her voice, reacting before thinking. And then she paused, looked away and up, looked back, sighed. "Okay. It's just . . . we're bound to fight eventually, Lucas. We always do."

Taking her hand, he tugged her to the side of the bed and sat next to her. He laced their fingers together, looking down at their hands. She could feel his caution, and she clenched her fingers around his. "There's no point in trying to be careful with me, Lucas. I'll know what you're thinking."

He looked up at her, his blue eyes bright. "All right, then, I won't be careful. We only ever fight about whether we should be together, Sylvie. That's the only important fight we've ever had. If you'd give us a chance this time, we might not argue at all."

Sylvie's mouth opened but no words came out. Finally, she snapped, "Me? Me give us a chance? I wasn't the one not giving us a chance in Milan." She pulled her hand free from his and stood, turning her back to him, walking the four steps away to the desk by the window, feeling her anger rising while the black chiffon layers floated with every quick movement.

"What are you talking about?" he asked, sounding authentically confused.

"Milan? When you didn't want things to change and I did?" She could hear the bitterness in her own voice and she tried to hold it back, to not let it spill out into her words.

"Again, what are you talking about?"

With the distance of the room between them, she turned to face him. "The last time we met? In Italy?" She didn't want to say the words but she couldn't stop herself from thinking them. *When you said that Dillon was better off with your parents? That they were better for him than we would be?'*

Lucas stood. "I didn't say that."

Sylvie arched her eyebrows at him.

"Well, not like that." He paused, frowning, and stuffed his hands into his pockets. "You thought I was a bad father. I wasn't."

"I didn't say that," Sylvie protested. She'd abandoned their child, so what right did she have to judge Lucas? On the other hand, he hadn't exactly been spending his time going to Little League games. She wouldn't have accused him of neglecting Dillon out loud. She hadn't meant to accuse him at all. But it was hard enough to control her unruly tongue without having to manage her wayward brain waves. "But you weren't any more of a father than I was a mother."

"Agreed." He shrugged. "I was fifteen years old when Dillon was born. You were seventeen. I still don't think you would have gone to jail, but you made a loving choice, Sylvie, when you let my parents raise him. All those things you wanted for him? He had them. He had the bedroom and the bicycle and the backyard and dinner on the table every night at six. And I made that choice, too. Sure, I could have dragged him to college with me and let a nanny raise him while I went to classes and studied, but with my parents, he had a home and love and security. And damned good parents, too."

Sylvie closed her eyes. Here they were, fighting about Dillon again. And the irony was, this time it didn't matter. Dillon was dead. Nothing she did could change that.

"Sylvie." Lucas's voice was husky, gentle. He had felt the moment her anger changed to grief, she knew. "We did the best we could."

'It should have been different.' For once, Sylvie didn't hide her pain. She let the hurt show. *'Why didn't you want it to be?'*

"I don't know what you're talking about."

Sylvie paused, uncertain, and then rested her hand on the desk beside her, feeling the cool wood under her fingers. This didn't make sense. Lucas seemed completely open, no hidden guilt, unlike her own. Some of the things she'd said in Milan had been cruel.

"Yeah," he agreed with her thought, his smile wry but his eyes serious. "But you weren't wrong. You'd been serving our country while I'd been playing the stock market. The stock market's way more profitable, but I think you'll like some of the ways GD's expanded in the last decade."

Sylvie frowned. "You expanded your dad's company?"

His smile reached his eyes as he said, "Into some areas that you might prefer, yes. Although we're still selective about the jobs we'll do.

I prefer FBI and police work, but we do the occasional job for the state department or the DEA."

"Lucas," Sylvie paused, not sure what to say, not sure what to think. She'd been scathing about the way Lucas was using his talents ten years earlier, but was he implying that he'd changed for her?

"Yes," he answered her.

'Stop doing that!' She was confused and having him two steps ahead of her made it worse.

He shrugged and looked away, his smile fading, and she took a step forward. *'I'm sorry,'* she thought. She forgot how hard it was for Lucas sometimes. He accepted his gift so calmly that it was easy not to realize how it isolated him. *'I know you can't help it.'*

He looked back at her and then stepped closer, bringing his hand up to touch her cheek. *'You have a beautiful mind, Sylvie. Clear and bright and direct. I love hearing it.'*

"Stop that," she murmured the words this time, feeling the traitorous heat stirring within her, loving the spark lit by Lucas's finger brushing against her skin, but fighting the distraction. "You're confusing me. I want to understand. Ten years ago, in Milan, you didn't want anything more. You didn't want things to change. You didn't want me to meet Dillon, you didn't want us to be a family. And now you—"

"Wait, what?" Lucas dropped his hand, his voice strong, rejecting her words. "That is so wrong. How could you think that?"

"You—you said so!" she protested. "Or thought it?" It was so long ago. She frowned, struggling to remember the details, the exact words that he'd said, but he was shaking his head.

"No," he said. "No. Definitely not. I might have thought that I didn't want anything to change, but that would have been about being in that hotel room with you." He stroked his hands up her arms, letting them come to rest on her shoulders, his eyes dark as they looked into hers. "I would have stayed there forever if we could have. But when we left, I wanted you with me."

Sylvie felt breathless, as if suddenly there wasn't enough air in the room. There was nothing in her feel of him that said he was lying, nothing. And yet . . .

"You said that Dillon was better off with your parents," she repeated stubbornly.

"Not wanting to disrupt Dillon's life didn't mean not wanting to be with you." Lucas was searching her face. The flow of thoughts and feelings between them echoed with regret. "Damn it," he muttered. "Did we really lose a decade to a misunderstanding?"

'Not just a decade,' Sylvie answered, tears springing to her eyes. All of her chance of knowing Dillon had been lost, too.

He pulled her close to him, wrapping his arms around her, and she tucked her head into the curve of his shoulder and let her grief flow. His chin resting on her head, he stroked her back as she sobbed.

'I'm sorry, love, so sorry.' The words were a murmur, aloud or in her head, she could barely be sure.

Minutes later, cried out and feeling like an idiot, Sylvie pulled away. "I'm getting snot on your tux," she muttered, wiping her face with the back of her hand. *'Probably mascara and smeared make-up, too.'*

"I'll survive." Automatically, Lucas glanced down at his shirtfront. *'And the hotel laundry will manage.'* The thought was dry.

"Lucas," she started, pressing her fingers to her eyes. She felt overwhelmed. She didn't know what to say, where to begin.

"It's still new to you," he answered her. "I remember." She felt him thinking about the days, the weeks, the months after Dillon had died. The desolation, the guilt, the self-doubt, the anger, the pain he'd felt. "But at Thanksgiving, he texted us jokes about turkeys while we were checking on the bird. What does a turkey's cell phone sound like? Wing, wing."

Sylvie blinked at him. "That is really dumb."

He lifted one shoulder, a smile tugging at his mouth. "But it was from Dillon."

"I've missed my chance for that, too," Sylvie said bleakly.

"Maybe for right now. But not forever," he told her gently. "He'll be back or we'll join him. You'll hear from him again. I promise."

"Turkey jokes, huh?" She breathed out a puff of laughter. Her face felt sticky and her eyes were hot. She was a mess, outside and inside. She'd been trying so hard not to think, to just live in the moment. But moments never lasted forever.

'Why didn't you look for me back then?'

'Ha.' His thought felt rueful. *'Zane loved his trip to Italy. But he couldn't find you. He thought you'd headed north.'*

'Germany,' she confirmed for him. *'I met up with my mom and stepdad there. And then Ty convinced me to join his security business.'*

"And you changed your name, didn't you?" Lucas asked. "I didn't expect that. I was still looking for you as Beth."

She nodded in confirmation, remembering what it had been like, how she'd felt leaving Milan—the anger, the hurt. If only she'd known. "Being telepathic ought to be more useful."

"My dad told me to stop looking, that I'd find you someday, but I never gave up. Do you know how many hundreds of women are named Beth Rodriguez?" Lucas's voice was light, but Sylvie could hear the pain that underlay it.

She tilted her head and looked at him, considering. "I hate to say it, but it wouldn't have worked back then anyway."

Lucas's denial was instant, but she put a hand up and covered his mouth before he could protest aloud.

"I was an unemployed high-school drop-out who felt like she'd wasted a decade of her life. You were a rich, Ivy League graduate with the world at your feet. I would have been jealous of your parents and a stranger to Dillon. Plus, I was angry at the world. We might have stayed together for a while, but we wouldn't have lasted."

"I would have lasted," he answered her.

"I wouldn't have." She waited, but he caught her meaning as quickly as always.

"Does that mean you might now?"

"I think it means I'd like to try," she said, as she stood on tiptoes to take his mouth with hers.

*****

Unsurprisingly, they were late to the party.

Sylvie shivered in the cold, waiting as Lucas spoke softly to the driver of the car that had brought them to AlecCorp headquarters, and then slipped her arm into his as he straightened and the car pulled away.

He smiled down at her, putting his hand over hers as they walked toward the low steps that led into the building. Automatically, Sylvie assessed the space. Three, no, at least four stories, with what looked like an open balcony on the front of the fourth floor. Multiple doors in the front wall meant too many entrances to easily defend, while pillars every ten feet or so could be useful hiding places or annoying visibility issues. On the left, the sidewalk sloped and the portico became a patio, a dead end unless you were willing to jump the railing to the street below.

"I don't think anyone will be trying to kill you tonight," Lucas whispered in her ear, stirring the soft hairs and sending a shiver down her spine.

She smiled at him, squeezing his arm in response, as they entered the building. *Habit.'*

A little thrill of excitement pulsed through her. With faint music playing in the distance and scents of fir and cinnamon in the air, the evening felt glittery and magical. Oh, sure, it was a really just a boring corporate party for a company she didn't much like and they were only here to see if Lucas could discover a link to the drug cartels. But she was wearing a beautiful dress with a gorgeous man next to her and she wasn't on-duty. And after the emotional wringer she'd been through earlier, it would be fun to relax and enjoy the night.

If they ever got in, that was. Sylvie craned her neck, trying to see what was ahead of them and why they were stuck behind a short line of equally well-dressed people. Ah, security. The ribbons and fir decorating the metal detectors were a nice touch, but the hold-up was typical for Washington events.

Beyond the short line, the lobby was sparsely populated. Off to the left, a temporary coat check had been set up. A few people stood there, outerwear draped over their arms, as they waited to turn their coats in to the woman who was carefully hanging each on an open rack. In the center of the room, a man sat behind a reception desk. Straight ahead, wide open doors led to the music, while to the right, a few people headed into the elevators.

As Sylvie reached the front of the line, she considered her choices. Then she dropped her black clutch on the moving belt and stepped through the archway of the security system.

Beep, beep, beep.

No surprise. Sylvie inhaled, feeling the comfortable weight of her gun held tight in the leather pocket across her belly. The Glock 36 was mostly made of a high-strength nylon-based polymer but it had enough metal in it for metal detectors to notice. Of course, she ought to just tell the guards she was carrying and show them her personal protection specialist license, firearms endorsement and concealed carry permit. At an AlecCorp party, half the guests had probably done the same. Still, getting past AlecCorp security without revealing her weapon would be much more satisfying.

A guard, dressed for the occasion in a dark suit and carrying a handheld wand, stepped forward, saying, "Excuse me, ma'am, could you step aside, please?"

"Of course." Sylvie kept her voice pleasant as she moved to the side of the machine, already planning what she'd say when the wand went off. Underwire bra? Metal studs in the leather? This wasn't the TSA, so she could refuse a pat-down.

Beep, beep, beep.

Sylvie glanced over her shoulder. Lucas, following her through the metal detector, looked mildly surprised and shrugged at her as the guard waved him over.

Beep, beep, beep. Beep, beep, beep. Beep, beep, beep.

"I think your machine might be malfunctioning," Sylvie said to the guard who'd stopped moving, wand held upright, as he frowned at the empty detector. No one was standing in it but the beeping continued.

The woman who'd been behind Lucas in line crossed her arms over her low-cut red evening dress, tapping her fingers impatiently. "It's cold over here," she called to the guard. "Could you speed it up?"

"It keeps doing that." The guard looked around, seeming helpless. The man behind the reception desk was standing up, Sylvie noted, and another in a black suit moved toward them from the elevators.

Beep, beep, beep.

The annoying sound continued. Lucas put a hand on Sylvie's shoulder and said to the guard. "You seem to have a problem. Could you finish up with me before taking care of that?" he asked, nodding toward the detector.

"Of course, sir." The guard responded with an automatic deference that had Sylvie's eyes narrowing. But as Lucas stepped forward, arms slightly raised, the guard waved the wand over him with reasonable care, ignoring the noise behind him. He then said perfunctorily, "Thank you, sir. Food's upstairs on the fourth floor, dancing through the doors, enjoy your evening," before turning his attention to the other two men and adding, "I don't know what's wrong with it. It keeps going off. That's the third time."

Sylvie couldn't decide whether to feel insulted or pleased. She'd gotten her weapon past AlecCorp security, but only because the guard had dismissed her as a threat when he realized she was with Lucas.

"If he read the newspaper, he would have known better," Lucas said to her as they moved farther into the lobby. She glanced at him. He was grinning at her, amused by her emotions, and she mock-scowled at him before laughing herself.

"What first?" Lucas asked.

"You have to ask?" Sylvie answered as she paused by the elevator. *'After nine and we missed dinner—I'll help you eavesdrop on some bigwigs, but you need to feed me first.'*

Behind them, another alarm started going off, and Sylvie glanced over her shoulder. The guard at the metal detector was gesticulating, frustration obvious, while the other two were looking away, one back toward the reception desk, the other toward the coat check.

"Fire alarm?" Sylvie asked. It didn't have the right kind of blare, though. It sounded more like the ringing of a security system when an emergency exit was opened.

"No," Lucas answered, frowning, as the elevator door slid open in front of them. "No, I don't think so." The words were slow, and his eyes were intent on the metal detector. Sylvie caught the flicker of a thought behind them.

"What?" she asked sharply, turning to look back at him as she stepped into the waiting elevator.

He followed her into the elevator without answering aloud. *'Check your phone,'* he thought. *'Just in case.'*

'You think it might be Dillon?' Sylvie opened her purse without waiting for a response, eager to see if she had a message, and checked her phone. *'Nothing.'*

Lucas was looking at his phone as well, and shook his head. *'Me neither.'* He tucked the phone back into his pocket.

"What are you thinking?" Sylvie asked the question, then felt silly. She ought to be able to tell. But she couldn't. Lucas was thinking more in impressions, fleeting memories and images, than in words. And the images flew by too quickly for her to catch them.

'Just a coincidence, I guess,' Lucas answered her silently, his expression abstracted for a moment before he seemed to shake off the mood.

There had been other people in the lobby, both arriving at the party and milling about, but they were alone in the elevator. Sylvie put her hand on Lucas's chest, sliding it into his jacket until she could feel the beating of his heart. *'You're okay?'*

He nodded, smiled, eyes dark, then bent his head and began kissing her.

CHAPTER ELEVEN

His parents were finally here.

And they looked amazing. His mom wore the cool black dress, her hair twisted up but glinting copper in the light, and his dad was in a tux, with a bow tie and everything.

As they came through the doors, his mom smiled up at his dad and Dillon's sense of guilt increased exponentially. He was letting—no, encouraging—Rachel to do something crazy. And all so he could get Sylvie and his dad to Tassamara. Maybe he should be leaving her alone instead. Maybe now that she and his dad had found each other again, they could work things out on their own. What good was talking to them going to do anyway?

But Rachel had been trying to kill herself, he reminded himself. He wasn't doing this just for his parents. He wanted to help Rachel, too.

Still, the whole plan felt like a huge risk. What if she got into trouble? What if she got kidnapped? What if some serial killer attacked her, like the one who'd gone for his mom? She wouldn't be able to defend herself and he'd be useless.

But it was too late now.

Rachel was determined. If he didn't do his part, she'd get caught right away and he couldn't do that to her. As his mom stepped through the metal detector, Dillon glanced at the clock on the wall above the reception desk.

It was time.

He and his dad stepped into the detector at the same moment. As always, it was strange but not uncomfortable to be standing inside another person, but as his dad stepped outside of the beeping machine, Dillon stayed in it, his eyes on the guard at the front desk. They needed that guard to look away from the monitor that scanned through the images from the building's security cameras for the next few minutes. Otherwise, the sight of a teenage girl using the emergency exit at the back of the building was sure to raise alarms. This way, Rachel's departure would still be recorded, but with any luck, they wouldn't find the recording until she was already on the train and halfway to Florida.

Beep, beep, beep.

There, the guard was getting up and heading this way. Perfect.

Dillon stopped paying attention to the guards and watched his parents instead. They were walking toward the elevators and his dad had his hand resting on the small of his mom's back. That seemed like a good sign.

As they disappeared into the elevator, he glanced back at the clock. Three more minutes and then he'd try to catch up with Rachel. No, not try, he corrected himself. He would catch up with Rachel. If she got into trouble, he'd be right there with her, even if all he could do was watch. He shuddered at the thought and stared at the second hand of the clock, wishing it would move faster.

Finally, at last, Dillon hurried out of the building. He turned up the tree-lined sidewalk, searching for Rachel as he rushed along the street, ignoring scattered pedestrians as he made his way toward Columbus Circle. With relief, he spotted her dark-haired figure waiting at a traffic light.

She'd already gotten rid of her velvet dress, he realized. She must have pulled it off and thrown it in the first trash can she passed. Her arms clutched around herself, she shivered in the cold, one hand clenched around her open GPS tracking device and the other holding the battery.

"I hope you're here, Dillon," she was saying under her breath. She'd left her phone behind so Dillon had no way to answer her. "Look for a cab that's loading up. When I walk by it, I'll put the battery back in my tracker. You make the driver's phone ring and I'll drop the tracker into the trunk. That way I'll know you're with me and I can get rid of the tracker."

Rachel was much too good at this, Dillon thought, feeling more anxious than ever. What if the driver noticed? What if he spotted the tracking device and stopped Rachel?

But it all went exactly as Rachel planned. As she hurried into the huge granite and marble train station, the cab driver was closing up his trunk, unaware of the small black object almost invisible against the dark trunk carpet.

Rachel's cheeks were pink. Dillon wondered whether it was from the chill or exhilaration. In his opinion, she was enjoying herself far too much.

As she passed hundreds of dollars in cash across to the ticket-taker to purchase the ticket she'd reserved online, the man gave her a sharp look.

"All by yourself, miss?"

"Oh, no," she responded blithely. "My dad's parking the car. He was worried I'd miss the train so he dropped me off at the door and sent me in ahead. He'll be here in a couple of minutes to see me off."

The cashier glanced at the clock, but didn't comment as he counted the cash and slid it into the drawer. Dillon looked, too. The train wouldn't depart for another half hour or so. It wasn't a totally implausible lie, but it wasn't foolproof, either.

"Awfully young to be traveling by yourself, aren't you?" The cashier still sounded skeptical as he printed out her ticket.

Rachel smiled at him. "I've been flying by myself since I was six," she lied. "My parents have joint custody so I visit Washington a lot. But this is the first time I've taken the train. Do you know how the food is? Should I get some snacks before I go? The little bedroom looks so cute, I can't wait to sleep in it."

She sounded excited and happy and not at all like a girl who was running away from home. Obviously reassured, the cashier smiled back at her. "Meals are included with the price of the room," he told her. "You'll get breakfast and lunch, but you can also get something at the snack car, if you like. Or the food court downstairs has plenty of options." He passed over her ticket and pointed out the direction to the train through the doorways on either side of the counter, then wished her a pleasant trip.

As she hurried away from the counter, Rachel's bright smile faded. She headed to the entryway on the right, avoiding the police kiosk on the left. "He might remember me," she muttered. "That's bad."

Dillon looked back, but the cashier wasn't watching her leave. He'd turned to deal with his next customer and Dillon suspected that he'd half-forgotten Rachel already. Oh, sure, if the police came by with a picture or her image made it onto the news, he might remember. But Rachel had soothed his suspicions perfectly.

For the first time, Dillon began to feel optimistic. Maybe this would work the way it was supposed to.

*****

The elevator doors opened with a ding. A slight cough let Sylvie know they now had witnesses. She pulled away from Lucas, breathless, and turned, cheeks flushed and head high, not meeting the eyes of the people who had been waiting as she stepped out of the elevator. She could feel amused appreciation, though, and the *'Lucky girl'* from the woman who had coughed came in loud and clear.

She glanced at Lucas as he followed her. His smile was just a little too smug. She batted him in the stomach with her clutch, but he only grinned wider and slipped his hand under her elbow.

Sylvie looked around. The lobby they stood in was decorated for the holidays, with a brightly-lit Christmas tree and festive red ribbons. Glass doors led onto the balcony that she had noticed earlier, while one open interior door clearly led to the party. She took a deep, appreciative breath. She didn't know exactly what she could smell, but it was food and she was starving.

She led the way into the party and wove a path straight to the buffet table against the wall, Lucas following her. Picking up a plate, she started filling it with abandon. Little cheesy things, check, she'd have two of those. Vegetables, sure, an assortment and some of that dip that looked as if it might be yogurt-based. Stuffed mushrooms, not a chance. Bacon wrapped around a mystery, definitely, although she hoped the inside was nothing too weird. Meat on a skewer, always an easy decision. She added three of the skewers to her plate and turned to Lucas with a smile.

His own smile was gone and he looked almost grim.

"You okay?" she asked, her smile fading. What was wrong with him? The easy joy was gone, replaced with a tension that made her want to wince. He was going to give her a stress headache if he kept that up, she thought crossly.

'Sorry,' came the thought in reply. *'It's just . . .'* The words broke off. His thought felt to Sylvie like the broken images of a spinning kaleidoscope, a whirl of colors and sensations.

She blinked at him then glanced around the room. To her, it seemed to be a typical corporate party: too many people, too small a space, voices too bright, stiff conversations and faked smiles, but also some genuine camaraderie and friendships. It was heavily tilted male and, in this room, upper echelon, which made sense for AlecCorp.

Most of the younger crowd would be downstairs dancing or, more likely, standing around getting drunk at the open bar.

There was no sign of Chesney, but he was probably holed up in a private office, sharing a whiskey with the other members of the board of directors. If Lucas hoped to discover any useful information, he'd want to stay here until the obligatory appearances and handshakes. Not that he was going to learn anything, anyway. It was ridiculous to think that Chesney would have anything to do with the cartels.

She and Lucas had agreed to mingle, though, and talk about Mexican vacations to see if anyone overhearing them let any unguarded thoughts slip free. If Lucas didn't pull it together, that was going to be tough to do.

Sylvie popped a cherry tomato into her mouth and bit into it, feeling a visceral satisfaction as the splash of liquid and tang of flavor hit her tongue. Lucas closed his eyes as if in pain. She waited for him to explain what was wrong, but he didn't say anything as she chewed and swallowed.

And then a dim memory floated to the surface of her mind. They'd gone to a movie together. Some summer blockbuster. Lucas had been strange in the line, but once in the crowded theater, he'd gotten worse. Sylvie held back her sigh, looking down at her plate. Did she have time to eat just a little more?

'*We forgot about crowds,*' she thought to him, deliberately trying to show him a glimpse of the memory.

'*Bring the plate,*' he thought back at her. If a thought could sound grumpy, his did. Turning, he led the way back to the door they'd entered through. Sylvie followed, nodding with a hint of apology to the people they were brushing past for the second time.

He went straight to the balcony. Outside, he took a deep breath of the crisp, wintery air as Sylvie shivered and moved to stand in the shelter of the building.

"How can you bear that?" he asked. "It's so—so chaotic. All those people. All their feelings."

Sylvie shrugged, picking up one of the chicken skewers. "You get used to it."

"How?"

She held out the plate for him to take some food as she thought about her answer. "Ever watched a home video of someone at the beach?"

He took one of the cheese puffs but didn't eat it right away, just holding it as he watched her, his blue eyes dark despite the light from the lobby. "Sure, probably."

"Sometimes the sound of the ocean is so loud that you can hardly hear the people. But when you're at the beach, you forget about it. You tune it out. It's like that for me."

"The woman next to us was worrying about a sick kid. The guy she was with is cheating on her. He was wondering if he could sneak away to his girlfriend tonight."

Sylvie nodded. She'd heard them, too. "I don't usually get their thoughts."

"I could tell you how every person in that room was feeling," Lucas continued. "Happy, sad, lonely, frustrated, bored—"

"I'd rather you didn't," Sylvie interrupted, voice dry. "I felt them, too." She took a bite of her chicken.

"The young guy by the door?" Lucas asked.

Sylvie swallowed before answering. "Depressed. Or maybe PTSD." She'd noticed him, too. Quiet, athletic, chatting comfortably to an older man, his polite smile not reaching his eyes. But for her—and for Lucas, too, when he was with her—the black cloud around him was practically visible.

"How can you stand it?"

Sylvie tried again. "It's like walking into a restaurant and noticing the smells of all the food. Five minutes later, you won't be able to tell that there's any smell at all unless you really think about it. You just have to stop paying attention."

"Neural adaptation." Lucas finally ate the cheese puff he'd been holding. "Like not feeling your clothes against your skin."

"Yeah, exactly."

"But it feels like sensory overload to me. As if I used to be blind and suddenly I can see. I don't know how to process all the emotions at once. It's too intense."

"We've never spent much time together in crowds. I guess I'm used to the feel of lots of other people. I've had plenty of practice." Being with Lucas added people's thoughts to the experience, of course, but it didn't seem to affect Sylvie like the emotions affected Lucas. It wasn't so different from overhearing conversations, after all. Besides, she could only hear the people closest to them. "Don't the thoughts bother you?"

He looked thoughtful. "I'm used to them. It's noisy, but I ignore it most of the time. It's like background music. I only listen when it catches my attention. You know, I wonder if there are others like you."

Sylvie raised a brow as she dipped a carrot into the yogurt and crunched down on it.

"Adapt or die, right? If you learn how to stop noticing the same way we all do with sounds or smells or touch, maybe you start taking it for granted. There might be other people who can do what you do who don't realize that they're unusual."

"Maybe," Sylvie agreed. "They probably get diagnosed with ADD. The inattentive kind."

"That sounds like the voice of experience."

Sylvie didn't answer out loud, just waved a hand dismissively before trying one of the bacon-wrapped appetizers. It tasted like pineapple on the inside, an odd but not unpleasant combination of salt and sweet. She lifted the plate a little. *Try one.*

'Changing the subject?' he asked as he took one of the bacon pieces.

"School wasn't my strong point." It was a reminder of how different they were. Lucas had probably never failed a test in his life.

"Hey." He stepped a little closer to her, his body almost touching the food that she held between them, and slid his empty hand around to the nape of her neck. "Don't do that. We're alike in the ways that matter."

She looked up at him and tried to smile. "Different in most ways."

"Different in only the best ways," he murmured, bending his head to hers. She opened her mouth to him, letting his searching kiss warm and reassure her, until the press of the plate against her abdomen reminded her of where they were and what they were supposed to be doing.

She took a step back. "We need to decide what to do."

He nodded, letting his hands drop and glancing into the building. "I don't want to waste this opportunity." His expression was somber. "I've been trying for months to find some evidence to prove Chesney's connection to the cartels. Or at least enough to get law enforcement on my side."

Sylvie raised a skeptical eyebrow. "I'm not sure the cops are persuaded by evidence that you find while breaking and entering."

He looked back at her, his grin flashing. "You'd be surprised. It's not my usual technique, though. I prefer to stay on the right side of the law, but this was an exception."

"Why?" Sylvie felt genuinely curious. Why was Lucas so determined to believe that Chesney was involved with criminals?

His smile disappeared and he paused for a long moment. His emotions felt mixed to Sylvie: a core of determination on the surface but underneath it, a sorrow flavored with a bitter anger. "I never wanted to get involved with drug cases. When I convinced my father that General Directions should expand into law enforcement, I imagined us finding missing people."

"A kid disappears, so you show up and read the minds of all the people who saw him last?" Sylvie could see how having someone with that ability on call would make the police very happy.

"Yeah, something like that. And we've done that a few times. But missing people sometimes overlap with drug cases and . . ." He shook his head and let the words trail off before starting up again. "Don't get me wrong, the war on drugs is a huge waste of taxpayer money. Prohibition didn't work in the 1920s, so why the politicians were stupid enough to think it would work when we tried it again is beyond me. As it turns out, no surprise, we've arrived at the same outcome. Prohibition led to organized crime and the war on drugs leads to the drug cartels."

Sylvie felt a trickle of unease. "You're not crazy enough to think you're going to take on the drug cartels, are you? Because that sounds like a fast way to get killed to me."

Lucas's chuckle held no humor in it. "No. That'd be an exercise in futility. They're hydras—chop one head off, two more show up. Breaking the Columbian cartels just made room for the Mexicans. But Chesney's a different story."

"How so?"

"The guy's not stupid. It's actually a damn clever business strategy. He supplies guns to the cartels on the one hand, mercenaries to the Mexican government on the other. He expanded AlecCorp during Iraq, but now that the war's over, he either cuts back or finds new markets. Instead, he's creating new markets. Like the world doesn't have enough problems."

Sylvie scowled. That sounded dangerously plausible. "Is the Mexican government hiring mercenaries?"

Lucas nodded. "They have no choice. The Zetas control more territory than the government does, anyway. It's war down there. And guess who funds it?"

Sylvie didn't have to think too hard. "We do?"

He smiled at her, but there was no humor in it. "Congress is spending billions to equip and train the Mexican military to fight back against the drug cartels. Most of that money goes straight to private military contractors."

Technically speaking, Sylvie was a private military contractor. She supposed she could even be considered a mercenary. Ty hadn't taken any contracts for training the locals in Iraq or Afghanistan, but he could have and she wouldn't have argued. But a good day for someone in her line of work was a boring day: one with no explosions, no bullets, and no injuries. From what Lucas was saying, Chesney was trying to make every day in Mexico an interesting day for his employees in order to get more of them hired and make more money.

That didn't sit well with her.

"All right," she said. She ate the cheese puff, picked up a skewer and nibbled at the beef teriyaki, then held the plate out for Lucas to take something. "We've got to go back to your original plan. Searching is pointless. Even if we got into Chesney's office, he's not going to leave proof of illegal weapon sales conveniently sitting out. We need to find out who he's working with. So we can either stay together and I'll do the listening while you concentrate on not letting the emotions get to you, or we can separate and you can listen to people on your own while I mingle and see if anyone has an interesting emotional response to the idea of Mexico."

"We stay together," Lucas answered firmly.

Sylvie tried to hold back her laugh, not altogether successfully. Had that been protective or possessive? In a mild voice, she said, "I am quite good at taking care of myself, you know."

"Not the point," he answered. Oh, possessive, definitely possessive, Sylvie realized, seeing the room they'd just been in through his eyes. Her focus on the buffet meant that she hadn't noticed the appreciative male gazes, but Lucas had.

Letting a slight smile play about her lips, she tucked her hand into Lucas's arm. "Lead the way then."

As they stepped into the building, Sylvie felt her muscles relaxing at the warmth. It wasn't bitterly cold outside, just brisk, but she wasn't dressed for the weather. "This floor first?" Then she paused, frowning.

Lucas glanced at her, sensing her sudden worry. "What is it?"

Moving quickly, Sylvie walked to the elevator door just as it opened and its sole passenger, Ty, disembarked.

"Thank God," he said with a sigh of relief. "Have you seen Rachel?"

"Rachel? Here? You've got to be kidding."

"Don't start, Sylvie."

"This party is totally inappropriate for a fourteen-year-old."

"I said, don't start. Chesney wanted her here." Ty rubbed a hand over the back of his neck, as if a stress headache was just beginning.

"God, that man is a lousy father," Sylvie muttered. Not that she had the right to criticize. It wasn't as if she'd been much of a mother. But she would never have brought a child to a party of mercenaries, much less a teenage girl.

"What's going on?" Lucas directed his question to Ty, not seeming to need introductions.

Ty glanced at him. Perhaps he recognized Lucas's potential usefulness, because he replied without hesitating, "Hourly check-ins. Her bodyguard hasn't answered."

"Lydia?" Sylvie asked. That wasn't like the older woman. Sylvie respected Lydia's ability and ethics, but calling her strict barely did her justice. Rigid and uncompromising were closer. Fortunately, she and Sylvie usually worked opposite shifts.

Ty nodded.

Sylvie frowned, but Lucas immediately followed up with another question. "Who've you got looking and where?"

"I've got four of us on duty tonight. Mark and me on Chesney, James at the car, and Lydia on Rachel," Ty responded promptly. "I've called James in already. I met him downstairs and he's searching, but it's crowded, noisy, and tough to see down there. Chesney's in his VP's office and Mark's with him there. I was about to start looking up here."

"Where was Lydia on her last check-in?"

"Downstairs," Ty answered.

"And how late is she?"

Ty glanced at his watch. "Twenty minutes now."

"We'll start downstairs then," Lucas stated.

Ty glanced at Sylvie. She hadn't said a word since asking if Lydia was the bodyguard on duty. She could see in the raise of his eyebrows that he was questioning whether this was okay so she smiled crookedly and nodded.

As the elevator dropped, she thought to Lucas, '*A little bossy, aren't you?*'

'*Sorry,*' he thought but without a trace of apology in his emotions. '*The first hours are the most important when someone's missing.*'

"Tell me about Lydia," he added aloud.

"Organized, responsible, reliable, uptight," Sylvie responded promptly.

"Not the kind to lose track of time?" Lucas asked, but Sylvie could tell that he already knew the answer. In fact, she was almost sure that he'd known the answer to his previous question, too.

She narrowed her eyes, looking at him intently. "Did you investigate us?"

He looked away from her, glancing at the floor number display as if checking how close they were to the ground. "Are you going to get mad when I say yes?"

She thought about it. It seemed like the kind of thing she would have gotten angry about ten years ago. Was it a sign that she'd grown up that she no longer felt that way? If she'd been capable of it, she would have found out everything there was to know about Lucas and the people around him. "Not this time."

"Good."

"Did you learn anything interesting?"

He grinned at her. "Nothing that indicated anyone was connected to the Zetas and that was all I was looking for. But your colleague James is an eclectic guy."

Oh, Sylvie so wanted to ask questions. James never talked about his past. But they'd arrived at the first floor and reluctantly she put the thought aside. First, they needed to find Lydia and Rachel and then they'd try to learn more about Chesney. Maybe after that she'd grill Lucas about James.

Finding Lydia turned out not to be difficult. James was hovering outside the nearest women's bathroom, cell phone pressed to his ear, talking to Ty.

"I don't know," he was saying, sounding exasperated. "There's a sick woman, that's all I've found out. I can't go in. It's the women's bathroom and there are at least two women in there. You want them to call the cops on me? Ah, here she is. Back in five." He stuffed his phone into his suit jacket pocket and turned to Sylvie with relief and a quick fire scrutiny of Lucas.

"No Rachel?" Sylvie asked.

James shook his head. "I asked a woman who was going in to look for them. She came back out for a minute, said no kid, but a woman who seemed sick or drunk, then went back in."

Sylvie nodded and didn't pause. Pushing the door open, she entered the bathroom. It was surprisingly empty for a women's restroom during a party. Two women were crouched on the floor at the far wall, talking to a woman half on the ground, half leaning against the wall.

It was Lydia. Her eyelids were fluttering and she was mumbling something, weakly trying to push away the hands of a woman who was trying to get her up. "You've got a friend waiting outside for you," the woman said. "Let me help you."

"Lydia, where's Rachel?" Sylvie dropped to the ground next to Lydia, assessing her quickly. Someone who didn't know her might say drunk. Really, really drunk. But Sylvie knew better. Could she have had a stroke? Or a heart attack? Or was she drugged?

Lydia tried to say something but the words were indistinct. Her head lolled sideways.

"She's trashed," the other woman said with disapproval. "She needs to sleep it off, but not in here."

"She needs medical attention," Sylvie corrected her. She was running scenarios in her head, trying to think through the situation.

Say Lydia got sick. A stroke. Would Rachel have gone looking for assistance? She might not have had her cell phone on her, but surely there would have been a woman here who could help her. Why was this bathroom so empty? Sylvie asked the question out loud.

"There's another restroom on the other side of the auditorium," the first woman answered readily. "It's closer to the dancing and bar. I was on my way upstairs so I stopped at this one."

The other woman nodded. "I came over here because the other one had a line, but it's not as convenient."

All right, so it was possible that no one was here when Lydia got sick. It still didn't make sense that Rachel would leave Lydia. The girl obeyed all the rules and abandoning her bodyguard was definitely not in the rulebook. But she'd been more rebellious lately, Sylvie reminded herself. There was the drinking and then the lie that took her to her mother's art show. Could Rachel have seen this as an opportunity for a little freedom, not realizing how sick Lydia was? Maybe she was out on the dance floor this very minute, flirting and pretending to be older than her age.

But what if Lydia was drugged? Not on drugs, not by choice, but deliberately drugged with the intent to knock her unconscious. Could Rachel have been kidnapped? From the women's bathroom in the middle of a party? That would almost mean a woman had to be involved. And maybe that Rachel went willingly.

Moving quickly, Sylvie hurried back to the door.

"She's here," she said to James. "But we need to get her to a hospital, ASAP. Call Ty and find out whether he wants us to call an ambulance or take her. And tell him there's no sign of Rachel."

James nodded, face grim, pulling out his phone before she'd finished the sentence.

Sylvie turned to Lucas. *'What do you know about Rachel's mother?'*

He looked a little startled, but answered, *'Almost nothing.'*

'New question, then—what can you find out about Rachel's mother and how fast?'

'You think she might be involved?'

'I think . . .' Sylvie paused and then finished out loud. "I'm not sure what I think. Except that this doesn't feel right."

CHAPTER TWELVE

The train stopped.

Dillon frowned. It had stopped several times already, but this felt different. There'd been none of the noise that indicated they were coming into a station, just a slow glide to a halt. Why weren't they moving?

Rachel propped herself up on her elbows and looked out the window into the dark night. She'd boarded the train and found her room without trouble. Both beds had already been made in the tiny train compartment and she'd promptly climbed into the top bunk.

Dillon had thought about lying down in the lower bunk, but it felt weird somehow. He didn't sleep any more, of course, and lying in the bed with the bunk on top of him, no view out the window, seemed too coffin-like for his taste. Instead, he perched on the closed toilet seat, so close to Rachel in the small space that if he raised his hand he could touch her leg.

Rachel pressed her face up to the glass. "There's nothing out there."

"Nothing?"

"And we're not moving." There was a hint of worry in her voice.

"Way to point out the obvious," Dillon responded and then immediately felt guilty. He shouldn't be mean, even if she couldn't hear him. But he was nervous and scared. He couldn't seem to stop worrying about all that might go wrong. Or all that might have already gone wrong. He wondered if Lydia was okay.

He'd realized, too, that he and Rachel hadn't talked about what she'd do after she got to Tassamara. They should have. She'd get off the bus and then what? He could go find Akira but he'd be leaving Rachel alone. Where would she go? What would she do? Tassamara was too small to have a bus station: it was just a stop. If she stood there and waited—a strange girl all by herself on the side of the road— someone would start asking her questions within a couple of minutes. They'd find out she was a runaway and before he could even text his mom, Rachel would be on her way back to Washington.

No, he had to make sure someone could meet her. But who?

If he texted Akira, he knew exactly what would happen. She'd call his dad and discover what was going on, even if he told her not to. Akira didn't like uncertainty. She'd want to know what he was doing and she'd take the most direct route possible to finding out. If he texted his uncle, Zane would tell Akira and the end result would be the same.

He could try texting his Aunt Grace. Of all his relatives, Grace was closest in age to him. She'd been his regular babysitter when he was little and if he asked her to keep a secret, she would. But Grace was always busy. She'd do it, but she wouldn't be happy about sitting by the side of the road waiting for a bus. His Aunt Natalya would wait for the bus, but would she send Rachel back to Washington the moment she found out who Rachel was? Maybe.

No, he could only trust one person to meet the bus and not ask questions. His grandpa. But how would Rachel react to that? Would she freak out if a strange old man approached her? Dillon felt his frustration level rising. Why hadn't he thought about this earlier?

Rachel shivered. "It's so cold. I hope it's warmer in Florida." Her black leggings and long-sleeved shirt weren't enough for the weather, but they were inside now. She should be warming up.

"You could turn the heat up," Dillon suggested. "The thermostat is right behind you on the wall."

She didn't respond, and he sighed. He understood why she'd had to throw away her cell phone, but not being able to communicate with her was driving him crazy.

The train still hadn't started up again, so Dillon stood, leaning against the bunk and peering over Rachel and out the window. He couldn't see anything except the reflection of the room in the glass.

Was it a mechanical problem? Something on the track? Or had they already found Rachel's trail? Was the train stopped waiting for the police to arrive and take her away?

"Brr." Rachel hugged herself. "It's freezing."

She looked cold, Dillon realized. Her cheeks were pale and her lips touched with blue. He glanced at the thermostat. It was set as high as it would go. Was it not working?

Oh, hell.

Dillon hated himself.

He hated being a ghost, he hated being unable to communicate, he hated being helpless.

And he especially hated that he was causing the temperature to drop because he was so worried.

"It's me," he told her, feeling miserable. He backed away from the bed, but the room was so small that there was no way for him to get far enough away from her that she wouldn't feel his cold aura. He needed to calm down. But how could he?

He pushed himself through the door and out into the train hallway. He'd promised to stay close to her and it felt as if he was breaking that promise. But he'd stay where he could see if she left the compartment and while he did, he'd text his grandpa. And he'd try to calm down.

But it would sure help if the train would start moving.

*****

Rachel was missing.

The words pounded in Sylvie's head like a drumbeat. She could feel the tension along her spine and in her shoulders, the rush of adrenaline pouring into her arms and legs telling her to go, go, go. But where was there to go? She kept her voice even as she said to James, "Someone needs to be at the hospital with Lydia to find out what's wrong with her. Ask Ty who he wants to go."

He nodded, speaking into his phone, and she turned back to Lucas.

"Fill me in on Rachel." He'd pulled his phone out, too, but he made no move to use it.

"Spoiled brat," Sylvie said succinctly. "Whiny, sulky, rude." Close protection security consultants got to know their clients intimately, but the good ones didn't talk about them. Under the circumstances, though, Sylvie would make an exception.

"The classic teenager?" His voice was serious but with a trace of amusement at her tone.

"More like the classic neglected rich kid," Sylvie admitted. "She's who you get if you raise a kid with high expectations but no love, affection, or attention. She's miserable so she does her best to make everyone else miserable, too."

"Harsh."

"But she follows all the rules, always does as she's told, gets straight As." Sylvie glanced back at the bathroom door, torn between going in to check on Lydia and thinking the situation through with Lucas.

"You think she might have run away?"

"From a party? In Capital Hill?" It sounded so unlikely. And yet Rachel was gone. "Where would she go?"

No, it made no sense. What were the options? Rachel could be in the building, looking for help for Lydia. But if that was the case, she should be back by now. She'd been gone for at least half an hour, since Lydia's missed check in. Even if Rachel had made the stupid choice of looking for her father instead of going straight to the security desk, she would have found him by now.

If Lydia had felt sick, would she have left Rachel alone somewhere? Could Rachel be waiting in another room for Lydia to return? That seemed unlikely to the point of absurdity. Maybe one of the other guards would have taken that chance at a closed party but Lydia? Never.

No, Rachel had left Lydia, not the other way around. But by choice or by force? She would have gone quietly with a gun on her. And she might have gone willingly if she was going with or to her mother. Could her mother have gotten into the party?

Sylvie shook out her hands, fighting the urge to move. Every cell in her body wanted to be doing, to be in action. She needed to go into the bathroom and help Lydia. She needed to head to the auditorium and start searching for Rachel on the dance floor. She needed to get to building security and see what camera coverage the building had. She needed . . . she turned back to James.

"GPS," she said. Rachel would have had her tracking device with her. It wouldn't necessarily tell them anything until they found it: if it was still in the building, it might mean that she or a kidnapper had left it behind.

James nodded and said as much into the phone.

"Or cell phone," Sylvie said. "Maybe we can trace her cell phone."

"The FBI will do that. They'll check messages, too, see who she's been talking to," Lucas responded.

"No FBI." It was Ty, stuffing his phone in his pocket, a little out of breath. He must have run down the stairs, Sylvie guessed. "And no ambulance."

"What?" Sylvie stared at him.

"Chesney doesn't want to risk any publicity."

"Ty!" Sylvie protested.

"Sylvie. It's the client's call." His words were an order and Sylvie, fuming, shut up.

"The FBI has the expertise—" Lucas started, voice mild.

"The client's call," Ty interrupted him. Sylvie could feel the frustration and worry simmering under his calm exterior and Lucas must have sensed it as well, because he didn't push, just stuffed a hand into his pocket. Sylvie suspected it was clenched into a fist. She stepped a little closer to him, resting her own hand on his arm.

"Mark's on Chesney," Ty continued. "Let's get Lydia to the car and—shit." He ran a hand through his short hair.

Sylvie raised her eyebrows in question.

"Not enough people, not enough cars. I'll call in backup, but it's Friday night. I don't know how soon anyone can get here."

"Rachel's GPS is on the move," James reported. His head was bent over his phone, fingers tapping away at the screen.

"Fuck!" Ty's frustration boiled over.

"I've got a car and driver here," Lucas offered. "Sylvie and I can take Lydia to the hospital."

Ty breathed a sigh of relief. "That would help."

"No." Sylvie shook her head. "I'm staying here." All three men looked at her with varying expressions of surprise, but Sylvie didn't bend. Rachel's GPS device might be on the move, but that didn't mean Rachel was with it.

What if this had been a crime of opportunity? AlecCorp hired dangerous men. Most would be smart enough to steer clear of an executive's young daughter, but alcohol turned even the smartest soldiers stupid. Sylvie wanted—no, needed—to make sure that Rachel wasn't in the building.

And if Rachel had been kidnapped, it had to be an inside job. This was an invitation-only party with security guards at the door. No casual kidnapper had stolen her from AlecCorp premises. She might be able to find someone whose emotions or thoughts would reveal their complicity.

Lucas, of course, was the first to understand, but Ty wasn't far behind. "Yeah," Lucas said, nodding. "That makes sense. But I should stay with you. I might be able to help."

"Can you really—" Ty started and then paused, but with Lucas standing so close to her, Sylvie had no trouble reading his thoughts. He was wondering if Lucas could read minds.

"Yeah," Lucas nodded briefly, answering Ty's question. "And if someone here is involved, they're likely to be thinking about it."

James looked from one man to the other, clearly mystified. "Someone want to tell me what you're talking about?"

"Later," Ty answered. "First things first. We get Lydia to your car," he said to Lucas. "I send Mark down to accompany her to the hospital. James and I chase the GPS while I call in backup. You and Sylvie search here."

Lucas nodded, already texting the driver of the car to meet them at the front of the building.

Ty turned to Sylvie. "You're not going to like this, I know, but I need you to sit on Chesney until someone shows up to relieve you. Then you can search."

Sylvie wanted to protest—what the hell did she care about Chesney when Rachel was missing?—but she gritted her teeth and managed a tight smile instead. "You got it. But get them here quickly."

*****

Chesney's emotions were all wrong.

Not that Sylvie had vast quantities of experience with parents of missing children. But she'd dealt with worried parents in Iraq and emotions crossed cultural lines. She'd understood how they felt. Not Chesney, though.

He didn't feel scared or even anxious. No, he was simply angry.

Sylvie stood outside the office door, wishing that Lucas had come upstairs with her so that she could eavesdrop on Chesney's thoughts. But Lucas was searching the rest of the building, a task they'd agreed couldn't wait.

Her phone vibrated in the clutch bag she had tucked under her arm and she quickly slipped it out. Lucas.

"Yes?"

"No sign of her," he answered. "But I got an update back on her mother."

"That was quick."

"It's not current information, just background."

"Go ahead."

"Lisa Sanger married Raymond Chesney in 1995. She was 22, he was 49. Rachel was born a year later. Three months after the birth,

Lisa was hospitalized. No details, but while she was in the hospital, Chesney filed for divorce and full custody. She didn't fight it. A few months later, she moved cross country to San Francisco where she became an artist. She's been moderately successful. No criminal record, financials stable but only barely verging on comfortable, never remarried."

"That doesn't sound like a potential kidnapper to me," Sylvie said slowly, trying to put the information together with the woman she'd seen at the art gallery.

"No," Lucas agreed. "I've got people tracing her current movements, but if she's in San Francisco and hasn't seen Rachel in years, she's unlikely to be a factor in this."

"She was in DC last week. We saw her on Sunday."

"What?" Ty would have been furious but Lucas just sounded surprised.

"Yeah, we . . . well, it's kind of a long story."

"You didn't think mentioning that earlier might have been helpful?"

The dry humor in his tone brought a smile to her lips as she responded. "Hey, I mentioned it. I told you to find out about her."

"I meant maybe mention it to your boss and your colleague. The ones who are currently chasing after Rachel's GPS?"

Sylvie's smiled faded and her mouth twisted. She should have told Ty the whole story last Sunday. And she definitely should have shared her suspicions downstairs. She wasn't sure why she hadn't, except that they'd been moving quickly.

"So do you think she's involved?" Lucas continued.

"It would explain a lot," Sylvie answered. She glanced at the door behind her. It was thoroughly sound-proofed; she hadn't heard a word from inside while she'd been watching, but she dropped her voice anyway. "Including why Chesney isn't worried."

"His daughter's disappeared and he's not worried about it?"

"No. Just angry."

"That does sound as if he knows more than he's saying. And might explain why he didn't want the FBI involved."

"Maybe."

"You don't sound convinced."

Sylvie shook her head, then sighed, wishing Lucas were close enough that they could share thoughts. She didn't want to say what she was thinking out loud, but the pieces weren't adding up to her. She would have pegged Chesney as the vindictive type. If he thought his ex-wife had kidnapped his daughter, wouldn't he use every power at his disposal to go after her, including the FBI and the full force of the law?

Instead he let Ty and James go racing off into the night without sharing whatever it was that he suspected.

It didn't make sense.

"Do you want me to keep searching?"

In the room behind her, Sylvie felt movement: two people coming closer to the door. "I've got to go," she said hurriedly. "Keep me posted." As the door opened, she was slipping her phone back into her purse.

Without even a glance in her direction, Chesney stalked past her, followed by another man. Automatically, Sylvie fell into step behind them, wondering where they were headed. She'd expected Chesney to socialize with the peons eventually, but that was before Rachel disappeared. Could he really be intending to shake hands and bestow jovial holiday wishes on the employees as if nothing was happening?

He headed straight for the elevator, however, and it wasn't until Sylvie followed him inside that he seemed to notice her presence.

"I won't be needing your company, Ms. Blair," he said, voice brusque.

"Sir?" She let her confusion show.

"Is there something wrong with your hearing? Your services are not required for the remainder of this evening," he said with a snap in his voice.

Sylvie glanced at the other man with them. He was tall, solidly built, but middle-aged and with a bit of a paunch. If he'd been military, he hadn't stayed in shape. He definitely wasn't a bodyguard.

"I'm afraid I'm not at liberty to disregard my orders, sir." Sylvie tried to keep her voice smooth but her mind raced with speculation. What the hell was Chesney up to?

"I'm your employer. I give the orders." His snap had upgraded to a growl.

"Of course, sir," Sylvie acknowledged gracefully. "Under the circumstances, however, I have no way to ascertain whether those orders are being given under duress. Should you depart the premises without your personal security, I'll have no recourse but to immediately contact the authorities and inform them of your daughter's disappearance and your own unusual behavior."

Chesney stared at her. He kept his expression as blank as hers, but she could feel his fury. She felt a laugh rising—was it hysteria?—and firmly suppressed it.

"How exactly do you think you'll be able to protect me, Ms. Blair? Are you even armed?" The scornful up-and-down glance would have annoyed Sylvie from a stranger. From Chesney, it enraged her and stilled the laugh that she'd been fighting.

"I was off-duty, sir." She avoided the question. "I can, however, serve as a liaison between you and the team searching for your daughter."

"And how will they know you aren't under duress?" He put mocking air quotes around the phrase.

"We have protocols for that, sir." Sylvie met his gaze, her own firm. She didn't know what was going on, but if Chesney thought he could find Rachel, she was accompanying him no matter how he felt about it.

If looks could kill, she'd be drawn and quartered and burned at the stake.

The elevator reached the ground floor and the doors slid open. For a moment, no one moved. The stranger looked uncomfortable, but kept silent.

"All right, if you feel you must." Chesney finally grudgingly acquiesced. He led the way out of the elevator.

"I'll get my car and bring it around to the front," said the other man.

"Fine, fine," Chesney waved him off. Sylvie followed him without saying anything more as he went to collect his coat from the coat check. She'd won. She should be content with that. Instead, she desperately wanted to ask questions.

Lucas stood by the security desk, talking to the guard who sat at the counter. Sylvie felt a wave of relief when she saw him. He turned at the brush of her mind against his.

'What's going on?' he thought to her.

'Fuck if I know.' Her return thought was fervent. *'Chesney's going somewhere. Without calling Ty. Without security. Usually, the man doesn't move without two guards half a foot away.'* Sylvie scanned the room, searching for threats, using all her senses to assess the risks but finding nothing.

'He must know something.'

'Yeah. But I don't feel good about this. Can you follow us?'

'Not unless you can delay. My car's still at the hospital.'

'Damn.' She should have known that. She did know that. She just hadn't wanted that answer.

'Slow him down,' Lucas suggested. *'I can get someone here in twenty minutes.'*

Sylvie didn't shake her head, but she knew Lucas could feel the negative. *'He doesn't want me to come to begin with. If I delay he'll leave me behind.'*

'Let him.' The thought was close to an order. Sylvie might have bristled but under the command lay concern and she was worried, too.

'Can't,' she replied briefly as she followed Chesney to the door and stepped outside. *Finish searching the building. If I'm gone too long, get Zane. Find me.'*

As soon as Sylvie was safely seated in the back seat of the car next to Chesney, she pulled out her phone and called Ty. She knew exactly how he was going to react to Chesney's departure from the AlecCorp building. Within the first thirty seconds of the call, she was handing the phone to Chesney, saying calmly, "He'd like to speak to you, sir."

She gazed out the window at the well-lit streets of Washington, trying to pretend she couldn't hear every word Chesney said as he argued with Ty.

"You don't need to know where I'm going." Chesney's anger was an almost palpable third presence in the back seat. "I don't give a damn what you think, Mr. Barton. You've lost my daughter. I want her found."

Ty's response was indistinct, but Sylvie had to press her lips together to stop her own grim retort. If Chesney wanted Rachel found, why was he making life difficult for them? Why this distracting road trip? And why not call the damn FBI? They needed more resources than half a dozen private security consultants chasing after a GPS.

"Yes, of course this excursion is related, but you don't need the details. Suffice to say that I know my enemies."

Sylvie had no idea what that might mean.

Enemies? Would he consider Rachel's mother an enemy? That seemed a harsh description for the woman she'd met in the art gallery. Victim felt more appropriate somehow.

But who else could he be referring to?

A drug cartel? Not a chance, Sylvie thought. The cartels might control Mexico, but kidnapping a teenager from a closed party in a secure facility in Washington? No way.

At least not without inside help.

Then could it be a corporate enemy? Sylvie had a low opinion of AlecCorp, but the idea of infighting among the executives leading them to kidnap their co-worker's children was insane. No, Chesney's actions made no sense.

"No, I don't need more guards. I want every person you have here in Washington, searching for my daughter."

That was the first reasonable statement Chesney had made. For a moment, Sylvie had a spark of sympathy for Chesney. He was putting Rachel's safety ahead of his own.

"Ms. Blair has insisted on accompanying me. Contact her when you know something," Chesney finished brusquely, pressing the disconnect button before handing the phone back to her.

Sylvie took it, not letting her annoyance show. She would have liked a slightly longer conversation with Ty herself. But the phone rang almost immediately and she answered.

"Do you have any idea what the hell he's doing?" Ty demanded.

"No."

"What the hell is he thinking?"

Ty's question was rhetorical but Sylvie almost opened her mouth to provide a flippant response before she thought better of it. If only she could have smuggled Lucas into the car. Under the circumstances, being able to read Chesney's mind would have been damn useful. "No idea."

"All right." Ty sighed and she could hear the worry. "We're still chasing down Rachel's GPS, but I'm not feeling good about it. It's looping around like whoever has it is going in circles."

Sylvie didn't respond immediately. If her first suspicions were correct and Rachel had gone willingly—or mostly willingly—then the GPS almost had to be a ruse. Rachel understood how the tracker worked. She could easily have disabled it if she wanted to. But they had to follow the lead and at least confirm that their fail-safe had failed. "What about her cell phone?"

"No," Chesney snapped. She glanced at him as he continued. "No one learns about this. Do not communicate with the cell phone company."

GPS tracking wasn't enabled on their phones. Too easy to hack, Chesney'd said, and Ty had agreed. Making your location continually visible to anyone with sufficient computer skills was poor security. The only way they could track Rachel's phone was with the service provider's assistance.

"Did you hear that?" Sylvie said to Ty, making an effort to keep her voice even.

"Yeah." The short answer held depths of frustration.

"Anything else?" Sylvie asked Ty.

"Take good care of Mr. Chesney," he ordered.

"You got it," Sylvie replied, disconnecting. She slid her phone back into her purse and set it on her lap. They were crossing the Frederick Douglass Bridge, she realized, so wherever Chesney was headed, it wasn't home or in Washington. As they sat in silence on the parkway, then headed south on Branch Avenue, Sylvie speculated. What did Chesney know? Could he have already received a ransom demand?

"Do you speak Spanish, Ms. Blair?" Chesney's words broke the heavy silence.

Sylvie considered her answer. She'd annoyed Chesney by insisting on joining him. His hostility toward her might get in the way of doing her job. Maybe she should make an effort to placate him. "I took it in the 9th grade," she said with a smile, trying to turn on the charm. "Senora Ramirez's class. But grammar got the better of me and I didn't pass."

He accepted her response with a grunt and leaned back into the seat.

"Do I need it?" she dared to ask.

"No." His abrupt response was a clear dismissal.

Sylvie didn't push. She looked out the window at the tree-lined roadway and tried to remember what was down this road. Andrews Air Force Base. But why would Chesney be headed there? Did he think Rachel's disappearance had something to do with AlecCorp's involvement in Iraq?

She glanced down at her hands, clenched on her bag, and with an effort, she relaxed her white-knuckled grasp. Maybe it was the reminder of Iraq, but she felt as if she were back on convoy duty: not sure when an attack would come or who the enemy might be.

But they drove past Andrews with only a slight delay from traffic congestion. Sylvie tried to relax but she still felt tense and watchful as they finally pulled off the road, turning into a short driveway. The driver—whose name she still didn't know—got out and opened a chain link gate, and then came back and pulled the car into a parking place.

"The lobby closes at five," he reported. "Do you want to wait in the car while I get the plane ready?"

Plane?

Chesney glanced at Sylvie. "Might as well. Ms. Blair's not dressed for the weather."

Sylvie looked down at her dress, with its black leather bodice and layers of black chiffon. "Sir, if you're intending a trip, I could call for back-up. We can get someone else here within the hour."

"I intend to be on a plane within the hour, Ms. Blair. Relax, you'll be warm enough at our destination."

Warm enough, maybe, but she was also going to be ridiculously over-dressed. She tried to keep her annoyance contained as she asked, "Where are we headed?"

"Florida."

CHAPTER THIRTEEN

Dillon spent a miserable night pacing the corridors of the train, which had finally started moving again.

When he stood still for long enough, tiny crystals of frost formed on the windows from all the energy he was stealing from the atmosphere because of his anxiety and stress.

Akira perceived ghosts who were beginning to overload with energy as having flickering pink edges. Like red auras, he'd once asked her, and she'd agreed that it was something like that. He couldn't see it himself but he suspected that if Akira were here, she'd tell him that he'd started to flicker and to cut it out.

He knew he could make it stop if he could calm down and quit worrying. But his thoughts were on a relentless track of circular paranoia. What if Lydia was dead? What if the train was delayed? What if Rachel missed her bus? What if the next bus wasn't until the next day? Where would Rachel spend the night? What if she got caught? Worse, what if she really got kidnapped? Even worse, what if she ran into a serial killer like Sylvie had?

He'd hit that point of the circle and tell himself that he was being ridiculous and stupid and he needed to quit worrying about things that he couldn't control. And then he'd remember that as a ghost he couldn't control much of anything, and he'd start worrying again.

But if he didn't calm down, he might be in big trouble.

Flickering was dangerous.

A ghost who took in too much energy could become what Akira called a vortex ghost. That had happened to his gran. When she'd died from a stroke, just three days after his deadly overdose, her despair and grief had left her trapped in a nether state, lost in some sort of energy sea. Desperately seeking a way out and unaware of the physical world, she became deadly to humans who were sensitive to the energy, such as Akira, and to ghosts. Dillon had been lucky his gran hadn't inadvertently destroyed him.

In the void, his gran had been able to see the auras of living humans. She'd grabbed Akira's iridescent blue aura and held on for dear life. Death. Whatever. In doing so, she'd pulled Akira's soul right out of her body. It hadn't been on purpose, though. It was just what happened to a ghost who'd lost control.

Dillon didn't want it to happen to him.

And all he needed to do to prevent it was relax.

Relax, relax, *relax*.

Would the night never end?

But dawn finally came and then daylight and the train trudged on, wending its way through South Carolina and Georgia and into Florida and finally, right on time, depositing Rachel in Palatka.

Dillon felt enormously relieved to be back in Florida. The yellow brick and red roof of the train station, the occasional palm tree, the dry grass, it all felt like home to him. And Rachel was almost to safety. Soon he could stop worrying.

The bus would arrive in twenty-five minutes. And then from Palatka to Tassamara was about an hour. Dillon hadn't texted his mom yet, but maybe he should do that now?

As Rachel took a seat on a bench outside the bus station, he looked around. The only person nearby was a skinny white guy, shaved head, zits, pacing nervously. Dillon was sure he'd have a cell phone but he looked skeezy. If Dillon had been alive, he would have avoided getting too close, maybe instinctively, maybe because of television stereotypes rooted deep in his subconscious. The guy fit his picture of a drug addict.

Dillon drifted closer, just as the guy's attention landed on Rachel.

"Hey, baby," the guy said.

Rachel looked startled. She didn't say anything in reply, just glanced at the man and then glanced away but Dillon saw her throat clench as she swallowed nervously.

"Yeah, I was talking to you."

Oh, hell. Dillon tried to think of what he could do. Set off an alarm? Make a phone ring? Then he scowled as he thought of another option. Something about it grossed him out but with a grimace, he stepped into the man.

The man shivered convulsively as Dillon's energy hit him. He looked around, as if searching for an air conditioning vent from the overhanging roof, before shaking his head and saying, "Cold out here today."

Rachel didn't look at him and the man stepped a little closer to her. "You look pretty cold, too."

Dillon followed him, feeling vindictively satisfied when the man shuddered again, until Rachel wrapped her arms around herself and tried not to shiver, too. Hell, he was too close. The cold was affecting Rachel. He stepped away, frustrated and angry at his own helplessness.

"So where you headed?"

Rachel kept ignoring him, but the guy kept talking. Dillon made his phone ring. The guy pulled it out, glanced at it, frowned, and stuck it back in his pocket. Dillon made it ring again. And again and again, but the guy paid no attention. He was telling Rachel his life story even though she still wasn't looking at him.

"Damn it, damn it, damn it," Dillon swore. If he set off a building alarm, people would come. But what if they asked Rachel questions? What if her picture was on the news already? What if they recognized her?

In all his years of being a ghost, he had never hated it so much. This sucked.

*****

Sylvie was still fuming.

Her gorgeous dress, which had made her feel like a biker princess such a short time earlier, now felt like a badge on the proverbial walk of shame. Not that she would ever have spent the night with Raymond Chesney by choice, but wearing a crumpled evening dress while waiting at the front door of a suburban McMansion in the shimmering mid-day Florida light felt tawdry.

It was a good thing Chesney couldn't read her mind or her emotions, or he would have fired her on the spot. She could barely keep her disgust from showing on her face. It was almost noon, Rachel had been missing for hours, and he hadn't even asked about her.

Sitting in the car with Chesney at the airport had been a nightmare. The plane had a mechanical problem, they needed a part, the pilot had to get the right paperwork . . . it had been one thing after another. But between bouts of spitting fury at the incompetence around him, Chesney had been on his phone, business as usual. During one particularly long conversation about some legislation that Sylvie knew nothing about, he'd actually relaxed. And then when they'd finally taken off, he'd slept on the plane as if nothing worried him at all.

Of course, Sylvie probably should have done the same. Instead, she'd had no sleep, and her eyes burned with exhaustion. At least the tiny airport they'd landed at had had an ample supply of free coffee. Sylvie had downed five cups while they'd waited for the rental car to arrive.

The door opened.

"Sir!" At the sight of Chesney, the man who'd opened the door stepped back, pulling the door wide and gesturing them inside. "Rosario didn't mention—"

"Rosario didn't know," Chesney interrupted, brushing past the man. "I need to talk to Mateo."

HOLY FUCKING SHIT. Every bad word Sylvie knew—and an extensive vocabulary of obscenities was part of a Marine's basic training—raced through her mind at light speed. She'd speculated on the plane, of course. Flying to Florida—okay, it was weird. Especially given that Lucas had made the connection between Chesney and the drug cartels based on a bust in Florida. And Chesney's question about whether Sylvie spoke Spanish troubled her. Still, even her conversation with Lucas at the party hadn't really convinced her that her boss was involved with Mexican drug dealers.

Rosario, though, wasn't a common name. But it was the name of one of Chesney's maids, the woman who'd left his office in anger last Sunday afternoon. Why would Chesney be visiting someone who knew his maid? Who called him sir? Who lived in a ritzy house in a Florida suburb? And all while his daughter was missing, presumed kidnapped? Sylvie hated the way the pieces were adding up, but she followed Chesney inside the house.

Two men were standing up in the spacious living room to the right, both Hispanic, mid-thirties, reasonably attractive and dressed well in casual jackets and shirts unbuttoned at the collar. Only the shorter man appeared to be carrying, his shoulder-holstered gun obvious. Sylvie wished she could blame the jittery feeling running down her spine on the coffee.

The taller of the two men scowled, asking, "¿Qué hace usted aquí?"

Sylvie had told Chesney she'd failed Spanish, but it wasn't because she couldn't understand the basics. Years of moving from neighborhood to neighborhood, many of them Hispanic, meant that she could get by, but with an accent that was a crazy mix of Caribbean Spanish—Puerto Rican, Cuban, Dominican—and Mexican Spanish. Her high school Spanish teacher had not approved. But she tried not to let her understanding show as Chesney responded, in his own heavily accented Spanish, "The bastards have kidnapped my daughter."

The man's face stilled, his nostrils flared, and he gestured to the door of the nearby office. "Come. We'll talk in private."

Sylvie followed Chesney, expressionless, trying to be the perfect blank automaton bodyguard who saw nothing, heard nothing, understood nothing. At the door of his office, the man paused. He gestured in her direction with his chin. "Who's this?"

Chesney waved off the question. "She's coordinating with the search team in Washington."

The man looked Sylvie over, his mocking gaze trailing up her body from toe to head, with a lengthy pause on the black leather cupping her full breasts. Sylvie gritted her teeth, trying not to flush and mentally cursing her fair skin, Chesney, and the asshole that stood in front of her. He raised an eyebrow at Chesney.

"We were at a party. She's not important," Chesney snapped.

The man shrugged. "Privacy is best."

"Wait here," Chesney ordered Sylvie in English.

She nodded and dropped her gaze. She wasn't scared, not exactly, but for the first time the balding, pudgy man in front of her felt potentially dangerous. He was angry, but there was determination behind his anger. She didn't want his attention on her, but as he turned to enter the office, she took an impulsive step forward. "Sir?"

"What?"

"Restroom?" she asked, trying to sound like a charmingly helpless girl. "And maybe some food? And then if I could get access to a computer, I could help Ty, Mr. Barton, with analyzing the security footage." Her heart was beating much too fast as she waited for Chesney's response. She could call Ty or text him, but a computer link and a reason for steady communication would make her feel a lot better.

Chesney looked to the man next to him. Tall guy nodded—he must be Mateo, Sylvie thought—and then gestured to the man who'd opened the door. "Ari, take care of her." He turned to the shorter man. That conversation lasted longer and strained the ability of Sylvie's Spanish to understand, but it sounded as if Rafe would find her a clean computer, no files on it, with a secure network connection.

In the bathroom, Sylvie stared at her reflection in the mirror. Her hair was almost back to its original color and it should have looked good: the copper with her blue eyes and pale skin had always been more flattering than the brown. But instead she looked tired and worried, with dark smudges under her eyes and pale lips. This was a mess.

What would happen if she walked out the door? Right now. Just walked out of the bathroom and then out the front door and down the street? She had her ID and her cell phone. She could call a cab. She wasn't sure where in Florida they were, but she could find a street sign.

Chesney had been rabid about not letting anyone know Rachel was missing, though. Would he trust her not to talk? And even if she hadn't already had reason to suspect Chesney's involvement with the drug cartels, she would have recognized these men as dangerous. No, leaving now wasn't an option. Not a good one, anyway.

She pressed her hand to her stomach, comforted by the solid feel of her gun hidden behind the layers of chiffon and the cell phone she'd tucked into the pocket next to it. Everything was going to be okay, she told herself, wishing fervently that Lucas were with her. Maybe she should call him? But the last two times she'd tried, her calls had gone straight to voicemail. And with Chesney within hearing distance, she hadn't wanted to leave messages.

Outside the bathroom, Ari had a sandwich waiting for her, while Rafe arranged a laptop at the dining room table, plugging it in, then sitting down in front of it while it booted up. Sylvie knew she should talk to them, smile, pretend to be friendly and sociable, but she couldn't bring herself to do it. She ate in silence until Rafe finished logging in and connecting to the network and stood, gesturing to her to take his seat.

"You look familiar," he said as she sat. "Have we met?"

"I don't think so," Sylvie responded. He was staring at her, curious but not concerned, so she tried to ignore the itchy sensation of his attention on her and focus on the laptop.

Ty and Lucas had updated Sylvie regularly through the night. Lydia'd had her stomach pumped in the emergency room—drug overdose, the doctor said. Ty and James finally caught up to the GPS tracker in a cab, but the driver claimed to know nothing about it or Rachel, and Ty believed him. Lucas and the others had worked the building, Lucas looking for anyone who was thinking about Rachel or Chesney or kidnapping, the rest trying to sound casual as they asked about a short, dark-haired girl. Eventually Ty had sent two people back to the house to set up a recording device on the phone and wait for a ransom call.

But without Chesney's help and unable to mention Rachel's disappearance, Ty had had a hell of a time getting the footage of the security feeds from AlecCorp. About an hour ago, he'd texted her that they'd finally gotten the feeds posted to a secure server and were reviewing them.

Opening a browser, Sylvie logged in to her account and opened a chat window. *You there?* she typed to Ty.

Yeah, came the quick response.

What've we got?

Inside/outside, eighteen cameras. Twelve hours each, from 7 to 7. Focusing on the doors for now.

How's it looking?

Nothing yet.

Sylvie hated that answer.

How'd you finally get the video? she typed.

Don't know. Pretty sure your boyfriend had something to do with it.

Sylvie could almost see the grin Ty would be wearing as he typed those words. Reflexively, she started to type a protest, and then paused. Boyfriend. Hmm. She felt her lips curving slightly and backspaced to delete, before typing, *He there?*

No, left a while ago. I'd been working my way through the list of AlecCorp head honchos, trying to find someone who'd answer their fricking phone on a Saturday morning when some guy showed up, flashed a badge, and told the dude at the front desk to give me what I wanted.

Sylvie frowned. Had Lucas contacted the FBI? Would Ty be upset about that? She wished she was in the room with him so she wouldn't have to guess how he was feeling. *Problem?*

No. There was a pause, and then another word followed. *Grateful.*

Sylvie thought she probably shouldn't write what she was about to write on a computer that was not her own, but she couldn't help herself. *When we get Rachel back, can we maybe look for a new job?*

Assuming we aren't fired?

Sylvie smiled. She could almost hear the dry edge to Ty's voice and as tired and worried and scared as she was, she felt much better knowing that he was there at the other end of the computer screen.

Unemployment would be nice, she typed. *But yeah.*

Afghanistan might be hiring. Poor Ty. Losing a client was any security consultant's nightmare. After coming back to the United States with a flawless record overseas, this must be killing him.

How about another egotistical movie star? she typed. Until they'd taken the steady job with Chesney last winter, they'd done a stream of short-term gigs, including some actors. The work had been inconsistent but given the circumstances that would be fine by Sylvie.

We'll see, he typed.

Good enough. Time to see if she could spot anything on the video.

Server log-in? Where do you want me to start looking?

Ty typed the codes that she could use for access to the video. As Sylvie entered them, she almost imagined she could hear their computer expert screaming at them for using an unprotected chat line to transmit confidential information. But she didn't give a damn if anyone else looked at video footage from AlecCorp and Ty apparently didn't either.

K, ready, she typed.

Ty didn't answer.

What do you want me to look at? she typed.

Still no answer. She waited and then tried again. *Where do you want me to start?*

Nothing.

For a little while, as she wrote to Ty, Sylvie had been able to forget where she was, to pretend that she was sitting at any desk anywhere. But with Ty not responding, the attention of the two men at her back pushed insistently at her awareness. She glanced over her shoulder. Yes, they were both looking at her. Ari, the door opener and sandwich maker, smiled but the other man stayed stony-faced and grim.

Sylvie turned back to the computer. *Ty?*

Sorry, popped up in the chat window and she felt a wave of relief. *James found something. Take a look.* He added a camera number and time stamp codes.

Sylvie clicked through the server looking for the right video. Her fingers tapped impatiently against the tabletop as she waited for it to stream until, deliberately, she stilled them. Five cups of coffee, she reminded herself. That was why she was jittery. Not because the attention of the men behind her was dangerous. She took a breath, feeling again the comfort of the weight against her belly, but resisted the impulse to touch it.

The video finally started streaming. Sylvie watched as Rachel walked toward a door, her hands held above her head in the traditional gun-at-one's-back position. Rachel pushed open the door and exited. No one else ever entered the camera frame.

Sylvie scowled and dragged the play icon to the left to rewind.

Smart kidnappers, Ty wrote. *Watched for the cameras. Someone must have been waiting for her outside.*

Maybe, Sylvie typed in response. She watched the video again. Then a third time. Then she typed, *Look at her legs. The bottom of her dress.*

What do you see? Ty asked.

Do you have the time stamps for when she arrived? Sylvie answered. She wanted a clearer picture of Rachel.

She had time to watch the video two more times before Ty sent her the codes she wanted. Then she watched the other video, looking at Rachel carefully as the footage showed her coming up through the basement parking garage with Chesney. Ty, Lydia, and Mark were close behind them, but James must have stayed at the car.

Rachel wore a long-sleeved, high-necked, full-skirted black dress. It was velvet and Christmas-y and not inappropriate, but also not her usual taste. Sylvie eyed it intently. Then she flipped back to the other video and watched again. "Clever, clever girl," she muttered under her breath as she realized what Rachel had done.

The chat icon blinked in the corner of her screen. *What do you see?* Ty had typed the question again.

See the dark line at her knee? Sylvie wrote. *When she raises her arms, her skirt lifts, too. She's wearing rolled-up leggings under her dress. And a shirt.*

You sure?

She looks heavier than usual when she enters. And she's sweating. She's got layers on. She waited for Ty's response. From the very beginning, Rachel's disappearance had felt wrong. It made no sense for a kidnapper to try to take her out of AlecCorp in the middle of a party. Kidnappers stopped cars, shot bodyguards, grabbed the kid and ran.

But if Rachel was running away? Sylvie glanced at the clock in the bottom-right corner of the screen. It was already past noon. Rachel had managed to delay a real search for something like fifteen hours. If she'd run away to her mother . . . .

We need to check plane tickets, Sylvie typed. *Ask Lucas for help.* Whatever reason Chesney had for not wanting the FBI involved, it was a moot point if Rachel had run away. Sylvie took a deep breath, relief washing through her.

Rachel was still at risk. A teenage girl crossing the country by herself? That was bad news. But no kidnapper would be cutting off her fingers to prove his possession. And if her mother knew nothing about Rachel's escapade, as seemed likely, she wouldn't get into trouble, but she might get to spend a little time with her daughter.

For a moment, Sylvie considered not saying anything to Chesney right away. It wasn't the same, she knew, but a few hours with Dillon would have been precious to her.

Upraised voices caught her attention. Behind the closed office door, Chesney was shouting in Spanish. Sylvie tried to make out the words. "The best defense is offense. We attack them!"

Sylvie looked back at the computer screen and tried to think. Chesney didn't want to contact the FBI. He'd come immediately to Florida. He believed he knew who his enemies were and that they had kidnapped Rachel. If he was involved in drug trafficking as well as weapon sales, could he possibly think that his enemies were the drug cartels?

Sylvie didn't know much about them, but she knew the Zetas were famous for kidnappings. She'd ruled them out as a threat because of the difficulty of getting into AlecCorp's party, but Chesney knew more than she did. Maybe he knew that there were others at AlecCorp who were compromised and that he could be vulnerable to attack from within.

She licked her lips, mouth suddenly dry. Was Chesney planning on attacking the Zetas? That seemed like a very bad idea to her.

"Lucas," came a voice from behind her, speaking unaccented English. "Who is this Lucas?"

Sylvie didn't quite jump. It was entirely unlike her to not notice someone moving up behind her, but she'd been so focused on her thoughts that she'd blocked everything else out. Rafe stood at her back, reading over her shoulder.

"A friend," Sylvie said stiffly, closing the laptop screen. She met his dark eyes with her own steady gaze, telegraphing as strongly as she could her best back-off message. He fell back a step or two, frowning.

Standing, Sylvie pulled the plug out of the back of the laptop and picked the computer up. She needed to show Chesney the footage and explain to him what she thought it meant. She pushed past the man standing in her way and crossed to the closed office door.

But she paused before knocking. "I don't care about the risk," Chesney was saying. Or maybe that word meant danger? Sylvie wasn't sure. But as she raised one hand, laptop tucked under the other arm, she heard more. "She's a stupid little bitch."

Sylvie's fist clenched and she knocked harder than she intended. Was Chesney talking about Rachel or her?

"She's your daughter," the other man said, before adding a sharp, "What is it?" That answered her question, but should Sylvie answer his? Would a response reveal that she understood Spanish?

She hesitated, then turned the knob and pushed open the door. "I'm sorry for interrupting, sir," she said to Chesney. "I have some video footage that I think you should see."

"What is it?"

"I'd prefer to show it to you and let you draw your own conclusions, sir." Sylvie glanced around the well-appointed office. To the right, Mateo sat in a comfortable-looking chair behind a wide desk. Two chairs were angled in front of it, but Chesney stood as if he'd been pacing. One wall was lined with bookshelves, but the other held a side table. She gestured to it and looked to the man behind the desk. "May I?"

He looked to Chesney who waved irritably and said, "Fine, fine."

Sylvie crossed to the table and placed the laptop on it. Her back was to the men, but while she opened up the computer, she tried to decide what they were feeling. Chesney was determined with a core of rage, but Mateo felt watchful, worried. She sympathized. She felt worried herself.

Once opened, the computer screen stayed dark. Sylvie pressed the power button. Nothing happened. Maybe the battery hadn't charged? "I need the power cord. I'll be right back."

As she walked through the living room and into the dining room, she tried to ignore the two men staring at her. Their heads were together, Rafe holding a phone as if they'd been looking at the screen. But their feelings had changed, Sylvie realized. The grim man was now excited, satisfied, while Ari's mild curiosity had turned to anxiety. By the time she gathered up the cord, Rafe had entered the office and was showing the phone to Mateo and Chesney, talking animatedly. She recognized a few words including *Washington Post*. He'd recognized her from the article. But so what?

Sylvie looked for an outlet, found one, plugged the cord in, shifted the computer closer, plugged it in, pressed the on switch, waited, all the while pretending to ignore the men behind her as she felt them react to Rafe's words. Her hands were trembling, she realized, and she tried to still them. Almost unconsciously, her right hand drifted under the chiffon layers of her dress.

"Go." The word was a command from Mateo to Rafe. Sylvie felt Rafe exit the room and heard the door closing behind him.

"We know the man in this image." He was speaking to Chesney now, his words slower. "He works for the government. Your woman is a spy."

Every cell in Sylvie's body felt focused on the scene behind her, her senses all poised for the slightest hint of information, even as she stared at the computer screen coming to life.

Chesney swore, fluently, the angry words almost covering up the sound of a desk drawer opening, but nothing could cover the sense of grim resolve she felt from the man behind the desk. Sylvie shifted position, hand reaching inside the concealed pocket in the leather of her dress, closing firmly around her gun.

"Not here," Chesney snapped. "And not that way. It has to look like an accident."

Sylvie moved.

No deep breath, no conscious thought, just movement.

Gun sliding out, she turned, saw the weapon in the hand of the man behind the desk, fell automatically into a proper shooting stance with both hands on her gun, and fired.

Once.

Twice.

As a pink mist of blood rose around him while a red stain spread across his chest and his eyes opened wide in shock, she flung herself at the door, found the lock, turned it, and backed into the corner of the room, positioning herself so that when the door opened, she'd have a clean shot.

No more than ten seconds had passed, and the man behind the desk was still gasping out his last breath while Chesney stood, jaw dropped and disbelief freezing him in place.

"First person through the door dies," Sylvie shouted over the ringing in her ears. She couldn't hear her own words, but the men outside would have been farther away from the shot. They should still have some hearing left. "Your boss is dead and I'm calling 911. If you move quickly, you may get away before the police get here."

It was a little too soon to say that Mateo was dead—he was trying to lift his hand, the gun held loosely. But it had been two good shots in easy range: he would bleed out long before an ambulance could arrive and aiming the gun and pulling the trigger should be beyond him. Even as she had the thought, his hand dropped and his head fell back, lifeless eyes still open and the feelings she'd had from him—regret and pain, mostly—faded away.

Sylvie stared at the door, willing it not to move. Locked or not, the men outside could kick it down easily enough. And her Glock 36 held exactly six bullets—four now. Out of the corner of her eye, she saw Chesney take a sidling step toward the desk and Mateo's weapon. Without moving her feet or changing her semi-crouched posture, she swiveled her hands so that her gun pointed directly at him.

"Don't even think about it."

She waited. She could feel the fear and the fury and the indecision from the men outside, and then they were moving out of her range. She took a deep, shuddering breath. It felt like her first in a lifetime.

Maybe a minute had passed.

Her heart was pounding, her ears still ringing, and the adrenaline coursing through her system was like ice water cooling her from the inside out.

She'd just murdered a man.

It wasn't the first time she'd fired her gun. She'd shot at people in Iraq. Maybe she'd even killed a few. But not up close. Not like this.

She turned toward Chesney, keeping her gun aimed at him. He was still angry, she realized, with only a trace of fear under a surface that was trying to look affable and conciliatory. His hands were half up, half making a placating air-patting gesture.

"What in God's name did you just do?" he demanded.

"Killed a man," Sylvie replied in her execrable Spanish.

"You speak Spanish?" Chesney stilled and his fear deepened. "I don't know what you think you heard, but this is a misunderstanding."

Sylvie stared at him, incredulous. He was going to try to brazen it out, she realized, to pretend that he hadn't just agreed to kill her.

"I would have stopped him. I wouldn't have let him harm you," he continued, words spilling one over another in his haste.

"The best defense is offense," Sylvie quoted the words he'd said earlier. Her heart rate was starting to slow, but her breath was quick and shallow, as if she were trying to sprint at the end of a ten-mile run.

Chesney's eyes narrowed. "You can't be wearing a wire. If you were, you wouldn't have pulled that trigger. Your back-up would be smashing down the doors."

Sylvie didn't answer him. Part of her attention was focused on the room behind her, on making sure that Ari and Rafe weren't returning, and the continued ringing in her ears made it hard to hear. She wondered if she'd done permanent damage to them, but the thought was fleeting.

She'd done permanent damage to Mateo. That felt much more important. He'd been going to kill her, but somehow she didn't hate him for it. Chesney was the one who had brought her here, walked her into this danger, created this ugly situation. Chesney was responsible; Mateo had just paid the price.

"You can't prove anything." Chesney glanced at Mateo's body, at his blood pooling on the floor beneath him. The fear she'd felt disappeared and he almost smirked. "Maybe I'm here answering a ransom demand. A phone call. No, a note left behind at AlecCorp ordering me to fly down here. Your crazy over-reaction could cost me my daughter."

Sylvie stared. "You can't possibly be serious."

He smiled at her. "Your word against mine and who's going to believe you?"

"You work for the Mexican drug cartels," Sylvie told him, almost as if he didn't know.

"I deal with the cartels," he corrected her. "And manage an organization of my own. And you work for the government and can't prove a thing. So feel free to arrest me. Nothing you've got will hold up in court." He radiated smug confidence.

"I don't work for the government."

For a moment, he looked startled, and then he shrugged. "Even better. You might as well walk away now. If you try to tell the police or get the FBI involved, I'll destroy you."

He was so calm, Sylvie realized, much calmer than she was. She was a Marine. She'd seen horrifying things in Somalia and Iraq and yet the sight of Mateo's body, the smell of his blood and waste, sickened her. Chesney was impervious.

"I work for you," Sylvie said. A strange numbness was taking over her body, a feeling like she wasn't really there.

Chesney blinked and scowled. His emotions felt clearer to her than her own. She didn't know what she was feeling, but he was irritated. She'd killed a man and his daughter was missing, in grave danger as far as he knew, but his reaction was annoyance at the inconvenience. And then she felt the calculation.

"Of course you do," he said smoothly. "So put the gun down and we'll work this out."

God, she wished Lucas was here. If she could read Chesney's mind, she'd know for sure. But she knew enough. She could see it in the coldness of his eyes.

"I don't think so. You hired me to protect your daughter," Sylvie said, each word sounding as if it came from a far-off distance, but her voice steady. "To keep her safe from anything that threatened her. So I'm going to do my job."

She pulled the trigger.

It was a perfect shot.

Or it would have been if she'd been aiming at his head instead of his heart. The bullet hole opened, dead center of his forehead, a mist of blood spraying, and he fell backwards.

"High and right," Sylvie whispered. "High and right."

She felt a bubble of hysterical laughter rising. It was what they said in the Marines when a soldier lost control.

She sat down, hard, on the floor.

She'd just destroyed her life, she realized. She'd murdered two men. She was going to spend the rest of her days in prison.

She should—what? What should she do now? She tried to think but a rush of exhaustion swept over her. She should call the police, she realized, and with shaking fingers, she pulled her cell phone out.

A text message was waiting for her. *Rachel's in Tassamara.* Sender *Unknown.*

Sylvie looked around her, at the two dead men, at the computer, at the shell casings by her feet. She could try to clean up, erase her presence here. But she wasn't going to spend the rest of her life running and hiding. She'd done what she'd done. She would have to deal with the consequences.

But first, she was going to find Rachel.

Someone had to tell her that her father was dead, and Sylvie should be the one to do it.

CHAPTER FOURTEEN

"Dillon?" Rachel whispered, barely moving her lips. "What do I do now? We didn't talk about this." She looked pale and stiff, standing upright as if her tension were pulling her spine into a perfectly straight line.

Dillon looked up and down the street, feeling a mix of desperate relief and frantic worry. Where the hell was his grandpa? He'd trusted Max to meet them. The bus had dropped Rachel off on the corner of Millard and Kerr, right in front of the gas station. Akira's house was only about four blocks away—an easy walk, but Dillon had no way to give Rachel directions. And he'd promised not to leave her.

Besides, he didn't want to see Akira yet. He knew that the moment she discovered Rachel had run away, she'd be on the phone to Washington. He'd texted Sylvie once Rachel was safely on the bus, but even if his mom caught the next flight, the earliest she could get to Tassamara would be evening. He didn't want Rachel sent home before then. And Akira wouldn't understand. She'd assume that Rachel's dad would be frantic about Rachel's disappearance and that telling him that Rachel was safe as quickly as possible would be the compassionate thing to do, as well as the responsible thing to do.

Of course, maybe he was and maybe it was. Guilt swamped Dillon and he closed his eyes. He should never have talked Rachel into this. He'd relaxed when the bus arrived and Rachel boarded, leaving the creepy guy behind, but what now?

"Oh, dear, did I miss the bus?" The voice behind him was as familiar as the sound of a summer rain on his tree house roof.

Dillon whirled. "Grandpa!" His hug passed right through the older man, of course, but Dillon barely cared. "I'm so glad to see you!"

"I'm afraid so," Rachel answered politely.

"Ah, well. Just by a minute or so. I suppose it won't have had time to go far." Max looked up and down the street, his blue eyes sharp with interest, and then taking a step forward, toward the road, cleared his throat and said to the empty air in front of him, "On behalf of my grandson, I'd like to welcome you to Tassamara."

"Um, Grandpa? Who are you talking to?" Dillon glanced out into the street, trying to follow Max's gaze. What did Max see?

"I'll do my best to ensure that your stay is comfortable. Please accompany me to Maggie's place. That's the restaurant about half a block that way." Max pointed toward the bistro, and began walking, leaving Rachel behind.

Rachel's eyebrows had drawn together in a slight frown and she was watching Max. Dillon shook his head. What was his grandpa doing?

"I suppose that you're here to talk to Akira?" Max continued. "It's the only reason I can think of that you might want to come to Tassamara. Not that it's not a nice little town, of course. I've lived here for years and love it dearly."

A slight smile started to play around Rachel's lips and she hurried to catch up to Max, falling into step behind him but close enough to hear him as he talked. Dillon sighed and followed, concentrating on sending a text to Max.

"I'm not sure how helpful Akira will be. My daughter Grace tried to get her to go see a ghost last week and Akira got a bit snappy, and said that she wasn't running a telephone service to another plane of existence. But perhaps Dillon can talk her into it. Unfortunately, she and my son are off on some sort of manatee-watching trip today."

Max's phone buzzed and he pulled it out of his jacket pocket, stopping so abruptly that Rachel nearly walked right into him. He read the message—*R behind u,* Dillon knew it said—and then turned.

"Oh!" he said, pulling back and looking startled at the sight of the young girl. "Are you—did you—excuse me, this might be an odd question, but—"

"Dillon told me to come here," Rachel interrupted him. The tension in her posture was gone and she smiled at Max with genuine warmth.

"You—but you—" Max looked taken aback. He scratched his head and then ran his hand down the back, smoothing his hair, before finally stroking his chin. Uh-oh. Dillon recognized those moves. They were Max delaying while he decided whether or not he was supposed to be angry.

"Is he here?" Max finally asked. "Dillon, I mean."

Rachel glanced at the phone, still clutched in Max's left hand. "I think so?"

He followed her gaze. "Oh, of course." He looked at the phone for a minute, almost as if he wanted to use it, and then turned back to Rachel, voice abrupt. "Could you wait right here for a moment? Right here, don't go anywhere, I won't go far." He was backing away from her as he spoke and as he reached the door to the restaurant, he turned so that he was no longer facing Rachel and whispered fiercely, "Have you lost your mind, Dillon? That's a little girl!"

Dillon almost laughed. *Keep her safe*, he texted. *And don't tell*.

His grandfather scowled at the phone. "Keep her safe? Keep her—" He shook his head and turned back to Rachel. She was rubbing one foot along the back of her leg, smile gone, and—much to Dillon's relief—Max immediately softened. He beckoned her towards him and pulled open the door to the restaurant.

"I'm afraid I was confused by Dillon's message," he said apologetically as Rachel hurried to catch up with him. "It didn't occur to me that he'd be communicating with, well, you know, someone with a heartbeat. You'll have to explain to me how you came to know him."

Max made his way to the booth in the back corner where he always sat, still talking, Rachel at his heels, but Dillon was stopped in his tracks when Rose bounced off a counter seat and rushed to hug him. "Dillon, it's so good to see you," she was saying as she wrapped her arms around him and squeezed, before hastily stepping back and adding, "But your grandpa's gone insane."

Dillon grinned at her. "I can't wait to tell you everything that's happened," he told her. Talking—really talking—was such a relief. "But the crazy's my fault. I asked him to meet my friend at the bus. I guess he thought I meant a ghost friend."

A waitress passed them, headed to the table in the corner with two plates of food: one, a barren platter holding nothing but a plain turkey sandwich on whole wheat bread, the other a mound of chocolate-chip pancakes piled high with whipped cream.

"Come on." Dillon grabbed Rose's hand and tugged her over to the booth, sliding in to sit next to Rachel.

Max sighed as he saw the plate in front of him.

"Maggie's mad," the waitress said, sympathy in her voice. She put the pancakes in front of Rachel, adding with a wink, "Here you go, sweetie. Enjoy."

"What's Maggie mad about?" Dillon asked Rose.

Rose patted Max's shoulder, careful not to let her hand pass through him. "He's been bringing ghosts here all morning. Not real ghosts, but he's been talking like there were ghosts and inviting them to stay. Maggie said she didn't want to run a haunted café and he told her it'd be good for the tourist business. She told him to cut it out and he told her not to be a stick-in-the-mud. She went back into the kitchen and hasn't come out since. He tried to apologize and she made Emma bring him decaf coffee. And you know he hates decaf coffee."

Next to them, Max and Rachel had introduced themselves and Max was saying, "So what brings you to Tassamara?" as Rachel dug into her pancakes.

"Dillon wants to talk to his mom."

Max stilled. "His mom? Sylvie?" He looked at Rachel intently, eyes narrowing, head tilting slightly to one side as if he were trying to solve a puzzle.

"Mm-hmm," Rachel mumbled through a mouthful of food. Dillon was glad to see that she was eating eagerly. He'd been anxious when she hadn't eaten on the train. He thought it was because she hadn't wanted anyone to see her, but he would have told her to take the risk if he could have.

"Ah, that's . . . well . . . hmm." Max glanced at his watch. He looked worried, Dillon saw, but before he could think too much about it, Rose distracted him.

"Your mom!" She clasped her hands together. "How exciting. How did you find her? Did you like her? Is she nice?"

Nice? Dillon didn't laugh, but his grin felt as if it would break his cheeks. He liked Sylvie a lot but nice wasn't how he'd describe her.

"Rachel." Max had his phone out and was typing in a number, the slow, old-fashioned way, frowning as he did so. His voice, as he spoke to Rachel, was urgent. "I need to warn you. In a few moments, some strange things may start happening. It's nothing you need to worry about. No harm will come to you. But it would be most helpful if you'd remain calm. If you get upset, Sylvie will get upset and then . . . well, then things will go downhill very quickly. Can you do that for me?" He finished what he was saying, finally looking up at Rachel and smiling although the expression looked strained, as he held his phone to his ear.

Rachel had stopped chewing, eyes wide.

"William, yes, it's Max. Yes, yes, no time for that. Do you remember the case I told you to prepare for—oh, it must have been a decade or so ago?" He paused and then chuckled. "Nag is a strong word. But I believe today's the day." As he spoke, he was sliding through Rose and off the seat.

"What's going on, Dillon?" Rose asked.

Dillon shook his head, watching his grandfather. Max was going around the room, plucking silverware off the set tables, still talking and nodding. He paused by one occupied table and pointed to a knife, appearing to ask if the patrons needed it, then picked up the knife and continued moving. Finally he stuffed his phone in his pocket and headed toward the kitchen.

As Dillon concentrated on sending him a message asking what he was doing, he heard Max calling out, "You were right, Maggie. Bad idea!" as he moved behind the counter and headed into the kitchen.

And then the glass door to the outside opened. For a moment, Sylvie stood in the doorway, backlit by the sun, her hair a corona of red-gold. Dillon wanted to stand up and cheer. Their plan had worked! They'd gotten Sylvie to Tassamara. He couldn't wait to tell Rachel, to tell her and to thank her for her help.

But as his mom stepped inside, his heart sank. Raymond Chesney, a malevolent scowl on his face, was right behind Sylvie. Why had she brought him? And how was he going to help Rachel with her father right here?

*****

The rental car had a GPS. Sylvie followed its instructions precisely; no shortcuts, no search for better routes, no detours down roads that looked more interesting.

Her mind didn't seem to be working the way it usually did. Instead of the constant risk assessment that was the usual silent soundtrack of her life, she found herself lingering over the sense of regret she'd felt from Mateo in his last moments and wondering what he'd been thinking when he died.

As she pulled into a parking place on the main street of Tassamara, the sight of the Christmas decorations—garlands wrapped around the lamp posts, tiny lights draped across the street—made her realize that she should call her mom. She needed to tell her she wasn't going to make it home for Christmas.

And Lucas.

She needed to call him, too.

She needed to tell him . . . but she couldn't bring herself to finish the thought. Thinking of Lucas, thinking of what she'd want to say, thinking of how bright their future had seemed just a few hours ago—her mind veered away and she latched on to the thought of Ty instead.

She should call him first. Last night, he'd told her to take care of Chesney. He was not going to be happy about how she'd interpreted that order. She stepped out of the car, automatically locking it behind her. Florida was a death penalty state, though, and for a double murder, she was going to want a good lawyer. Ty would send Jeremy.

And then there was Rachel. She needed to tell him she'd found Rachel.

If, that is, she had. She looked up and down the street. Despite the holiday décor, the small town looked much as it had twenty years earlier. Some of the shops had changed: the old drugstore was gone, replaced by an antique shop, and the store next to it with all the dangling crystals in the window had to be new. Mostly, though, it had the same quiet, dusty feel that she remembered.

Where would Rachel be?

"Oh, my." The voice came from right behind her and Sylvie whirled, the black layers of chiffon in her skirt floating up around her. The tiny woman standing on the sidewalk shook her head, saying, "Your aura, my dear." She tsked with disapproval. "You should drink some tea. Lavender, perhaps. Very good for anxiety and nervous exhaustion."

Sylvie's smile in response was more of a crooked twist of the mouth as she answered politely, "Hello, Mrs. Swanson. If I get a chance, I'll give it a try."

"Maggie will have some for you." The woman gestured to a storefront a few doors up the street, then cocked her head to one side and narrowed her gaze, staring intently at the air next to Sylvie's head. "She's new since you were last in town, but she fits right in. Sylvie, isn't it? Does Max know you're visiting?"

Sylvie held back her sigh. Within twenty minutes, half the long-time residents of Tassamara would know she was in town; within an hour, it'd be all of them. But it was genuine worry she felt from the old woman, with not even a hint of malicious interest. Still, Sylvie needed to find Rachel and get her to safety and quickly. Maybe the restaurant would be a good place to start.

"I'm sure he will," she responded as she backed away, nodding and smiling. "Good to see you again. Take care now."

She opened the door to the restaurant and stepped inside. It took a moment for her eyes to adjust to the change in light. By the time they did, Max was already moving toward her.

Sylvie froze.

The last time she'd seen this man, she'd been leaving her baby behind.

Forever.

A rush of grief—for Dillon, for Lucas, for the life she could have had, for all that might have been—swept over her. She would have stepped back and away, but Max was taking her hands in his and saying, his voice warm, "Hello, Sylvie. Don't worry. Everything's going to be okay."

She frowned. He looked so much like Lucas—older, of course, with his hair touched with gray and the laugh lines around his intense blue eyes more deeply engraved—that instinctively she wanted to trust him. But what a ridiculous thing to say. Nothing was going to be okay.

She opened her mouth to snap at him, but he forestalled her, raising a hand and saying, "I know you don't believe me right now, but that doesn't matter. You don't need to. But Sylvie, please—I beg of you—please don't hit the sheriff. I promise I'll take good care of Rachel."

She blinked at him, and then looked around the restaurant. It was half-full of people, many of them watching in fascination, but no one who looked like a sheriff. She looked back at Max.

"He's not here yet."

Sylvie sighed. Twenty years and despite the gray hair Lucas's father hadn't changed. "Is Rachel here?"

He stepped back, indicating a booth in the corner, where a dark-haired head peeking around the edge of the seat ducked back immediately.

Sylvie took a deep breath, bracing herself. She should have planned this conversation during her drive, she realized, but she hadn't. She felt curious eyes on her as she made her way to the corner booth and slid into the seat across from Rachel.

The girl was staring at the table, a slight flush on her cheeks and her chin set stubbornly. "I don't want to go home," she muttered without looking up at Sylvie. "It's not fair."

Sylvie stared at her blankly. What was Rachel talking about? And then she shook her head at her own stupidity—of course that's why Rachel thought she had come—and said, voice gentle, "I'm not here to take you home."

Startled, Rachel looked at her directly, eyes wide. And then her eyes grew even wider. "Sylvie? Is that blood on you?"

Sylvie looked down. She hadn't realized it before but she'd been hit by spatter. Little tiny flecks of red-brown dotted the leather of her dress and the pale skin of her cleavage. "Oh, God."

She shuddered, feeling nausea rise. Was it Chesney's blood or Mateo's? Had she come to Rachel wearing her father's blood? She was horrified at the thought.

"Are you hurt?" Rachel stood up, her emotions an immediate churn of worry and fear, glancing around the room for help.

"No, no," Sylvie reached for her, putting a hand on Rachel's arm and then quickly pulling away. She shouldn't touch Rachel, not when she'd just murdered her father. She tried to smile reassuringly. "It's not my blood."

Slowly, Rachel sat back down. "Whose blood is it?"

"I—" Sylvie swallowed and then admitted the truth. "It might be your father's."

The silence felt as if it lasted forever, but it was only a few seconds before Sylvie found the courage to continue. "I wanted to be the one to tell you this. I wanted to—"

"Is he dead?" Rachel interrupted her.

Sylvie stared.

"Because the way you're talking, that's not right. That's not how it's supposed to go. You're supposed to say, he's fine, don't worry, but you're not saying that." Rachel's eyes were bright. "And if what you want to say is something that you wanted to tell me, you specifically, then it's because you thought I'd be upset. So you ought to be telling me he's going to be okay even if he's not right now, but you're not saying that either. So is he dead?"

Rachel had been talking so quickly that Sylvie wasn't entirely sure what she'd heard. But she'd gotten the gist of it. She said flatly. "Yes."

"Yes, he's dead?" Rachel asked.

Sylvie nodded.

Rachel didn't say anything. She picked up her fork and poked at the dissolving whipped cream on the pancakes in front of her.

Sylvie waited.

Rachel traced a pattern in the white with a tine.

Sylvie stayed silent. She knew she needed to tell Rachel the rest, but she could feel Rachel's distraction. Maybe the girl needed a little time to come to terms with her loss first, she told herself.

Finally, Rachel asked, voice tiny, "Is it my fault?"

"No! Absolutely not." Sylvie hesitated. Was Rachel ready to hear all of it?

"He didn't die because I ran away?"

"No," Sylvie said firmly. Okay, Chesney wouldn't be dead if Rachel hadn't run away but she wasn't going to expend any energy analyzing cause-and-effect. "But . . ."

"I'm not sad," Rachel interrupted her. She looked up and her eyes met Sylvie's. "That's wrong, isn't it?"

Sylvie paused. She wasn't sad, either. Not about Chesney, anyway. But then he wasn't her father. Picking her words carefully, she said, "I think sometimes it takes a little time to understand your own feelings when you lose someone. And that you shouldn't worry about how you feel right now. It's okay to not feel sad."

Suddenly, a photograph on the wall next to them slid down and landed on the table with a crack. Both Sylvie and Rachel startled, and then Sylvie shook off the surprise with a little laugh. "I have to tell you, though, Rachel—" Sylvie started as Rachel set down the fork that she'd been playing with and picked up the photograph. She leaned it against the wall.

Her fork slid across the table and onto the floor.

Both Sylvie and Rachel glanced at the fork and then Sylvie, shaking her head, slid out of the booth and bent to pick up the fork. She set it on the table and turned back to Rachel.

"I'm really not sad," Rachel announced. She picked up her fork and eyed it critically. "I think I'm happy. May I have a clean fork, please? I want to finish my pancakes."

Sylvie paused. Okay, that was unexpected.

Rachel smiled at her. "Can we stay here for a while? Dillon wants to talk to you but the girl with the funny name who talks to ghosts isn't here right now. Dillon's grandpa was telling the ghosts about it. Except I think he was just confused."

Sylvie stared. And then, "Ow," she yelped as something hit her in the back of the head. What the hell? She turned around. A spoon was on the floor by her feet. She bent to pick it up as the door to the café opened and a man in uniform walked in.

"Rachel," Max called from across the restaurant by the counter. "Remember what I told you? Now's the time."

Rachel looked puzzled and then she yelped as her plate skidded across the table, away from her and toward Sylvie. Sylvie felt a burst of fear from the girl and quickly straightened, turning in time to catch the plate before it flew off the table and onto her.

"Rachel?" she asked.

Rachel was staring at the table. "It's okay, it's okay," she said under her breath. "It's okay. Nothing bad will happen. Dillon's grandpa said so."

People were starting to notice what was happening and move, craning to see, standing up, beginning to talk and point.

"Colin," Max called out cheerfully to the man at the door. "Lovely to see you, how's the family? Let me introduce you to Sylvie."

"Max," the man drawled, his voice low Southern honey. "I'm taking a pretty big chance here. Lucas swore on Maggie's apple pie that the SWAT team could stand down."

SWAT team. Lucas. Ah, hell. And she still hadn't told Rachel. The worry and tension and fear coming from the man at the door, Max, and Rachel were like a pounding beat under a pop song of curiosity and confusion created by the other restaurant patrons.

Sylvie laid her hands flat on the table in front of her but didn't otherwise move. Two more minutes, that was all she needed. Enough time to admit the truth to Rachel and then to reassure her and make sure she knew she'd be okay. She felt her muscles tightening as Max and the other man approached.

The light over the booth crackled, popped, and with a burst of sparks, broke. Bits of shattered glass from the light bulb fell to the tabletop.

Sylvie's jaw dropped. Rachel's eyes widened. Their eyes met and Sylvie knew that they were both thinking the same thing.

"Rachel, get under the table," Sylvie ordered.

Rachel shook her head. "I probably shouldn't have said that about not being sad, huh?" she said faintly. And then she set her lips and crossed her arms and leaned back in her seat. "But I'm not."

"Rachel!"

Rachel shook her head. "Dillon's grandpa said not to be scared."

Dillon's grandpa was insane, as far as Sylvie was concerned. Always had been. But behind her she felt Max and the sheriff approaching and inside her she felt the rising urge to strike out and she knew that at least this time Max had foreseen a possible future correctly. She took a deep breath.

"Ma'am?" The word was gentle and Southern and Sylvie gritted her teeth. This wasn't the same man who'd been sheriff twenty years ago but she hated him anyway, just on general principles. "Will you come quietly?"

She sighed. "Yes." She turned to face him, feeling the relief from Max as another light bulb, slightly farther away, exploded.

"Wait, what?" Rachel stood, sliding out of the booth.

"Stay with Max," Sylvie ordered. "He'll take care of you until Ty gets here." She glanced at Max, knowing that he recognized the order in her voice, and he nodded slightly, putting a hand on Rachel's shoulder and then ducking as a spoon came flying at his head.

"What the hell?" muttered the sheriff, putting a firm hand under Sylvie's elbow.

"Just a little ghost problem," Max told him. "Nothing to worry about."

"Where are you taking Sylvie?" Rachel demanded. "What's going on?"

Sylvie opened her mouth, then glanced at the sheriff and closed it again. She'd heard Jeremy rant about his idiotic clients far too many times to tell Rachel the truth in front of law enforcement. She was going to accept responsibility for what she'd done, but she wasn't going to be stupid about it.

"She's gonna come answer a few questions, that's all," the sheriff replied.

"Sylvie?" Rachel might have claimed that she wasn't scared but her panic was close to the surface.

"You stay here with Max, Rachel." Sylvie glanced around the room, at the lights, at the scattered silverware, at the people watching them. And then she grinned at Rachel. "And Dillon. And don't worry. If there's someone else here, he's probably pretty pissed off, but it's not at you."

CHAPTER FIFTEEN

His mom slid into the booth, passing through Rose, her gaze intent on Rachel. Rachel didn't look at her, just muttered something sulky.

"Is this your mom? She's so pretty. Younger than I would have expected. And I love her hair." Rose frowned. "Can't say as I think much of her accessorizing, though."

"What do you mean?" Dillon asked. He couldn't contain his smile as he looked at Sylvie. They'd done it. They'd gotten her here. He wished she hadn't brought Chesney, who was standing at the edge of the table glaring at Sylvie and his daughter, but maybe Max could help distract him. Or maybe even teach him something about how to be a father.

"The blood," Rose said, her voice matter-of-fact. She tipped her head to one side as if to get a better look, leaning closer to Sylvie and examining her dress.

"What blood?"

"She's sprinkled with blood." Two little creases appeared on Rose's forehead as her mouth formed a puzzled moue.

"My blood," growled Chesney.

Dillon did a double-take, but Rose barely blinked, her expression smoothing. "Oh, that explains it. You must be new in town."

Chesney bared his teeth in what might have been meant as a smile, but his eyes never wavered from Sylvie. "You could say that."

"Um, Rose, this is Raymond Chesney, Rachel's father," Dillon said, feeling nervous and eyeing Chesney. How had Chesney suddenly become a ghost?

"This is your daughter?" Rose asked. "How lucky you are to be able to see her. Some ghosts are trapped where they die, you know."

"Lucky?" Chesney snapped. "Lucky? There's no such thing as luck."

Rachel and Sylvie had been talking when suddenly Sylvie said, "Oh, God," and shuddered.

Dillon looked back at them as Rachel said, "Are you hurt?" and stood.

"Ha!" Chesney snorted. "Not her."

"It's not my blood," Sylvie told Rachel.

"Of course it's not, you bitch." Chesney clenched his hands on the edge of the table.

Dillon shifted uncomfortably. Rose looked at him, raising her eyebrows and tilting her head in Chesney's direction as if to suggest he do something. Dillon gave a slight shrug, opening his hands. What did she want him to do?

Rose rolled her eyes at him, and then tried to console Chesney. "Being a ghost isn't so bad, you know. You might get to like it after a while."

He looked at her and for the first time seemed to truly notice her. His eyes raked her up and down, taking in her blond curls, full skirt and sleeveless top. "You've got to be kidding me." He dismissed her, lip curling with scorn, and turned his attention back to Sylvie and Rachel, his eyes hot.

Dillon felt anger stirring. Ghostly Chesney was as much of a creep as the living Chesney, he thought, as Rachel asked, "Yes, he's dead?"

Sylvie nodded.

"Oh, how sad she must be," Rose said sympathetically. She propped her chin on her hand and watched Rachel as the girl stared at the table, playing with her food.

There was a silence that felt awkward to Dillon. He didn't want to talk to Chesney; he wanted the man to go away. But finally he said, reluctantly, "How did you die? Was there an accident?" just as Rachel asked, "Is it my fault?"

"No, absolutely not," said Sylvie firmly as Chesney answered, "Accident! It was no accident."

"He didn't die because I ran away?"

"Damn straight I did," Chesney retorted.

"No," Sylvie said.

Chesney exploded. Foul words spilled from his mouth, expletive after expletive cursing Sylvie and Rachel and the entire world. Rose sat up straighter, her eyes opening wider and then blinking rapidly as Chesney went on and on. He turned and strode away from the table, walking through other tables, then turned and stormed back.

"Maybe you should cover your ears," Dillon suggested to Rose.

192

"Do you know what he's saying?" she asked him. "I've never even heard most of those words."

His smile was wry. He was not going to be the one to teach Rose bad words. Maybe Akira would pay for HBO.

"It's okay not to feel sad." Sylvie finished what she was saying just as Chesney turned back to the table.

"The hell it is!" Furious, Chesney flung out his arms as if his rage had become too great for him to contain. Across the table, a photograph on the wall bounced and then fell.

Dillon and Rose exchanged glances, Rose wide-eyed. Dillon stood, sliding out of the booth. "Calm down," he told Chesney. "You're dead. Get over it."

Chesney snarled with fury. Rachel's fork slid away from her and toward Chesney. He tried to grab it, but his fingers went right through it as the fork dropped onto the floor.

"I may be dead, but I'm going to make her pay." Chesney turned to a nearby table. He tried to pick up a glass without success. Then he narrowed his eyes and scowled. A spoon flew off the table and across the room, hitting the back of Sylvie's head as she straightened from picking up the fork.

"Cut that out," Dillon snapped.

"Not a chance!" Chesney looked around as if trying to find another object to hurl at Sylvie.

Dillon felt his simmering anger start to boil. He reached for Chesney, grabbing at his arm. The bigger man shoved him, and Dillon fell back. Ghosts sometimes faded away, but Chesney was solid to him, so he wouldn't be fading any time soon.

"Dillon, be careful," Rose said, sounding worried. She also slid out of the booth and came to stand between the two ghosts. "Mr. Chesney, this isn't going to help you."

Max called something to Rachel, and Dillon looked back at the table. Rachel looked scared, he realized, and the sight of her fear made him even angrier. Chesney had done nothing to help her when he was alive and he was upsetting her now. He stepped forward, next to Rose, between Chesney and the booth, but the man ignored him. Behind him, Dillon heard a plate moving across the table and his mother gasp.

People were moving, looking their way, some standing up. A man at the door said something but Dillon was focused on Chesney. "Nothing you do can hurt them now." His fury pulsed through him, a throbbing energy that burned.

"Want to bet?" Chesney's eyes narrowed. Dillon could see the calculation as the man added, thoughtfully. "You recognized me. And you know them."

He looked behind Dillon at Rachel, still seated, and Sylvie, standing by the edge of the table, before finally letting his gaze stop on Rose. "What did she say?" He gestured at Sylvie with a jerk of his head. "That's your mother?"

Dillon glared. "That's right."

"Well, kid, I'm going to make her life hell." His voice held a vicious edge.

"Right, by throwing spoons at her?" Dillon scoffed, but his rage was like a choking cloud around him, a fog that he had to fight to see through.

Chesney closed his eyes and clenched his fists. Behind them, a light bulb popped and glass shattered.

"Leave her alone," Dillon yelled. His hands curled into fists. Another light bulb crackled and shattered.

"Dillon, don't," Rose protested. "That was you. Stop it."

Chesney stilled, but he was watching the people at Dillon's back, ignoring Dillon. Then he laughed. The sound grated like the shriek of an owl. "Yes! That murdering bitch will fry."

Dillon looked behind him. Colin Rafferty, the sheriff, had his hand on Sylvie's shoulder and she was turning to accompany him, tossing a wry grin at Rachel. "What's going on?"

"He's arresting her." Chesney chortled with mirthless glee. "For my murder. We'll see how the bitch likes jail."

The words hit Dillon like a bucket of ice water pouring over his head.

Jail?

His mother had killed Chesney. He wouldn't be able to talk to her. His parents wouldn't be together. His mother wouldn't be safe.

His father wouldn't be happy.

"Dillon, please." The urgency in Rose's voice broke through his shock. "You have to calm down."

"Run, Rose," he answered, although his voice didn't sound like his own. "Run."

Anger, frustration, despair, grief. His emotions were a whirlpool, pulling him down, down, down.

And then the restaurant was gone. Walls, tables, chairs, people, all had disappeared. The ceiling and the floor were lost, vanished into an infinity of space and endless nothing.

*****

'Sylvie. Sylvie.'

The voice was insistent, demanding. Sylvie rubbed her nose against her arm, squeezed her eyes shut a little tighter, and tried to ignore it.

'Sylvie. Love. Wake up for me.'

Wait. Was that Lucas? She forced her eyelids up, feeling the stickiness of sleep and the burn of not enough of it in her eyes, but not moving as she came slowly alert. 'Lucas?'

Head still resting on her folded arms, she tried to remember where she was. The interrogation room at the police station, of course. She'd been so tired that when they'd left her alone in here, she'd put her head down on the table and gone to sleep like a first-grader at quiet time. How long had it been?

She pushed herself upright and rubbed her face. The room was still empty, but she could have sworn she'd heard Lucas talking to her. "Lucas?"

'I'm here. Behind the glass.'

Sylvie looked. The wall across from her held a window that was dark glass. A one-way mirror. Still half-asleep, she said, "Your dress saved my life."

On the way to the police station, sitting in the back of the sheriff's car, she'd been thinking about the phone calls she hadn't had a chance to make, the words she hadn't had a chance to say. She'd wanted to tell Lucas that even though she'd destroyed their future, she wouldn't be alive without him.

'Shhh. Not out loud,' he thought. 'I don't want Colin to know that we can talk.'

She blinked and then shook her head slightly, trying to come back to full consciousness. Now that she was awake, she could feel Lucas's presence. But he wasn't alone—at least two, maybe three other people stood with him.

One of them was the sheriff. Sylvie's lips curled in a reluctant smile at the sound of his grumbling thoughts. 'I'd say he suspects.'

'Yeah.' Sylvie could almost see the resigned shrug Lucas was giving in the face of the sheriff's glare. 'He's an old friend. It doesn't matter as long as he doesn't try to kick me out. If he does . . .' He let the thought trail off, but the threat was implied.

'I'm sorry.'

'Don't be.'

'Not about that. About all of it.'

'It'll be okay.' His thought held a calm assurance that almost made Sylvie laugh. It was so Lucas. And so wrong.

'Lucas,' she protested. Didn't he understand? Did he not know why she was here? 'I killed two men.'

'I know.'

Sylvie's eyebrows drew down as she frowned. How could he sound so sure? He hadn't been there. And what was he doing here? She glanced around the room, wondering. Was she really awake? This wasn't a dream, was it? But the cool air, the hard chair, the antiseptic smell—it all felt real.

'Once I knew you were headed to Florida, I caught an early flight. I thought it'd be faster than getting a company plane sent to Washington to pick me up. But we got stuck on the runway.' Regret and frustration at the memory tinged the words as Lucas answered one of her questions.

'But how did you know . . .' Sylvie let the thought trail off.

'We had the house under surveillance.'

Sylvie winced. Hell. If she'd known that, if she'd known that Lucas was on his way and that help was so close at hand, would her choices have been different? Probably.

'I wish I'd known. I wish . . .' Sylvie couldn't find the words to express her regrets. 'I'm so sorry,' she repeated instead.

'Don't apologize. You have nothing to be sorry for.'

Why didn't he understand? 'I'm going to prison, Lucas. Probably for a very long time.'

'No, you're not.'

Sylvie wasn't sure whether she wanted to laugh or cry. She pressed her lips together to stop herself from doing either. 'Florida's a death penalty state. I'll be lucky if they call it manslaughter, not murder.'

'Trust me on this.' His thoughts sounded so calm, so reasonable.

Sylvie closed her eyes. 'Even if you're friends with the police here, Lucas, you can't be sure of that.'

'That has nothing to do with it.' His thought felt slightly offended. Sylvie almost felt relieved. She didn't want to go to jail, but she also didn't want any part of a corrupt investigation.

Then he added, with a tone that was more amused than anxious, 'Besides, I've waited twenty years for you, Sylvie. I'm not going to stop now.'

'Lucas,' Sylvie tried to protest. 'You're insane.'

'Admit it, Syl. It's the same for you. What we have is special, worth waiting for.'

Sylvie stared at the glass. She wished she could see Lucas's face, wished she could touch him and know that he was next to her. He hadn't sounded worried about whether or not she was going to prison, but was there a trace of anxiety in his last statement? Was he asking a question?

'Yes,' she admitted. 'Why?' Maybe it was his uncertainty or her fear that this might be the last chance she'd have to share her thoughts with him for a very long time, but she felt as if she were opening a door. He'd always been Prince Charming—rich, attractive, smart, the world at his fingertips. But she'd always been Cinderella. What did he see in her?

His answer was a flood of memories and then he stilled his thoughts. She could feel him picking his words. 'People wear masks. I see beneath them. Do you know what's under your mask, Sylvie?'

She scowled. Good God, was he going to get all complicated and weird and metaphorical on her? And then her frown deepened as she felt him laughing.

'That's what's under your mask, Sylvie. Honesty.'

'I don't wear a mask.'

'No, you don't. And . . .'

It was feeling he sent, no words, but she understood the message because it was how she felt, too. Without Lucas, she was alone. Aware of other people in a way they couldn't reciprocate, understanding but not understood. Lucas, though—he saw her, the real her. He understood her. And she gave that back to him.

She'd never admitted it, not even to herself, but that link had always scared her a little. Lucas had exploded into her lonely adolescence like a dangerous narcotic, one that could far too easily take her over.

'Ha.' He was listening as she thought, of course, and responded with a picture, a memory of the exotic, mysterious older woman he'd seen her as when he was fifteen.

She smiled but sorrow was rising in her throat. They could have made it work this time. They could have.

But it was too late. She'd ruined everything.

'Stop that.'

She'd made so many mistakes in her life, but this one was—but the thought of her mistakes reminded her. 'Dillon's back.'

'What?' That was surprise, but also quick joy she felt from Lucas. She smiled and leaned back in her uncomfortable chair.

'I believe our son is a bad influence.' She wasn't sure when she'd realized that Dillon had to be involved in Rachel's appearance in Tassamara—maybe it was the moment she'd gotten that suspicious text—but events at the diner had confirmed it. She let Lucas know what had happened with Rachel and felt his sense of relief and amusement.

'I think Chesney's there, too,' she added.

Lucas's amusement changed to alarm. 'Tell me.'

Sylvie frowned. What was Lucas worrying about? But she told him the rest of the story and waited.

'I'm going to go find out what's happening and where Akira is,' Lucas responded. 'I'll be back soon. Be good.'

Sylvie raised her eyebrows. 'Is there another option?'

'Colin's a friend. Don't torture him too much.'

Sylvie shook her head. Lucas had a strange idea of what was happening here. She was under arrest. His 'friend' was going to send her to prison. But she tossed a wry, two-fingered salute to the window and felt Lucas chuckle in response before he moved away.

Then she waited.

Before too much more time had passed, the sheriff entered the room. He dropped a manila folder on the table and took a seat across from her. She met his gaze evenly, assessing him. He was young, probably in his mid-thirties, with sandy brown hair and blue eyes. He looked vaguely familiar. She wondered if he was related to the old sheriff. Tassamara seemed like a place where law enforcement jobs would be handed down, generation to generation, and she'd really hated the old sheriff.

"Every year, second Saturday in December, my gramma has a tree-trimming party," he told her. "Tinsel, eggnog, gingerbread cookies.

Little kids running around all over the place, screaming and yelling. Big kids sulking 'cause they're not off with their friends. Grown-ups getting into stupid arguments about football and politics."

Sylvie held back her smile. He made it sound unpleasant, but she could tell that he didn't feel that way.

"I'd really like to get there before it ends. Not so much because I mind missing it, but if I'm a no-show, I'll hear about it for the next five years."

"Is my lawyer here?"

"Got a great lawyer waiting in the outside office for ya'. He's been here since before we got here."

Sylvie crossed her arms, urge to smile gone. They'd had this conversation before. "I'll wait for my lawyer," she told him.

He scratched his head. "He won't be licensed in Florida, you know. He's going to need local help."

"I'll let him tell me that."

"All right. Well, maybe you'll change your mind about that when I tell you what I've got."

Sylvie stayed silent.

He opened the folder. "Let's see. Two dead bodies, but you know that. Shell casings at the scene. I'm guessing that our ballistics guys are going to match them and the bullets inside our two dead vics to that pretty little Glock you had on you."

With an effort, Sylvie refrained from tapping her foot. It wasn't as if she didn't know there was plenty of evidence. What was he trying to achieve?

"Fingerprints came back a match, so I know you were at the house. Of course, I knew that already because I've got eyewitnesses who put you at the scene."

Sylvie didn't say anything. The eyewitnesses might have been a surprise if Lucas hadn't already told her that the house had been under surveillance.

"We've got the blood on your dress. We're sending that off to the lab but since you're not injured, we can say now that the blood's not yours. It'll be a match to one or both victims. And then there's the gunshot residue on your hands."

He leaned back in his chair, his face somber. "I'd say we've got an open-and-shut double homicide here. You sure you don't want to tell me your side of the story? Once I send this off to the DA, there won't be much I can do for you."

He waited.

Sylvie tried not to glare, but she knew her disgust showed. Did he think she was an idiot? "I'll wait for my lawyer, thanks."

He grinned at her. "You don't remember me, do you?"

The unexpected question startled her. She looked at him closely, puzzled, and then shook her head. Should she remember him?

"Eh." He waved his hand, dismissing her forgetfulness. "You never saw anyone except Lucas, anyway."

She frowned, but he continued without waiting for her recognition.

"Ready for what else I've got?" he asked her.

She didn't answer, but her eyes narrowed.

"Eyewitnesses: one who was surveilling the house, but two who were in it. One of those is willing to testify that you were a dead woman walking. The other's keeping quiet but he's got an ugly record."

They must have picked up Ari and Rafe. Sylvie didn't comment.

"That's not all, though. The DEA was happy about getting into that house, happier when they found the drugs and guns, and really, really happy when they found files. Lots of files. Computers, too."

Sylvie shifted in her seat. Where was he going with this?

The sheriff continued cheerfully. "I hear, though, that the folks in Washington are even happier. They executed a search warrant on Chesney's house and office about twenty minutes after they got the news, and are busy cleaning out AlecCorp as we speak."

He glanced at his watch.

"Is that it?" Sylvie asked. She felt confused. She didn't understand. Okay, so Chesney was a criminal. But that didn't change anything. She could call Mateo's death self-defense. He'd pulled a gun and he'd intended to kill her. But Chesney had been unarmed. She could have—should have—called the police. Instead, she'd shot him.

"Oh, not entirely." His grin was lop-sided, and she could feel a faint hum of annoyance coming from him. "Five messages—already—from the Commonwealth Attorney's office back in Virginia. Apparently someone warned them that they might lose a key witness in a serial killer case?"

It was a question, but Sylvie shrugged in response. She hadn't even called her mom, much less the Virginia police.

"Then there's the lawyer sitting in my office." Colin drew a deep breath, his annoyance level jumping. "You've passed on him but your lawyer won't be so stupid."

Sylvie scowled. She didn't like being called stupid. "How so?" she asked, her voice dangerous.

"William Piero. Criminal defense attorney and an expert in Florida's self-defense laws. Your lawyer will probably recognize the name. It makes prosecutors wince. Anyway, he takes a lot of pro bono cases. It turns out he's been on retainer for Max Latimer for over a decade."

Sylvie blinked. A decade?

"Do you know much about Florida law?"

Sylvie shrugged one shoulder, feeling vaguely resentful and unsettled. This conversation wasn't going the way it was supposed to. But of course she didn't know anything about Florida law. She wasn't a lawyer and she hadn't lived here for twenty years.

"Put it this way." The sheriff closed the folder, picked it up and tapped it against the table. She could feel that he was looking for the right words. "We're a little more liberal than most states."

"Liberal?" Sylvie protested, cocking her head to one side and letting her disbelief show. "Florida?"

"Well, only when it comes to murder." The sheriff's smile showed a flash of white, even teeth. "If you'd confessed, I might have something to hold you on." He sounded regretful, but Sylvie could tell that he didn't really feel sorry.

She narrowed her eyes. "I don't understand."

"Florida state law: a person is justified in the use of deadly force and does not have a duty to retreat if he or she reasonably believes that such force is necessary to prevent imminent death or great bodily harm to himself or herself or another or to prevent the imminent commission of a forcible felony." The sheriff rattled off the law at top-speed.

Sylvie swallowed. She should point out that Chesney hadn't been armed. But Jeremy's voice echoed in her head: 'Never, never, never tell the police anything without a lawyer present.' She kept her mouth closed.

"Nice thing is—well, for you, anyway—Stand Your Ground isn't a defense."

Sylvie didn't say anything but the sheriff grinned at her. "You're not going to ask, are you? Lucas told me you wouldn't say anything." He stood, pushing the chair back.

"We do have to get your statement, so if you won't talk without your lawyer, you're going to have to wait for him to get here. But the Stand Your Ground laws provide immunity from prosecution. If this is what it looks like, and what your lawyers will undoubtedly argue it is, the DA can't prosecute you."

Sylvie didn't let her mouth drop open, but she knew her eyes widened. She almost wanted to protest. Sure, she'd hoped a jury would be on her side, but she'd killed an unarmed man! Were they just going to let her go?

"Ready to talk?" he asked, sounding hopeful as he glanced at his watch again.

Sylvie shook her head. "I'll wait for my lawyer." She knew she sounded wary, but she felt it.

Wary and mistrustful, but with a spark of hope.

Maybe her worst fears wouldn't come true.

CHAPTER SIXTEEN

His worst fear had come true.

This was hell, Dillon thought. It was the only thing that made sense.

He felt unmoored, cut loose from the ties of gravity and lost in a darkness punctuated by clouds of color and swirling light.

Had Rose heard him? Had she had enough time to get away? Akira had told him that turning into a vortex pulled other ghosts into the energy. They never came back. She thought they were destroyed. Had he destroyed Rose? The grief and fear grew until it was lightning running against his skin, fire surging around him.

He tried desperately to make sense of what he saw, to still the shifting whirls and streams, to find solid ground, but it was impossible. The energy tossed him about like ocean waves lifting driftwood.

A mottled gray cloud streaked with muddy red and sickly green flew toward him. Was this the vortex? Was he drawing it in somehow? Pulling it toward him? Frantic, Dillon tried desperately to scramble away from the diffuse shape but it drew closer and closer until it was oozing up, over, and around him, a slimy miasma.

What could it be? It was disgusting, slick yet grimy against him. And then he realized.

Chesney.

The cloud was Chesney. His spirit sizzled against Dillon, searing like a chemical, like the touch of ammonia. As the cloud reached his face, Dillon panicked. As a ghost, he hadn't needed to breathe in a long time, but it felt as if the cloud was trying to suffocate him.

He tried to push it off, scraping at it with his hands. But it wasn't solid. It flowed between his fingers and back toward him, clinging where it touched. It was trying to swallow him, he thought. To cover him up and drown him in its gray poison.

Revolted, Dillon lashed out at it. His energy crackled around him, red and flashing in the darkness. It bit into the cloud, sparks flaring where they touched, then disappearing as the ooze surrounded them. Was it absorbing his energy? Eating it?

Desperately, he fought harder, smashing against the cloud with all the power he could muster, forcing his energy higher and higher until it was lightning, smashing the air around him, filling the void with the rumbles of thunder.

He hated Chesney. Hated him, hated him, hated him.

For an endless, timeless space, his hatred of Chesney was all-consuming, the essence of his existence, the pure drive that kept him burning.

And then the cloud was breaking up, the ooze splitting into chunks and wisps of gray and green that drifted away on the energy sea. As the pieces became smaller they dazzled with light like sparklers on a summer evening and then fizzled out and were gone.

It had been over five years since Dillon had taken a shower, but he desperately wanted one now.

He was pretty sure that he'd just broken Chesney's ghost into a million pieces. He thought he ought to feel guilty, but he didn't have room for it: he was too consumed with hate and rage.

He stayed angry, floating in nothingness, oblivious to his surroundings, until a little whisper of thought broke into his fury.

It wasn't Chesney's fault.

He shoved the thought away, but it crept relentlessly back.

Chesney hadn't been a nice person. But what had he done really? Ignored his daughter? Wanted revenge on his killer? Was that such evil?

Chesney hadn't convinced Rachel to run away, putting her in danger from any creepy stranger who might accost her.

And he hadn't shot himself. Dillon didn't know why Sylvie killed Raymond Chesney, but it wasn't the other way around: Chesney hadn't murdered his mom.

Chesney hadn't even plunged them into this void world. Even if he had, it wouldn't have been deliberate. He couldn't have known the risks of overloading on energy. But Dillon had known. Had known and had let it happen anyway. If Rose was gone, it wasn't Chesney who had destroyed her.

As his anger started to fade, Dillon's guilt and grief grew. What had he done? He'd screwed up. Again.

Reluctantly, he thought back to his last big screw-up. Not the time he asked Akira to visit his gran and got her killed: although that one was big, he didn't really blame himself for it.

No, the time before that.

He'd been angry then, too. All his friends were headed to the midnight movies—for the third time that summer—and as always, he wasn't allowed to go. His curfew was ten o'clock. Fifteen years old, on summer vacation, and his gran insisted he be home by ten. It just wasn't fair, he thought, but the words were rote, the resentment long since gone.

He'd stolen the pills, snuck off to the car so no one would hear him if he got sick, and died. No psychic gift. No shortcut to adulthood. Just day after day of monotony as the world went on without him.

The choice he'd made meant living—well, existing—with the consequences ever since, both for him and for the people who loved him. He could never go back and change what he'd done.

But that's what he'd been trying to do, wasn't it? He'd wanted to erase time, to make his parents be who they'd been before him and before he died.

To make his father be who he was before Dillon died.

He thought back to that day by the car, when Andy got the police to pull Sylvie over. His dad had smiled at her. Really smiled, the way he used to smile. That was what Dillon had wanted: for that smile to come back and erase the grim look that Lucas usually wore.

Sylvie—she was cool. He liked her, and he wished he could have gotten to know her. But making his parents come to Tassamara hadn't only been about her, and maybe it wasn't even mostly about her. He'd wanted his dad to be happy; happy the way he had never been since Dillon's death. He'd wanted his dad to laugh again and he'd thought Sylvie could make him do it.

In the darkness, he closed his eyes as the sadness overwhelmed him.

And then that little voice was back, pushing up from his subconscious.

Maybe his mom would go to jail for killing Chesney and maybe she wouldn't. He'd bet she had a good reason for doing it. But whether she went to jail or not, if his dad lost Dillon again, this time to a vortex of ghostly energies, he was definitely not going to be happy.

Dillon couldn't change the fact that he'd killed himself. That was over and done and nothing could make that better. And he couldn't change what he'd done to Chesney's spirit. But his gran had escaped from the void. Maybe he could, too.

If he'd destroyed Rose, though, he wasn't sure he wanted to. Did he really want to keep on existing if his actions had ripped her spirit apart? But he hadn't felt her, not like he'd felt Chesney. Maybe she'd had time to run away.

A whisper of thought told him to stop worrying about Rose and concentrate.

He frowned. His subconscious seemed a little unreasonable: Rose was his best friend, he could worry about her if he wanted to.

This time the whisper was more of a growl. *Concentrate*, the voice ordered him. It was time to think of a way out of this mess.

Slowly he turned, trying to make sense of everything he saw. With his fear suppressed, the tossing felt more like floating and the chaos of swirling lights in the darkness separated into distinct glows. His gran had recognized the lights as people. Could he do the same?

Closest to him was a pillar of white. Seeing it made him feel better, safer, as if he wasn't alone in the darkness. He drifted a little closer to it and basked in its warmth. He had no idea who it might be, but he liked it.

Other lights were sprinkled around him; yellows, greens, a pale blue, a deep royal blue. And in the distance, far off, a sparkling blue iridescence. It called to him like sunlight on a stormy day, like firelight on a dark night. Without thinking, he started pushing himself against the waves, trying to reach it. And then he froze, stopping himself and hurriedly retreating back to the white light.

That blue had to be Akira. He understood why his gran had wanted to grab her aura and hang on to it. It had a kind of solidity about it, as if it might be a life raft instead of a star. But tugging at Akira's aura had killed her. He wasn't going to do that again. No, he'd think of something else.

But what?

*****

Ty and Jeremy had brought Joshua. Sylvie felt tears spring to her eyes at the sight of the toddler leaning against Ty's leg in the waiting room, babbling happily as his father tried to read him a book. She blinked them back furiously.

With Jeremy on one side and the lawyer sent by Max Latimer on the other, her interrogation—if it could even be called that—had been swift and painless. Rachel's disappearance, the circumstances of how she'd been at a suspected drug trafficker's house, her lack of knowledge of Chesney's business—the only moments they'd glossed over were the actual shootings.

Had Chesney threatened her? Yes, she'd answered truthfully, he'd said that they needed to make her death look like an accident and that he would destroy her. Had she believed her life to be in danger? Yes. She didn't clarify the timeline or the source and the police didn't ask. And her lawyers refused to let her respond to some questions, so she told no lies. Her reasons for shooting Chesney and whether she'd considered alternatives stayed off the record.

The sheriff politely requested that she stay in Florida while the investigation continued, but with that he'd let them go.

Behind her, Jeremy and William chatted.

"How do you like diminished capacity from lack of sleep?"

"Not as good as post-traumatic stress disorder."

"We'd need a documented history for that."

"No, she was attacked by a serial killer last week. She's definitely still in the window of trauma response."

"Nice."

Sylvie glanced over her shoulder at them. "You're planning a defense. Am I going to need one?"

Jeremy shrugged, but William shook his head and said, sounding almost regretful, "Not a chance. You might get charged, but we'd assert immunity pre-trial based on Stand Your Grand, and we'll get it."

"You seem pretty confident."

"A decade ago, when Max hired me to defend this case, it would have been different. You'd still have a damn good chance of getting off with an eyewitness willing to testify that they were planning to kill you. But the way the law currently stands, you won't go to trial."

"You—what? A decade ago?" Jeremy blinked in surprise, shoving his hands into the pockets of his suit jacket.

Ty shook his head as he stood, smiling in wry greeting. "Don't ask. Sylvie's told me about this place."

"Ty," Sylvie started before stopping. How could she ever possibly apologize enough? She'd killed their employer. The reputation of Ty's company, so carefully nurtured, would be destroyed. Every one of his employees would be out of work. And at Christmas. She'd ruined so much.

"Cut it out, Syl," Ty said mildly. He scooped up Joshua who leaned toward Sylvie with a joyful yelp. "You're doing that black hole thing, I can see it. Planning for the worst is great, but expecting the worst is a waste of time. Besides, all I care about is that you're okay."

This time a tear overflowed. Sylvie brushed it away, embarrassed, and reached for Joshua. "Shooting the client isn't going to be good for business."

"Working for a drug cartel? Also not good for business. At least not the kind of business I care to have." Ty released the toddler who pressed both hands against the side of Sylvie's face and gave her a sloppy kiss as Ty pointed to a duffel bag on the ground. "When we got to your boyfriend's plane, your luggage was waiting. I guess he sent someone to your hotel in DC and checked you out. You want to change before we get out of here?"

Sylvie's laugh was still slightly teary. She looked down at the blue scrubs she was wearing. She hadn't minded when the police took her dress as evidence and let her clean up, but it would be a relief to wear her own clothes again.

Joshua was talking to her, long sentences of toddler babble that made no sense at all. She took a deep breath before dropping a return kiss on his cheek and then asking Ty, "Joshua?"

"No sitter. And we didn't know how long we'd be here. Rachel?"

"With Max Latimer."

"Let's go."

Sylvie managed a smile as Ty tried to disentangle her from the complaining toddler but Ty saw something in her face.

"Problem?" he asked.

Should she tell him about the ghosts?

"Nope, not at all," she answered, scooping up her bag. "I'll just change."

*****

"Christmas in Florida is strange," said Jeremy. "Do they usually throw midwinter street parties?"

They were walking down Millard Street from the sheriff's office. The temperate night air smelled of Florida, humid and fragrant with a strong undertone of moldy swamp, and in striking contrast to the twinkling holiday lights and Christmas decorations. But Sylvie didn't think the people gathered on the street and sidewalks were celebrating. Excitement, curiosity, uncertainty, doubt—the flavor of the crowd was mixed, but she knew it wasn't a party.

She glanced around, looking for faces she recognized, pausing on the people with the strongest emotions. A young Asian woman had her arms crossed across her chest, almost hugging herself, the strength of her worry not showing on her calm face. Another woman on the other side of the street was facing away from Sylvie. From the back and in the dark, Sylvie could see only that she had dark hair but her emotions were a mix of joy and terror. As Sylvie walked by the door to the restaurant, still searching the crowd, she tasted sheer annoyance from someone inside.

Finally she spotted Lucas. She walked straight into his arms, lifted her lips for his kiss, and let herself get lost for one long glorious moment in the touch, taste and feel of him.

Then she pulled back and said, "What the hell is going on?"

He smiled down at her, his eyes even bluer than usual under the glow from the street lamp and the sparkle of the holiday lights. "The fire marshal kicked everyone out of Maggie's place while he inspects the electricity." He slid his arm around her, nodded at the two men, smiled at Joshua, and turned his attention back to the door of the restaurant.

"Electric problems?" Jeremy asked, looking toward the restaurant.

"Where's Rachel?" Despite the boy in his arms, Ty stayed focused on the job.

Without looking, Lucas nodded toward the sidewalk on the other side of the street, safely away from the crowd. Sylvie glanced that way and then frowned in recognition at the sight of the scared but happy dark-haired woman. "Is that—" she started.

"She's with her mother," Lucas confirmed.

"Her mother?" Ty and Sylvie said the words almost simultaneously.

"I had her sent for as soon as I heard the news. She got here about twenty minutes ago." Sylvie could tell from his distracted tone that Lucas was still mostly focused on what was happening inside the restaurant.

"Why?" Ty demanded.

"Pre-emptive strike," Lucas answered absently. And then he must have felt Ty's response, because he finally turned his attention back to them.

"Against who?" Ty must have tightened his grip on Joshua, because the little boy started to fuss.

"Not you." Lucas put a hand out and patted Joshua gently on the back, drawing his attention. "Child protective services here in Florida would have Rachel in foster care faster than you could blink if they knew her custodial parent was dead. The same should be true in DC. Unless you want her in state care until an executor is found and Chesney's estate is settled, she needed an emergency guardian."

"I could have—" Ty started.

"With Sylvie's involvement in her father's death?" Lucas interrupted him. "Under the circumstances, you wouldn't get temporary custody."

"The authorities had no reason to know that Rachel needed anyone to have custody." Ty's voice got quieter.

Jeremy must have recognized the danger signs, because he reached for Joshua, firmly taking the boy from his husband's grasp, and saying, "Come on, Joshua, let's go look at the pretty lights."

"Raymond Chesney's death is under investigation and Sylvie's future is at stake. We are not covering up Rachel's unaccompanied presence here." Lucas's voice also got quieter, but gentler as well.

"Stop it," Sylvie snapped at both of them. If they kept this up, in two minutes one of them would haul off and punch the other. "Go meet Rachel's mom," she ordered Ty. "Reassure yourself that Rachel will be safe with her. And be nice—she loves her daughter but she's scared."

Ty scowled at her and she narrowed her eyes at him and added, "She's Rachel's mother."

With only a minor grumble but a strong feeling of annoyance, Ty turned and headed across the street.

"As for you . . ." Sylvie punched Lucas lightly on the arm. "Efficiency is nice. I appreciated the clothes. But Rachel was my problem to worry about. Don't be so damn managing."

Lucas's smile was crooked. "Rachel's situation was a very small problem. We have bigger issues."

"The police?" Sylvie's heart sank. She'd known that was all too easy.

"No." Lucas shook his head quickly. *'Dillon.'*

'What about him?' Sylvie responded wordlessly.

'He's in trouble.' He nodded toward the worried woman Sylvie had noticed earlier. *'Akira can explain.'*

Taking her hand, Lucas tugged her toward the woman. As they got closer, Sylvie recognized the man standing with her as Zane, Lucas's younger brother, all grown-up now. She couldn't help a quiet hum of appreciation.

'Hey,' Lucas protested, slightly indignant but also amused.

'He looks just like you,' she told him, an unrepentant grin on her lips, and then she sobered as Lucas introduced her to Akira. They exchanged greetings and then Sylvie turned to Akira and asked, "What's going on?"

"I wish I could see better." Akira's eyes were back on the restaurant storefront, almost as if she hadn't heard the question. And then she said, softly, "I can't be sure."

"About what?" asked Sylvie, confused.

"A ghost has taken over the restaurant," Zane answered.

Sylvie shook her head. She didn't understand. Why was it a problem for Dillon to be in the restaurant? Or was Chesney making trouble still?

"As I understand it," Lucas said, picking his words carefully and glancing at Zane and Akira for confirmation, "a ghost can get so upset that it loses control and becomes sort of a vengeful spirit."

"Like on *Supernatural*?" Sylvie asked, feeling doubt rising within her.

"Like on what?" Lucas responded.

"The television show?"

He shook his head. "Never heard of it."

"Ah. Well." Sylvie shrugged. Somehow she didn't think that she and Lucas would be curling up together to the adventures of the Winchester brothers any time soon. "Go on."

Zane took over. "When our mom died, she became a ghost, too. But she couldn't communicate and her ghostly energy was . . . dangerous." He stopped.

"Not to everyone. But she killed me," Akira reported matter-of-factly. "Killed me and possessed my body. It's what vortex ghosts—the ghosts that have lost control—try to do. And they destroy other ghosts." She sighed and started chewing on her lower lip, still watching the restaurant.

"You seem pretty alive?" Sylvie's tone made the tentative words a question.

Akira waved a hand dismissively without looking. "Defibrillator. Resuscitation. No permanent damage. That time, anyway."

"So do you think Chesney's one of these vortex ghosts? Could he have destroyed Dillon?" Sylvie's horror was like vomit rising in her throat. She would rather have gone to jail for the rest of her life, for eternity, than learn that Chesney had taken his vengeance out on Dillon.

Lucas put his arm around her shoulders and pulled her close to him, but Akira shook her head.

"I'm not sure." Akira uncrossed her arms and put her hand on her stomach. "There's a lot of energy there. I can feel it from here. And Rose is gone, too."

"Rose?"

"The other ghost that lives in Akira's house," Lucas told Sylvie quietly.

"I can't tell what's happened. And I can't . . ." Akira let the words trail off as she stroked her hand up and down, across her shirt.

Sylvie recognized the gesture, putting it together with a memory of Lucas babbling in the coffee shop. "You're pregnant."

Akira nodded. Zane put his hand on the nape of her neck, his love obvious in the touch, and she leaned into him.

"And you can't get close enough to help Dillon because the ghost, whoever it is, might kill you," Sylvie said flatly.

Akira nodded.

Sylvie took a long deep breath. For an instant, she desperately wanted to go for a run. Not to run away, but to hit the rhythm where she could block out the world and let her brain go numb. It had been a very long day. And then she firmly suppressed the desire and pulled herself back to the moment at hand.

"What can we do?" she asked.

The men looked at one another. Akira's arms went back up, crossing herself like a hug, and Zane shifted so that he stood behind her, his head resting on her hair, his arms around her protectively.

"I used to think the ghosts were literally a vortex, like a whirlpool pulling other ghosts in, but I'm not sure about that anymore," Akira said.

"What do you think it is now?" Sylvie asked.

"A portal to another universe," Zane answered for Akira, his voice touched with enthusiasm. They all looked at him, Akira turning her head up so that she could see his face without moving. He shrugged and his arms tightened around Akira. "Admit it, it'd be cool."

"Not another universe," Akira corrected him. "Another dimension." She looked over at Sylvie, almost as if Sylvie had voiced her skeptical response. "Do you know anything about quantum physics?"

Sylvie's eyebrows rose, but she didn't smile. "No."

"Human beings are limited by our ability to perceive the world only through our senses. Physicists have known for decades that ordinary matter," Akira stamped a foot on the ground, as if to indicate its solidity, "makes up less than five percent of our universe's mass. We can see from the ways the stars and galaxies move that there has to be a lot of mass out there that we aren't able to perceive."

"Okay." Sylvie nodded. What did that have to do with ghosts?

"Particle physicists call the missing matter 'dark matter' and are searching for a subatomic particle to explain it. Proponents of string theory, specifically M-theory, postulate instead that there are dimensions that we can't see or experience. The dimensions would exist only at the quantum level, but they might contain energy that could affect the dimensions that we do see." Akira paused, eyebrows raised as if to question whether Sylvie wanted her to continue.

"Okay," Sylvie agreed. "So . . . the energy inside those dimensions moves the stars?"

"Exactly." Akira sounded pleased.

Sylvie didn't want to diminish her enthusiasm by asking what quantum physics had to do with Dillon, but she was lost. She glanced at Zane.

"Ghosts are energy," he said. "Energy that most human beings don't have any way of seeing."

Sylvie frowned and looked back at Akira. "Are you saying that ghosts are dark matter, then?"

"No, no." Akira spread her fingers wide as if to say stop, and then closed them. "Well . . . ." She tilted her head to one side as if to consider the idea and then glanced back at the restaurant window. She shrugged, her dark eyes thoughtful, and leaned back into Zane. "I'll have to think about that one."

Sylvie waited, but apparently Akira was planning to think about it right now. Her thoughts were a jumble, none of the words adding up to anything that made sense to Sylvie, while the silence lengthened and dragged on. Finally Sylvie broke into Akira's thoughts impatiently, "Okay, but what do we do?"

Akira shook her head slightly. Sylvie could feel her unhappy worry but she didn't say anything.

"There must be something," Sylvie prompted.

At the restaurant door, a man who had to be the fire marshal emerged with Max Latimer. They were talking and the man shrugged. Max shook his hand, clearly thanking him. Inside the restaurant, the lights came back on.

And then suddenly Akira's mood changed. Sylvie glanced at Lucas to see if he felt it, too, as joy swept through Akira.

"What just happened?" Lucas demanded.

Akira ignored him. "Rose, Rose!" she called out, her smile unforced and grateful. She pushed herself onto her toes and waved at the door. "Rose!"

"At least one ghost made it out," muttered Zane.

"What happened? How did you break free?" Akira was talking to empty space in front of her as if someone were there. "Did you—but—all right, that doesn't make any sense." Akira frowned. "Rose, I've seen this before. The vortex should have—what do you mean you're not really a ghost anymore? That's . . . oh. Well . . . ." Akira glanced at Sylvie and shrugged. "Sure, that should be all right."

"What's happening?" Sylvie's frustration built. She'd been focused on Akira but even with Lucas present, she couldn't understand what the other woman was thinking.

"Rose wants you and Lucas to go into the restaurant. She says that Chesney is gone, but that Dillon is stuck and she thinks that if he sees you, he might be able to figure out how to get unstuck."

Unstuck? Sylvie was so ready for a nice straightforward white light to show up.

"Is it dangerous?" Lucas asked.

"Who cares?" Sylvie responded, grabbing his hand and starting to pull him toward the restaurant door. Other people were going inside and it didn't matter to her if it were dangerous. She wanted to know what was happening to their son.

"Not to you," Akira called after them. "You'll be fine."

CHAPTER SEVENTEEN

The lights were moving around.

When the white light moved away from him, Dillon yelped in protest. He liked that light. He wanted it to stay near. But it was moving toward the iridescent blue that had to be Akira, and he knew that he couldn't go near her.

He stopped himself from moving after the white light with an effort and tried to think.

The lights were people. He couldn't talk to them and he couldn't hear them, but he could see them. He wondered what his light looked like to them, but then he realized that none of them would be able to see him. He'd never been able to see these glowing images when he was alive.

Maybe Mrs. Swanson, the old woman who claimed to see auras, would know what he was looking at. But he couldn't talk to her to find out what she knew.

He looked around him again. The void was endless. It went on forever. He understood why his gran had despaired because the thought of staying here filled him with horror. But he had an advantage that she hadn't had; he knew what had happened and he knew that it was possible to escape.

But not by taking over Akira's body and killing her in the process. He wouldn't do that, not even if it was the only way out.

Energy.

That had to be the solution.

He'd fallen into this void by overloading on energy. What would happen if he tried to get rid of the energy?

Lights were coming closer, shifting and bobbing around him. Two seemed to pause next to him, one a warm fiery red, the other a golden red. He felt as if he should recognize them, but the colors didn't mean anything to him.

The white light moved back toward him, too, and Dillon relaxed. The white light soothed and encouraged, its warmth comforting. As long as it was close, he thought he could search for a solution without fear. He wondered who it could be.

The little voice in the back of his head gave a disgruntled harrumph.

Dillon's eyes narrowed. His subconscious was annoyed at him? That seemed . . . odd. Okay, so maybe his mind had plenty of reason to be disgusted with his emotional actions, but that voice had felt like a response to not knowing who the white light was. Was he being stupid?

He waited, but his subconscious was silent.

Dillon shook his head, dismissing the idea, and stared at the red auras. Who were they? He should be able to figure it out, he thought.

Listen.

That was the voice again.

Concentrate.

A slow smile turned up the corners of Dillon's lips. He closed his eyes, the better to focus on his ears, and with all his heart, all his soul, listened as hard as he could and concentrated even harder.

And then the smile turned into a grin.

*****

"Dillon?" Sylvie spoke out loud to the restaurant, not caring what people might be thinking. "Are you here?"

She ignored the curious gazes directed her way. People were taking seats, obviously expecting to order food, eat dinner, move on as if nothing had happened.

"Think how much you'll save on air-conditioning." That was Max Latimer, calling out to someone in the kitchen.

Sylvie glanced at Lucas, asking the question without words.

"Cold spots, remember?" he told her. "Ghosts absorb atmospheric energy and make the temperature drop."

She nodded, then closed her eyes and tried to feel if a cold breeze was coming from any specific direction. It was cold. But not so much so that she could say that one direction meant more than another. "Dillon?" she tried again.

No answer. She hadn't expected one, not really.

She took a deep breath. Did she care about the people watching her? No, not after the day she'd had.

She took another step forward. "I told you why I left," she said. "But I didn't tell you this. I love you. I don't know you. I chose not to be part of your life because I thought it was best for you. But I would do anything for you. You . . ." She swallowed hard, feeling the tears springing to her eyes again. She was too tired, too exhausted to be thinking clearly. But did she need to? Did it matter?

"You were the most beautiful baby. When I looked at you, I thought that I had never seen anything so wonderful. I've seen the pictures since. I know it was hormones, and me being a mom. You were a little lump of baby, just like every other baby, but to me, you were the world. I loved you with all my heart. And you still have it. I will do anything for you. Whatever you need, I will give you if it is in my power to give. And if it's not, I'll find a way to get it. Dillon . . ." She let her voice trail off and then strengthened, she kept going. "Find a way to tell me what you need. I will get it for you. I will make it happen. You just have to tell me how."

She waited.

Behind her, she felt Lucas.

'*Love.*' His thought was a whisper, filled with grief. '*He would answer if he could.*'

'*He will answer,*' she told him back, her response fierce. '*He will answer.*'

And then her phone rang.

*****

Akira slid into the booth, her face alight with happiness.

Sylvie looked up from her phone. "We disagree on *Buffy the Vampire Slayer*," she reported. "I'll have to watch it again, but I don't know. I thought it was pretty damn hokey."

"So I hear," Akira responded. "I'm supposed to tell you that it's a statement of feminist empowerment."

"All that fake karate? Please." Sylvie rolled her eyes. And then she paused. "Does that mean—"

Akira nodded. "I've been waiting outside. The energy around the restaurant started slowly diminishing a while ago, but Zane wanted to be cautious." Akira rolled her eyes, but Sylvie could tell from the amusement in her smile that she didn't really mind.

Sylvie leaned back, letting her head rest against the booth. She closed her eyes.

Lucas tugged her closer, until her head was resting against his shoulder. She could feel the warmth and joy emanating from him.

"Our boy is okay?" For some untold time, Sylvie had been talking as text messages appeared on her phone. They'd started with personal history but had quickly—very quickly—devolved into television, books, movies, politics, even a touch of religion, if Joss Whedon worship could be considered religion.

Ty, Jeremy, Rachel and her mom were sitting at an adjacent booth, Joshua having long since dropped into an exhausted sleep on Jeremy's shoulder but Rachel still bubbling over with excitement. Max, Grace and Natalya were at a third booth, poking at their desserts and talking desultorily, with Zane just taking a seat with them. Otherwise, the restaurant was deserted, the hour long past any reasonable closing time.

"He's fine," Akira reported. "He's been pumping his excess energy into texting, but he's fully back in this dimension."

Sylvie sighed with satisfaction and turned her face into Lucas's shirt front. "Good," she mumbled.

He stroked his hand down her hair and her back. She lifted her face and looked up at him. *'Happy?'* she thought.

'Happy,' he confirmed. And then he bent his head and took her lips and she stopped thinking entirely.

*****

Christmas Day

Dillon didn't care about presents any more, but watching his family exchanging gifts, teasing each other, being silly, and celebrating the holiday felt like the most fun he'd ever had.

His mom had gotten the phone call from the sheriff the day before. She was free to leave the state if she so desired. The district attorney had decided no charges would be pressed. In another hour, she and his dad would catch a plane to North Carolina to spend part of the holiday with her family.

"So is Rose really . . ." Akira started.

"Don't say it," he told her. "She gets weird about that word."

"But, Dillon," Akira protested.

"I'm serious," he said. "She thinks it makes her sound like a goody-two-shoes or a Christmas tree ornament. She swears if you ever say it again, she's going to turn into a poltergeist just to make you stop."

"But . . ." Akira began to complain and then stopped herself. "All right, I won't say it. What about you, though?"

He glanced at her. "What do you mean?"

"Are you going to head through a passageway sometime soon?"

He looked over his shoulder. No passageway had appeared. He shrugged. "I don't think so."

Akira frowned. "Are you okay with that?"

Dillon spread his hands. "I wanted my parents to be together and to be happy. They are. But I guess this dimension needs something else from me before it's ready to let me go."

Akira sighed.

Dillon grinned at her. "Aren't you curious to find out what it is?"

AUTHOR NOTE

If you enjoyed reading about Dillon, Sylvie and Lucas, please consider leaving a review at your favorite online retailer. For any author, but especially those of us self-publishing without marketing budgets or PR people, Reviews = Sales = Money = Time = Stories making their way from our imaginations to your screen. Your support makes all the difference.

Find me on the web at **sarahwynde.blogspot.com/** or **www.facebook.com/sarah.wynde** or on Twitter as wyndes.

Thanks for reading!

ACKNOWLEDGEMENTS

Some writers write because the act of putting words to paper is like oxygen for their souls. I write because it's less expensive than playing *World of Warcraft*. (Unemployed graduate-school dropouts need cheap hobbies.) That said, I could not possibly have kept writing through this incredibly difficult year (see: *Dedication*) without the encouragement of all of the people who wrote reviews for *A Gift of Ghosts*, sent emails, and posted comments to my blog. This book literally would not exist without you. Thank you so much.

I'd also like to thank everyone who reviewed *A Gift of Thought* as it was posted on fictionpress.com, with special thanks to Luckycool9 for his helpful insight and to Caroline Humphries who got me writing again when I wasn't sure I ever would.

Rachel Sager cheered me on every step of the way. I owe her more than I can repay. I hope she lets me return the favor someday.

The folks at Project Team Beta (projectteambeta.com) emailed me and asked if I wanted beta readers: saying yes was an easy decision and I'm grateful I did. My thanks to the beta readers who read early chapters, but especially to the wonderful and talented Shellynne Waldron and Jordan Walterman for their insight and commentary and all their help with those pesky commas. Mike Kent found the first chapters of *A Gift of Ghosts* on critiquecircle.com, loved it, told me so, and gave me the confidence to self-publish it. And then he offered to beta-read *A Gift of Thought*. I greatly appreciated all of his suggestions (even the ones I ignored—the world needs more parentheticals!) and his help making *A Gift of Thought* a better book. Heidi Eckstein found the first draft, "meh, but entertaining": her honest criticism was much appreciated and truly useful. Stacy Taylor read the first draft and posed great questions; I'm grateful for her help. Finally, I had an incredible stroke of good fortune when Yvie Burleson agreed to beta read: her knowledge of DC and legal issues improved every reference to the city and made the police scenes more realistic (all errors are mine, of course), while innumerable sentences are cleaner, stronger and shorter because of her suggestions. Thank you all!

My wonderful aunt, Marcia Newton, walked the fine line between unconditional encouragement and making smart suggestions for change beautifully, while my wonderful sister, Karen Lowery, stayed firmly on the unconditional encouragement side. I'm very grateful to them both and to all of the rest of my family for their support and enthusiasm.

Finally, special thanks and love to my brother, Werner Sharp, and my friends, Pam Hartman and Suzanne Courteau, for being here for me during a very dark time. You are the safety net that keeps me from falling too far and helps me bounce back up when the drop is over.